SNOWBOUND IN
WINTERBERRY FALLS
ANN BRODEUR

SNOWBOUND IN WINTERBERRY FALLS
by Ann Brodeur

ANAIAH SEASONAL
An imprint of ANAIAH PRESS, LLC.
7780 49th ST N. #129
Pinellas Park, FL 33781

First Anaiah Seasonal print edition November 2020

Edited by Candee Fick
Book Design by Anaiah Press
Cover Design by Laura Heritage

Anaiah
Press
Books that Inspire

To Martin, I couldn't have asked for a more godly husband or a better encourager. This book happened because of you. Je t'aime fort mon amour. (James 1:17)

To God, all the glory is Yours.

ACKNOWLEDGEMENTS

To my Lord and Saviour who gave me the love of story as a young child. It is You who has given me the talent and ability to tell a story and who has led me on this writing path.

To the amazing team at Anaiah Press – each of you have made this debut experience an easy one. Thank you especially to Candee Fick, for believing in my story and for coming alongside to make Jason and Stephanie's story so much stronger. To my fellow authors at Anaiah, I'm so happy to be a part of a family who cheers each other on. Laurie Wood, you are a wonderful resource and have a beautiful gift of encouragement. Thank you for all the advice and emails.

To all the Seekers in Seekerville—you women are amazing. It is because of your blog I found Candee and Anaiah Press. Please never stop investing in those of us who have a dream of someday sailing off the island. Much of what I have learnt about the craft has come from you.

To my best bud, Heather—everyone needs a friend like you! You gave me the kick in the pants I needed to jump headfirst into writing years ago, and I blame you for my overflowing bookshelf of writing craft books. It's no wonder I wrote in a character with the same kind of candidness as you.

To my husband, Martin—what a gift you are and I'm so blessed to have you in my life. Thank you for your understanding, for cooking meals and being papa to our girls when I was on deadline. For kicking me out of the house to write at the library or in a quiet place for a few hours at a time, so that this dream of mine could come true. For believing in me when I doubted my abilities.

To my girls—oh how blessed I am to be your Maman! You all have been so understanding and patient while I've been working on this book. And your prayers. There's nothing sweeter than listening to you pray for my work. Now that I'm finished, we can have that ice cream party we were talking about.

ONE

This wasn't how she was supposed to die.

Stephanie Clark's pulse accelerated, her screams sticking deep in her throat as she wrestled the wheel and spun across the ice crusted asphalt. The white of swirling snow blended with streaks of evergreens beneath the long beams of the headlights. A sickening crunch of metal and the snap of wood jarred her nerves and jolted her head back before the world stopped spinning.

An eerie stillness followed, marked by the hiss and sputter of a cooling engine and the ragged tempo of her breathing. The front end of the driver's side folded like a Christmas ribbon around a dark heavy shadow that seemed to bend with the wind. She squinted and leaned forward. A much too large wooden signpost had stopped her dizzy spin, stranding her in the middle of nowhere, but left the right side of the car untouched. The remaining shaft of light on the passenger side flickered and faded to a dull glow, marking the trail of towering trees beyond the crumpled front of her car.

Her lips trembled, and heat pricked her eyes.

Thank God she was alive.

It had been a gamble turning off the main highway in this weather. Both the interstate and US highway had been closed due to a multi-vehicle crash and the storm still brewing outside her windows, but this route would have taken her to Saratoga Springs. A place where a warm bed, hot shower, and buffet breakfast waited for her. And after the weekend of skiing alone in Vermont, heading home early to spend the rest of her two-week vacation with family seemed the most enticing idea. All it would take to get there was an overnight stop before the long drive back home to D.C. tomorrow.

Stephanie's throat swelled, and the throbbing in her temples increased with every beat of her heart, a not so subtle reminder blood still flowed through her veins. Blood that was likely getting low on insulin, thanks to the winter's idea of playing curling with her car. It was an adrenaline rush she could have done without.

"It had to be here, didn't it God? It couldn't have been somewhere in New York?" She sucked in a mouthful of icy air and let the tears come.

She didn't need to read the letters on the embedded sign to tell her she'd arrived at the one place she swore she'd never go to again. Little good it had done to press harder on the gas through the backdrop of a disaster that still haunted her twelve years later. Winterberry Falls, Vermont was just a blip on the map, a small black dot isolated on Route 30, but it might as well be jail.

Her chin jutted out and a quick breath escaped through her nose. As if she needed one more thing to worry about. Crashing into her past mistakes couldn't possibly be the answer to her prayers regarding Daniel Walker's offer to lead his PR team for next year's Attorney General elections. If this was God's warning sign not to take the job, then Daniel's campaign was destined to fail with Stephanie at the helm.

"Sometimes the sign God gives us is the one we least expect to receive." It was no wonder the flash of an old memory surfaced now. This was Jason's town.

Shaking the ache from her fingers, Stephanie pried them loose from the steering wheel and smothered her whirling thoughts with the soothing rhythm of falling sleet on the roof.

Her neck twinged, and her body throbbed with the dull stirrings of pain. She vaguely remembered tossing a bottle of ibuprofen in her bag before setting out on this vacation-turned-nightmare. She stretched across the console and swept some of the contents of her overturned purse into a pile, scanning the items as she stacked them up. The glint of a gold bracelet, a gift from Daniel on her last birthday, caught her attention. Stephanie unhooked one of the delicate chains snagged in a wayward stitch of her cuffed sleeve, the pain momentarily forgotten.

Accepting the PR position would be a smart move career-wise, giving her the credentials to launch her own firm, but being the center of attention turned her into a ball of nerves. Heaven knew she would be if Daniel had his way. Any woman seen with D.C.'s most eligible bachelor on more than one occasion would be noticed. Not that things were like that between them…

She pushed aside the distressing thoughts, grabbed the painkiller bottle, and thrust the remaining items into her purse. Stephanie wrestled the lid open, shook out a small white pill onto her palm, and shoved it into her mouth. She wrinkled her nose, the swig of coffee cold as it washed the pasty tablet down. Capping the lid, she tossed the bottle into her bag and fished around for her phone. Her fingers brushed the device and freed it from a wad of receipts. She glanced at the display. No signal this far out from town, but plenty of juice.

Stephanie moaned. Everything she knew about what to do in a snowstorm was not an option right now. Abandoning her car to find shelter was the least of her worries. Her blood sugar was low, and she didn't have enough food or water to wait out the storm, and with the falling temperatures, her insulin supply would freeze in no time. Then there was the itty bitty problem of not having a cell signal to call for help…

She leaned back against the head rest and dropped her phone onto her lap.

"God, help me find help before…" She squeezed her eyes shut. She would not let fear immobilize her.

Resolving to trust God, a challenge at the best of times, Stephanie unbuckled the seat belt and rubbed her aching shoulder, shivering beneath the crisp draft of the night air whistling through the cracked windshield. She'd need more layers if she was to have half a chance out in that storm. The metal fastener of her purse pocket opened easily, and Stephanie slid the phone inside before moving the leather bag to the floor. She turned and positioned her knees beneath her, bracing her spine against the steering wheel. Spots bolted past her vision and slowed as she gripped the back of the seat with her arms. She leaned her chin against the headrest and let her long lashes rest against her cheeks. *Breathe.*

Opening her eyes, she spotted a blue duffel bag occupying the middle spot in the back with the rest of her ski vacation gear. She rifled through the bag and pulled out black snow pants and ski gloves, tossing them on the seat next to her. Spying her heavy boots peeking out from beneath the passenger seat and her woolen hat next to them on the floor, she grunted from the effort of pulling them up and then dropped the boots on the mat of the passenger side. The thick wool was soft against her forehead as she slipped on her hat, the warmest one she had. With a few gymnastics moves she hadn't used since seventh grade, she clambered over the console, dressed, and ready to face the storm outside.

Ice fell from the stubborn door and snow crunched beneath her boots as she emerged into the cold. The rush of frigid wind against her exposed cheeks sent a shiver through her. Was this the best thing to do? Stephanie shook off the hesitation and leaned back into the escaping warmth of the car, draping her purse across her shoulder. She dragged two bags from the backseat containing her clothes and everything she'd packed for the ski trip, her diabetic kit neatly tucked in one of them. Her hand pushed against her chest, checking she hadn't forgotten something important. The pendant of her medical ID necklace dug into her skin beneath the layers of clothing. She swallowed down the lump of nerves. Someone would need to know she was diabetic if God forbid, she collapsed somewhere along the darkened road. Shoving the thought away, she pressed against the bulge of a flashlight in the deep pocket of her jacket. At least she'd have some light for the unplanned late night stroll, however small and strong the beam.

With the straps of the bags arranged across her body, Stephanie surveyed her surroundings. Nothing but a curtain of snow against a black backdrop encompassed her and her sorry-looking vehicle. The teetering sign whined and hovered above the hood of her sedan, bending to the demands of the wind.

She had to be off her rocker to think this was a good plan.

Stephanie gritted her teeth and braced her hands against the car, shoving the door closed. Metal struck against metal, spraying powder across her face and leaving clusters clinging to her scarf.

Her ears clogged with the shallow heaving of her lungs. She was taking too long. The tire tracks her car had left behind would be fading fast, and her internal compass wasn't exactly reliable, especially in the kind of dark that swallowed people up.

"Now what?" She choked back the prayer.

Move.

Stephanie pushed back from the vehicle and inhaled a long draw of air thick with pine and ice. Should she rethink her decision? Maybe she should get back in the car and wait things out, taking care to ration what few snacks she had and hope someone as crazy as she would roll by and help.

Move.

Tucking her gloved hands into her pockets, the barrel of the flashlight reassured her there would be a way to light her path. A second horrifying crash of wood and glass sent Stephanie reeling back, nearly landing on her backside in the snow. The oversized plaque inhabited the space where her windshield once had been, her vacated seat now occupied.

Stephanie's eyes misted, her pulse erratic at the impossible situation.

"'You could do with a vacation', they'd said. 'Take some time off.'"

Her incredulous laugh echoed across the desolate road as she lifted her arms in the air. "Really? This is what I needed?"

Adjusting the crisscrossed straps of the bags over her shoulders, a prayer for safety and anything else she could think of whispered from her heart. She pulled the flashlight from her pocket and clicked it on, thankful for the strong beam that sprung to life. She took one last look at her poor car and spun on a clunky heel with an air of confidence she'd lost somewhere on US-7.

Tread back to the place she hadn't managed to leave unscathed twelve years ago? Or, die alone in the worst storm she'd seen in over a decade?

Maybe she could ask for a do-over for today. Mondays were always overrated any way.

Her breath hitched. "Just move." Stephanie's snow-covered boots heaved through the accumulating snow as she shuffled along the lonely set of tracks her car had made when heading from town. The deep grooves of winter tire treads filled with a steady stream of fat snowflakes and would all but disappear if she didn't hurry. It was another half mile to the edge of Winterberry Falls. With the heavy blanket of snow falling, there was no telling how long it would take her to reach the Christmas-ready tourist trap. Just her luck. Santa's big day wasn't for another two weeks, landing her precisely in the middle of the month-long Christmas festival.

Stephanie adjusted her scarf and pulled off a glove. She unzipped the pocket of her purse, opened the stash of raisins she always kept there, and popped a handful into her mouth. She'd need to find shelter soon, a place where she could check her sugars and rest.

She floundered as her boot skidded across a patch of ice, the weight of her bags shifting with the sudden movement. Her eyes grew hot, and her breath curled a wispy cloud into the cold night. She slowed her pace on the isolated highway, the grand hallway of trees closing in. She sniffed. Only the whispers of wind wrestling ice from twigs and the steady *swish* of her snow pants brushing together followed her. Turning her face upward, she squinted through the maze of white leading to an indigo velvet sky beyond her reach.

Did God really see her there?

Stephanie tugged her hat lower. Skiing in Vermont was supposed to be the catalyst for change. She loved her job at the *DC Affairs* magazine, but it was time to move on and spread her wings. Daniel's offer gave her the chance, didn't it?

Her stomach twisted and gurgled.

"What do You want me to do?" Her voice cracked as she scanned the heavens above. Shaking her head, she puffed a heavy sigh.

He hadn't answered the last fifty times she asked the same question, why would He now?

Stephanie rubbed her eyes and stared at the cluster of shadows ahead.

Was that a flicker of light?

The dark moved and seemed to sway in the wind, springing hope to life. She stared harder.

But the light was gone.

Perhaps the effects of shock were kicking in.

Thwack. She jumped at the distant sound from the forest. With pulse racing, she plunged her feet forward. No way she wanted to meet whatever lurked behind the dark covering of the forest. And she wasn't about to become the victim in a sensational article she'd always dreamt of writing.

If there was one thing she should focus her attention on now, it wasn't whether or not God was answering her prayers.

It was how to survive her worst nightmare.

#

It couldn't possibly get any worse.

Jason Miller flicked the light switch on and moved toward his cluttered office desk. He flopped into the swivel chair and leaned his head back before releasing the frustrations of a typical Monday through buzzing lips.

Who was he kidding? If only it were a typical Monday night, he wouldn't be here.

Emily, his news editor, had decided to elope two weeks before Christmas and emailed him her resignation before she fled the storm with everyone else in the office. Avoiding family squabbles was always a good plan, except when it came to leaving him in a lurch. Finding a news editor ASAP at this time of year was like trying to find Santa's workshop. Emily would be flitting six weeks of accumulated vacation time away with her new husband while Jason scrambled to find a permanent replacement. Pay day was around the corner, and he'd lost an ad sponsor earlier today. Small ducks in a big pond, but money nonetheless. Money his family-run regional newspaper desperately needed to stay afloat.

Jason grimaced. He was too young to develop ulcers, but at the rate the issues were piling up, he wouldn't be surprised if Doc Hudson demanded he take time off to look after himself.

He massaged his forehead, pushing the fog from his brain and tempering the dull hammering in his temples.

The large window behind his desk rattled, drawing his attention from the overcrowded desk to the blustery storm outside. The trees surrounding the old newspaper's office building sagged under the weight of amassing snow and ice and seemed to quiver with cold. Perfect conditions to knock out power and push him further behind.

He huffed.

There was only one person he trusted to fill Emily's shoes, but he'd lost the right to contact her years ago. She'd never forgive him if she knew the whole truth. She was better off believing he'd left on purpose because he hadn't loved her. Or whatever lie she'd been told.

Thoughts of Stephanie Clark, his best friend and the most talented reporter he knew, belonged buried in the past. Along with the huge clump of guilt that plagued him every time his mind wandered to her.

He still deserved coal in his stocking for what he had done.

Jason leaned forward, squinting through the streaks of snow falling outside his window. What kind of light was by the road? It looked like someone needed a headlight replaced. It was crazy to be out in this weather at this time of night and this far out of town.

He rubbed his eyes and searched the distance again. He must be seeing things. Despite the unplanned cat nap in the break room after the last of the employees had left for the day, he needed more sleep. Even more so now that he was down one staff member and handling her portfolio, too. A good night's sleep was for people who had normal jobs, not people still working at nine p.m. and surviving on reheated coffee.

Jason brushed a stack of papers aside and glanced at the notes scrawled across his desk calendar, bold red circles popping from the page. He shoved back the panic of looming deadlines, preferring not to think about the town's anniversary edition the council was anxious to see.

His fingers clattered across the keyboard of his laptop. The help-wanted ad would have to go in Saturday's edition since tomorrow's issue had gone to print already. Jason rubbed his neck and rolled his shoulders back. He'd just have to buck up and survive the week without his righthand woman during the busiest reporting season of the year, thanks to the town's Christmas festival. He wouldn't even think about the time it would take for applications to roll in, interviews to be conducted, and a person hired.

"God, I need a miracle." He rubbed his scruffy jaw. The shallow prayer fell flat. When was the last time he'd read his Bible and prayed, let alone darkened the door of church?

Shaking the shameful questions from his mind, Jason sat taller in the chair.

Since Dad's stroke a year ago, Jason had found himself in the unwanted position of publisher and editor-in-chief, plucked from an adventurous photojournalism career, though it was only to be a temporary position until his dad was well enough to come back. The office still looked very much the same way as his dad had left it, and Jason felt like a regular imposter.

He was a hard-worker and had spent weeks poring over the business aspect of his father's pride and joy after the stroke. Days had rolled into nights until he found himself sleeping at the office more than in his loft apartment above his parent's garage. The hours helped him forget… things. Hiring more staff hadn't been high on his priority list, and he didn't want to make major changes without his dad's input. Since he'd been able to manage with a skeleton staff and his long hours, he hadn't worried. Until now.

The sound of freezing rain tapping against his window made Jason involuntarily shiver. He pitied anyone who was stuck in that nasty weather. Most people were already home, warm and safe from the storm while he sat here shivering and breathing in fresh ink and paper. But this was his life, the only part he understood.

The office chair wheezed as Jason pushed to his feet. Someone had to pick up the slack Emily left behind. At least she was organized to a fault. It'd be easy to track down the information he needed in her files. Ignoring the framed photos on the wall, especially the one on the bottom right of the woman he'd loved but never told, Jason moved around the boxes one of his staff members had brought up from the basement records storage that morning. It had been a curious decision for Emily to direct the boxes into his office at the time, but now it all made sense. She'd been planning her escape while he'd been trying to retain sponsorship dollars, and Jason had been none the wiser. A worn-looking file box marked 'Archives' in black marker looked promising.

The stench of yellowed paper and faded photos from the past editions of *The Winterberry Falls Independent* wafted from the box as he pulled off the tattered lid. He wriggled his nose and sifted through the pile of newsprint and an album of loose photos. He frowned. There was no sign of negatives anywhere. He'd have to be creative with the less than stellar photography of years gone by. That was the travesty of hiring anyone who needed a job and handing them a camera. They'd come a long way since his father's early days of running the paper. Now that Jason was in charge, the quality of the photos was decidedly different. Not that the average subscriber would notice, but Jason did. And that's what mattered.

The town's 200th year anniversary loomed, and of course the paper was running a special edition in its honor at the beginning of the new year. Emily's special project. Proceeds were ear-marked for the library's refurbishment fund, a stone building in dire need of upgrades. There was no way the paper could produce the funds expected without releasing the edition.

Jason leaned back on his heels and ran his fingers through his hair.

Yet another reason he desperately needed help. The new year was three weeks away, and this was the first time anyone had made an effort to sort through the archives to prepare the issue. He cleared his throat, wishing the distressing thought as far away as possible while he hunkered down to tackle the special edition.

Shifting positions on the floor, Jason opened the lid of another box and thumbed through the contents. A corner of a white envelope jutted between two yellowed papers, its contents squished near the bottom of the box. He tugged on the corner and removed it from its place. Jason slid his finger under the flap and pulled out a USB key. He flicked the small flash drive between his fingers, curiosity pulling at his tired brain. If the drive contained image files, there had to be a photo or two worth using.

His joints cracked as he rose to his feet. What he wouldn't do for a hot shower or sauna right about now to work out the knots in his shoulders and back. He stretched and gazed out the office window. The sleet had stopped, but the snow continued to fall like powdered sugar on Christmas morning donuts.

Jason flopped in his chair and reread Emily's last email. His eyes honed in on the final paragraph containing a file name on the shared server. He pulled up the indicated file and scanned the documents. *Bingo.* At least she'd started the project, but there was still much to do, and hopefully, the USB key contained what he needed to create a compelling edition.

Jason rubbed his hands together. Perhaps he was a bit too optimistic that the drive would have what he needed. The USB inserted easily into his laptop, revealing a trove of picture files to transfer to the server.

Maybe God was on his side after all.

Jason's vision blurred, the mindless task of copying and pasting lulling him nearly to sleep.

Something snapped outside his window and pulled Jason from layouts and content. Likely another branch had given way in the yard. He stared at the glass, the warmth of the room wrapping around his weary body and cajoling his burning eyes to give way to slumber.

Coffee!

Jason stood and zigzagged through the maze of silent and darkened cubicles until he entered the decent-sized break room. Another casualty of their limited funding since it could do with a good cleaning.

The percolator's light indicated warm coffee, and Jason smiled. At least one thing was going his way. A cup of coffee, even one brewed hours ago, would provide just the jolt he needed before he could break for another uncomfortable night on the staff room couch.

Jason reached for a clean mug, filled it with the last of the amber liquid, and stirred in a healthy dose of sugar.

Gone were the days of espressos and photography adventures only to be replaced by cheap coffee and small town gossip. Good coffee exchanged for bad. He shook his head.

Chasing that story had cost him too much.

"What am I doing here?" His shoulders sagged.

Quiet moments like this brought back the memories of Stephanie and the colossal mistake he'd made. They'd had a great thing going, and then he ruined it.

Like he'd been given a choice.

Jason lifted the mug and sipped the sweetened brew. He wrinkled his nose and scooped more sugar into his cup. Not enough sweeteners existed in the world to mask the taste of a pot left too long on the burner.

Even though more than a decade had passed, the desire to gain what he had lost left an unpleasant aftertaste and a belief that somehow God had failed him.

Most regrettably, he'd failed her. It didn't matter how hard he tried to type THE END to their story, the ghosts of the past lived on.

A *thump thump* at the back door followed by a steady banging reverberated throughout the empty break room.

Who'd be coming in at this hour and in this weather?

"Help! Please help me."

The desperation of the muffled cry on the outside pushed him into action. Leaving his mug on the counter, Jason dashed to the door.

"My car... I need help. Please!"

"Just a second." He raised his voice, flipped the deadbolt, and yanked open the door.

A blast of December wind rushed at his face as the unexpected visitor slouched next to the frame. "Thank you."

The timbre of the feminine voice seized him, causing his muscles to tense as the snow-clad figure moved to cross the threshold. A pair of deep set eyes peeked out from the tangle of wool across her face and forehead as she grappled her things through the entry.

Jason stepped back. How was it possible to want to push her back into the cold and pull her into his arms at the same time?

A deep cold slithered through his veins. God had stopped answering his prayers long ago, yet here she was. In the flesh.

The woman pocketed a flashlight and lifted her purse over her head, staggering with the motion. Jason braced her arm and steadied her. A strap slid down her arm as she tried to wriggle free of the bags entangling her. Jason removed it, relieving her of the weight that seemed to pull her down. How had she managed to trek through the storm with those bags hanging from her tiny form?

He rubbed his arms before shutting out the frigid wind.

Maybe God *had* been listening earlier.

She shook the storm from her coat, her breathing audible and shallow. The purse in her hands landed with a *thud* in a puddle of melting snow, splattering his pant leg.

"Sorry…" She turned to look at him.

Jason dropped his hand from the brass handle. This was no ghost in front of him.

Her eyes grew wide, a flash of recognition igniting beneath long, wet lashes. Her gloved hand moved in one swift motion, tugging down the scarf.

Her lips parted. "Jason?"

TWO

The hammering of Stephanie's heart against her ribcage rattled her whole body. Despite trudging through snowdrifts and fighting fears in the night, a cool sweat beaded her brow, and a chill seeped into her skin.

Really God? Jason?

Her hands shot out, bracing the wall beside her before her vision blurred and the room spun.

The old building pitched and something caught her. No, not something, some*one*. Her body sunk into something cushy, and her muscles relaxed.

Stephanie was safe. Jason had seen to that.

"Here, try and drink." The hand that lifted her head was gentle and strong.

Her eyes focused on the plastic bottle Jason held up to her face. Parting her lips, she let the cool liquid slide down her throat. An old memory stirred, and a wave of comfort rushed over her. His name had been synonymous with this feeling. And then he'd disappeared.

Her breath hitched. Too much remembering wouldn't help her rest tonight.

Jason slid a soft object under her head. "How's that?"

Stephanie released a breath through her nose, leaning into the fabric he'd positioned behind her. His long fingers brushed across her forehead and down the side of her neck. She relaxed beneath his touch. She lifted heavy lids and nodded once, too weak to manage more. His face had matured beyond his age since she'd last seen him, but maybe it just looked that way with his clenched jaw and jagged lines bunching together on his forehead. The color of his eyes was just as deep as she remembered, though she couldn't be quite sure. He stared at her neck.

Jason popped to his feet, leaving her cold and confused.

He was good at that. Leaving her.

She followed him with her gaze. Jason bent and rummaged through her bags. He must be searching for her kit. Stars darted across her vision, and she shut her eyes, willing the pain to stop and Jason to figure out what to do.

"How much do you need?" Jason's voice wavered next to her ear.

Stephanie's eyes opened.

He knelt next to her, the diabetic kit in his hands. Jason stared at her, his face etched with concern.

"No insulin… Glucagon." She was exhausted with the effort to speak even those few words. If only she could drift away.

Jason leaped from the floor, the stomp of his rushed footfalls taking him away from her.

God, please show him what to do. I shouldn't have let myself get so stressed. Show him. Please!

Hurried footsteps brought him back again, a phone pressed to his ear. The pounding in her head skipped to double-time, and her muscles strained with the turn of her head. Her focus grew fuzzy as she watched him through tiny slits.

Glucagon.

"Doc, I'm putting you on speaker phone." He placed the handset on the table and picked up a needle and vial from the opened case.

A melodic but steady voice drifted from the speaker, instructing Jason. He jabbed the syringe in the end of the uncapped vial and pulled back the plunger, filling the barrel with glucagon. He rolled the bubbles away and recapped the end.

Stephanie struggled to pull the zipper of her coat the rest of the way down. The faster she could remove it, the faster he could inject her. She dropped her hand against her stomach, the attempt too much.

The weight of her torso pinned her to the faux leather finish of the couch, the lure to sleep stronger.

Jason's knees cracked as he crouched and guided her to a seated position. The room spun, and her stomach churned, but Jason's soothing tones and the gentle strokes of his hand on her back eased the nausea. He would take care of her. He had to.

Stephanie shivered as he pulled her jacket from her arms. The speaker on the other end of the phone continued to give directions as Jason rolled up Stephanie's sleeve.

"Stay with me, Steph!"

Stephanie's lashes fluttered as the cool of the needle pricked her skin.

Glucagon would help. It always did.

Thank you, God! The prayer raced through her mind before she slipped beneath the darkness.

\#

Dr. Hudson's reassurances Jason had done everything possible for Stephanie's comfort did nothing to ease the tension squeezing his neck and shoulders. He leaned back on his heels and watched the even rise and fall of her chest and listened to the unlabored breaths slipping through her parted lips. Doc would come when it was safe for her to venture to the newspaper office. In the meantime, she'd continue to check in by phone.

His gaze fixed on the soft features of Stephanie's face and the coils of chestnut brown hair splayed across the makeshift pillow. Her lips trembled and breath stilled before a wimpy snore wheezed through her nose.

He smiled.

Someone had been looking out for Stephanie tonight, and Jason was glad he'd been stuck at the office. Funny. He didn't remember her being diagnosed with diabetes in college. She'd always been careful with her diet back then because of her family history with the disease, but as far as he could remember she'd been fine. Good thing he'd seen the alert pendant on her necklace before it was too late.

Jason surveyed his surroundings. Puddles of melted snow had followed his feet to the couch, and wet snow gear was heaped by the door, Stephanie's duffle bags and purse spilling out their contents from his hasty search. The used syringe had rolled across the table, a Christmas floral arrangement blocking its path to the stained tiles below. The glucagon vial stood upright, its plastic cap angled on top. The table was strewn with his discarded phone, the half bottle of water Stephanie had consumed, his mug now cold with sludge, and the opened diabetic kit. Evidence of a dramatic arrival.

Stephanie moaned. "Jason?" Her voice was hoarse. Her dark lashes fluttered, and her gaze settled on him.

He slid closer on the floor next to her, the last of the slush seeping through the knees of his cotton pants.

"Hey…" He kept his words low. "You certainly know how to make an entrance."

Stephanie snorted and grimaced as she ran her fingers through her tangled hair. "How… Where?"

Pain crossed her face, and sympathy squeezed his heart. "From the little you said, I think your car crashed close by."

She closed her mouth and exhaled through her nose. "Yeah." The whisper drifted across her lips. She draped her free arm across her eyes, her head still resting on the makeshift pillow he'd placed beneath her. "Help me up?"

Jason slid his arms beneath her back and guided her to a sitting position, her feet still sprawled on the couch. Her breathing was heavy, but not shallow like it had been before.

"Here." He grabbed the water bottle, uncapped it, and handed it to her.

Stephanie sipped what was left in the bottle, and Jason yawned. Her eyes twinkled with the familiar spunk from their college days. She was laughing at him.

"I don't know about you, but I for one could go for coffee. If I make a pot, do you want some?"

Her nod was barely perceptible.

Jason stood and stretched his legs. He swiped his mug from the table and dumped the contents into the sink. It looked like he was in for a longer night than he'd bargained for. He'd have to give up the lumpy

26

couch and settle for cat naps in his office chair. It was the best he could do under the circumstances.

Exhaustion swept over him like the whirling snow outside. His eyes burned. Sleep. Too many more workdays like today would leave him collapsed on the floor. He poured the water from the glass carafe into the machine, placed it on the burner, and flipped the switch. Fresh, hot coffee was better than the sludge he'd been drinking any way.

He glanced behind him. Stephanie sat with her feet now on the ground, head clasped between her hands.

"Won't be but a minute."

She lifted half-closed eyes and offered a weak smile, her skin as pale as the falling snow.

The coffee perk hissed and sputtered.

The last time he'd seen her this ill had changed his life. He rubbed his eyes, pushing the memory away. He couldn't afford to relive the past. It was bad enough her presence revived this sense of protection he had toward her. If only it wasn't mixed with years of regret.

"Thanks." She cleared her throat. "I don't know what happened out there. One minute I'm driving like an old granny and the next…" Her voice faded, and her expression grew pensive.

"So rather than ringing me up, you decided to crash your car instead? Even I'm not smart enough to come up with that one." He grinned, and Stephanie stuck out her tongue, just the kind of reaction he was going for.

Jason reached into the cupboard and pulled down a clean cup for Stephanie. He looped a finger through the handle of his used one and carried them to the table along with cream and sugar.

"I was on my way to D.C. and the storm hit. I wasn't expecting it." Stephanie's brow furrowed.

"Light flurries and a high of thirty-two." He mimicked the weatherman's tone as he returned for the full pot and filled their cups on the table. "Could feel the storm in the air at lunch time. Didn't believe the report this time. It might as well have been Christmas Day for all the cheers I got when I sent my staff home early. I'd hoped to finish up a couple of things before heading home to miss the storm, too, but…" Emily had decided to drop her bomb.

Stephanie's weakened laughter wrapped around his heart like a finely tied Christmas bow as he replaced the pot on the warmer.

"Don't you ever sleep?"

Jason chuckled. "It depends. Tonight's the exception though. I managed to catch a couple of winks earlier. When I woke up, it was pitch black in here." It was a wonder he was able to make his way back to his office through the maze of desks and chairs. He should consider installing night lights or fix the exit lights that seemed to be on the blink.

Stephanie wobbled to her feet and moved at a snail's pace to the table. Jason hurried to her side and pulled out a chair, ready to steady her. She gripped the back of the chair and leaned against it before sitting. He slid the mug closer to her, and she looked up at him with big round eyes.

"Stuff is still spinning, but much slower now." Her smile was uneasy.

Jason glanced across the table to where he'd left the phone. Doc would be checking back soon and maybe—

"I'm okay. I've been worse off than this." Stephanie gripped his wrist and sat taller. She released her hand and wrapped her fingers around the Christmas themed mug. "I could use a glass of juice, if you have any."

Jason pulled a juice box from the fridge and set it next to her mug on the table. He'd seen some soda crackers in one of the cupboards before, one of those little packages that came with takeout soup. *Jackpot*. He tossed the little packet on the table, and she smiled. How he'd missed that smile.

"What's keeping you here this late on a Monday night?" Stephanie pulled out from her small black zippered bag what looked like a mini remote control with a display screen and slid a thin plastic strip into the end. She pricked her finger with another device and coaxed a small bubble of red to the surface before pressing the tab to her skin. "I mean, what was keeping you here, wherever here is, before I crashed your party?"

Jason raised an eyebrow as he studied her face.

Still direct like I remember.

"Oh, the usual. Meeting deadlines, planning special issues, and trying to find a news editor since mine quit today because she decided to elope before Christmas." He paused for dramatic effect. "And trying to keep *The Winterberry Falls Independent*, my dad's newspaper, from running aground."

Jason lifted the steaming cup to his mouth, and her eyes grew wide.

"If that's the usual, I'd hate to see when you're busy."

He grinned and took another sip of coffee. She had no idea.

Stephanie replaced the devices in her kit before poking the straw into the drinking box and sipping the juice.

Jason settled in his chair, widening the space between them. "And what takes you to D.C., especially in weather like this?"

She fingered a gold chain around her delicate wrist, her face pensive. The wall clock counted the seconds of silence between them before Stephanie's dark eyes captured his. "I need to call Daniel."

A swirl of something gripped his gut, something he'd rather not acknowledge. Stephanie deserved to be happy, and a boyfriend or husband in her life was better than having her parents know exactly where she was, or rather whom she was with at the moment. He never wanted to lay eyes on any one closely related to her again. One look from her father would uncover everything he'd worked so hard to bury.

Stephanie turned in her chair toward the heap of bags he'd left on the ground by the door. If she was looking for her cell phone, she'd be unable to use it any way.

Jason slid the phone across the table, keeping his grip on the cordless handset he'd brought from his office earlier.

"You'll not get a signal in this storm. It's spotty at best out here even in good weather. Dial nine to get out."

The throbbing in his temples started again.

"Daniel is an old family friend and is hoping I'll come work for him." Her eyes and mannerisms gave nothing away.

How old was old?

"He's running for Attorney General in the next election and wants me to head up his PR team."

Jason crossed his arms and leaned back in the chair while Stephanie lifted shaky fingers to scoop back a handful of hair. His pulse sped up, an unbidden memory of wishing he could more intimately explore the exposed nape of her neck and the curvy lobe of her ear unsettled him.

He averted his gaze and studied the worn out numbers on the telephone from years of usage. Yet another item to put on the growing list of things to replace around here.

He resented his attraction to her. She was a beautiful woman from the inside out and a talented reporter, a skill he could only match in photography. Someone with her abilities could solve his Emily problem. When they were in college they had always talked about someday.

But that wasn't today.

He needed distance. Stephanie didn't belong in his world anymore, and the sooner he got that through his thick head, the sooner he could kick his attraction all the way to the North Pole.

"And how does your husband feel about that?"

If Stephanie were married, she would be easier to resist. He could leave her family secret buried deep beneath the snow-covered ground and relinquish his promise to protect her at all costs.

But if she were married, he could hardly expect her to dig him out of the mess he had created.

"My husband?" Her brow furrowed for a moment before she shrugged. "I suppose Daniel would be thrilled if I said 'yes' to both his propositions."

Jason's hands fisted. Perhaps Daniel wasn't so old after all.

He lifted his mug and swished the coffee around in his mouth.

He studied his companion. He hadn't been on speaking terms with God for quite some time, but if he was, he'd likely ask why Stephanie was really here.

He swallowed. While she was an excellent reporter, he couldn't see her happy writing promotional and marketing copy designed to make someone look good, especially if she believed her client wasn't being truthful. And Stephanie didn't exactly thrive on being front and center in a large crowd of people. "And how would you like working PR? It's not exactly reporting the truth." The connection of her family history with the current situation dripped with irony. His shoulders stiffened as memories wriggled free from the place he stored unpleasant thoughts.

Stephanie's glare pierced through the protection of his composed façade. He wouldn't be the first one to break the imploding silence. Let her glare all she wanted. He owed her nothing. Especially after saving her life tonight.

Jason's impatience swelled along with the desire to barricade himself behind closed doors. Her penetrating gaze drove him to his feet, the legs of the chair screeching in protest.

He'd made a promise. And the longer he sat across from her, the more liable he was to break his word.

"I'll be in my office if you need anything."

And for the second time in his life, Jason left her alone without turning back.

THREE

Stephanie cradled the portable phone long after the line disconnected her from someone who had become the voice of reason in her life. *Whenever in doubt, talk to Daniel.* The conversation hadn't helped one bit. Then again, she probably shouldn't have left out tiny details like she'd nearly died and likely totaled her car. The information would have made its way to her parents who would insist on calling in the army to bring her home. Besides, Daniel had been more obsessed with her ETA than anything else. After all, there was a campaign to think about. One she wasn't sure she should be a part of. If she'd had doubts before she landed on Jason's doorstep, they were expanding like a rising lump of dough. Just thinking about it made her head hurt.

Stephanie grappled her snow boots off and slid off her snow pants. She grimaced and leaned back in the chair.

Her calves burned, and her shoulders ached, but with each new prick of pain came the terrifying reality of how close she'd come to death's door. God had spared her and dropped her where someone could help. She should be shouting praises of thanksgiving, but instead, anger bubbled beneath the surface.

She reached for her diabetic kit left on the table. A second blood glucose check was required after that shot of glucagon and the bits of food she'd eaten. Two more tests on the hour to measure her sugars would be enough to indicate they were successfully controlled. She touched the test strip to the blood on her finger. The crackers, juice, and coffee had stayed down so she was optimistic something more substantial to eat would, too.

Her levels were just fine.

She breathed in potpourri from the arrangement on the table and the lingering aroma of brewed coffee and wrestled the storm of emotions back into place.

Lord, how did I end up here? Why him of all people?

Stephanie pulled the cuffs of her sleeves over her palms and hugged her arms across her middle.

This had to be punishment for something, for growing impatient with unanswered prayers. Jason was a coward who had dissolved their friendship at her most vulnerable time, and she would've been perfectly happy to never cross paths with him ever again. It had taken years to get over his betrayal, not to mention her ability to build trustworthy relationships had taken a massive blow. With time, and a whole lot of help from God, she finally learned how to trust people again.

The scratched refrigerator in the corner clicked as if chastising her for her thoughts. She was being unfair and she knew it, but seeing Jason... What was she supposed to do with that? How was she to forgive him for using her?

Stephanie eased up from the table, tested her limbs, and limped to the vending machine in the corner. The wall was cool beneath her hand as she braced herself and did a gentle quad stretch while eyeing the selection. A bag of peanuts and popcorn looked promising, but after tonight's episode, she wasn't eager to try any of the rest. She leaned her forehead against the cool glass and closed her eyes.

Her stomach rumbled.

"It works best if you put change in it."

She pushed away from the machine and turned to see Jason towering over her. "Yeah, well I think there's some change in my car." She frowned, dried lips cracking. There had been change in her cup holder from the five dollar bill she'd used to buy her coffee and snacks before setting out that evening, but it was likely covered in snow by now.

Jason leaned against the door frame, his hands in his pants pockets. His eyes, the same intense color of the sky, glinted at her, and his infectious grin released an aggravating flurry of flutters in her midsection.

"I guess you'll be needing some money then." He freed a fist from his pocket. "Some things never change."

Stephanie's heart beat faster at his nearness. Her feet refused to move, and her nose tickled from the dark hairs on his forearm as he reached in front of her face. His muscles tensed, and his fingers paused next to the coin slot.

Her anger over his past desertion dissipated with every excruciating second he stood next to her, replaced by something she was loathe to admit.

"What do you want?" His pitch dropped a notch, and Stephanie's throat tightened. She inhaled mint through her nose and froze.

No, no, no. We are not going down this road again.

She focused on the terrible vending selection of snacks, willing her racing heart to slow. Stephanie slid her hand across the smooth surface and stopped in front of the bag of peanuts. She tapped a manicured nail against the glass. "C twenty."

The coins clinked, and the machine grumbled as the spirals rotated and spit out the selection, tossing the snack-sized bag to the bottom of the machine with a *clunk*. Change clattered in the return as Jason's hand disappeared into the belly and reappeared with

Stephanie's peanuts. He straightened, the snack clutched between his fingers. Stephanie licked her lips and then reached for the bag on his opened palm. His fist closed, trapping the item, his skin brushing the side of her hand. A trail of tingles tracing its way up her arm left a wake of goose bumps. Stephanie swallowed hard.

"Truce?"

His fist remained closed, and when she finally looked up, gone was the cold hard stare from earlier. The magnetic pull of his sincere gaze captivated her, begging her to set aside their differences.

Stephanie's trembling fingers flew to her chest, covering the medic pendant nestled in the collar of her sweater. She could never forget the past, but she could be thankful he rescued her tonight. "Truce."

Jason relinquished the snack as she mustered a polite smile. She snatched the bag from him and steadied herself against the vending machine, the room closing in on her. Maybe she should take it easy.

"Okay?" His examining gaze disturbed the neatly packaged parts of her heart.

Forget it, Stephanie. He's bad news, and the sooner you remember that, the better.

"Yeah." She tore her gaze from his and ripped open the bag, shaking a few peanuts into her palm before changing the subject. "Daniel is glad I'm safe." Stephanie shoved the handful into her mouth, careful to avoid touching him again no matter how she itched to push back the stray strands of hair from his forehead. Salt tingled her tongue but did little to soothe the rumbling in her stomach or to distract her.

Jason eyed her peanuts and headed for the fridge. "There's food in here if you need something more substantial than that. Help yourself." Jason closed the door with one hand while the other held a shiny red apple.

Stephanie's mouth watered as she glanced from her peanuts to Jason's apple.

He quirked a brow as the apple glinted under the dim lights of the kitchen. Smiling, he dragged the lovely red piece of fruit to his mouth.

Her eyes narrowed. No doubt he did that on purpose.

The crunch of the first bite drove her toward the fridge. Her stomach growled again.

Jason chuckled between bites. "When you're finished, I'd appreciate your opinion on something, if you're up to it."

Stephanie nodded, the savory smell of the apple spritzing the air. He rapped his knuckles along the counter as he sauntered away, leaving her to examine the contents of the fridge. She smiled. There was enough healthy stuff inside to lift the last bit of fog from her brain.

With hands full, Stephanie dropped to a chair and relaxed. She spread out her selection on the table and said a quick prayer before piling cheese and fruit on

SNOWBOUND IN WINTERBERRY FALLS

her plate. Her mind cleared with every taste of the peace offering from Jason. A vague memory of his family owning a newspaper wiggled its way to the surface, but the harder she chewed on the crisp, juicy mouthful of apple, the more the details grew hazy. She may not be happy she landed at the back door of *The Independent*, but she was more than thankful help had been on the other side. And deep down, she knew God had a purpose in all of this.

There is a time for everything…

She frowned at the passage weaving through her mind before sliding a slice of cheese into her mouth.

No wonder the words brought little comfort to her now. Nothing was in her control. Life surely had taught her that.

And when it was God's time to do something, there wasn't a thing she could do to stop it.

#

The soft shuffle of Stephanie's feet stopped just outside his office door.

Jason peeked over the top of the laptop, her presence more interesting than the weather report on his screen. Though from the looks of things, they were both bound to be stuck at the office longer than either of them wanted to be. "Better?"

Her face brightened with a smile. "It's amazing what a little glucagon and some food will do." Her gaze rested on the only other seat in his office, buried beneath a mountain of files that seemed to grow on a

41

daily basis. Two months' worth of expense reports, vacation approvals, and a bunch more items he'd forgotten about, which had seemed urgent at the time they got placed there. He'd been meaning to get through them. Sometime.

"Let me get that." Jason popped up and gathered the files. His shoulders slumped under the weight of the documents in his hands, and his ears grew hot while searching for a spot to move them. He deposited them on the ground next to his desk and extended his hand to the vacated seat.

Stephanie chuckled. "Some things never change."

He'd forgotten she could be witty. "Touché." Jason eased himself behind his desk.

Why had God dropped her at *The Independent* in the middle of the worst snowstorm he'd ever experienced living in this small mountain town? The weather station agreed with his assessment from all accounts posted online. They hadn't had this kind of snowfall in over a decade. Years ago he'd stopped praying that God would bring her back so he could explain everything. Now that she was finally here, he didn't know where or how to begin.

Maybe she'd forgotten all about it.

Jason rubbed the heat from his neck.

Likely not.

"Are you still writing?"

Stephanie's head tilted, seeming to consider his question. "Not as much as I used to. My job now doesn't give me much time to write, except for the stories I want to take." She shifted her position and drummed her immaculately painted fingernails across the top of her knee.

"But?"

A shadow crossed her face. "It's politics. And you know how much I love politics." She held her hand across her heart, fluttering her lashes and sighing dramatically.

Jason laughed. "What about the PR position? It'd be a change and might be interesting."

A hint of humor colored those deep chocolate eyes framed by equally dark lashes. "Not reporting the truth?"

That tone was definitely teasing him now.

He offered a shrug, and the humor faded from her eyes. If he were a betting man, Jason would say she looked defeated.

Her gaze strayed from his, and she pressed her lips together. Stephanie's expression intensified, and despite himself, he wished he could help.

"I keep asking God what I should do, but it seems He's not answering me these days."

The soft reply shouldn't surprise him. Her profession of faith in college had been genuine after all. Not a ploy to grab his attention. At least that would explain why she didn't punch him out the first moment she got, but had agreed to a truce instead. At the same time, her words plunged a dagger into his heart, his own guilty thoughts accusing him.

Jason picked up a pen and rolled it between his fingers, ignoring the prodding of his conscience. "So if it's as busy as you say it is at... Where is it you work?" He rolled the pen faster.

"*DC Affairs.*"

He stopped the pen midroll. She'd made it to the big times and here he was stuck in this out of the way town, running a bitty regional newspaper that ran twice a week on Tuesdays and Saturdays for his sick father.

A paper he'd already saved once.

He cleared his throat. "If it's as busy as you say at *DC Affairs*, how is it you ended up stranded outside my door in Vermont? Two weeks before Christmas to boot."

Her face brightened like the soft glow of candlelight. "Me time." Her sigh was full of contentment. "I haven't had any time off in the seven years I've been there so I took two weeks off. The magazine closes the week of Christmas so I've got until New Year's Eve. Three full weeks to myself. There's so much to do and see at this time of year, and I always missed out while working at the magazine. Plus, with everything else going on, I just really needed some time to myself." She cast a crooked grin his way. "That, and my editor said I needed to take some vacation time or he'd dock my pay."

Jason set the pen down. "I'm pretty sure he can't do that."

She nodded. "No, he can't, but it was his way of forcing me to slow down and take care of myself."

Jason started. Had she been sick again?

She waved her hand as her eyes locked on to his. "I'm fine, Jay. He was right. I needed time to myself."

For once, he trusted her on that one. She looked content. If that was the case, he was happy for her.

"So, how'd you end up here?" Stephanie turned an inquisitive stare his way. "I would've thought you'd be halfway across the globe chasing your Pulitzer by now."

"About a year ago, I was in Morocco doing a story on Moroccan architecture when Dad had a massive stroke. With Brandon serving overseas and Megan still in school studying business to eventually take over the paper..." Jason let his recollection fade, the burden of responsibility weighing like a snow-bogged evergreen on his shoulders. His dad's stroke really hadn't given him a choice in the matter.

Stephanie's lips parted, eyes wide with concern. "Is he okay?"

Jason's throat swelled. Compassion wasn't something he was used to, but it was like home coming from her.

"He's doing much better, but it will still be a while before he's ready to come back. And when he is ready, there's no telling how much he'll be able to handle."

45

Jason heard the frustration in his own voice and chided himself for being so transparent.

He grasped the pen again and clicked it open. "In the meantime, there are bills to pay, stories to print, staff to hire, and a myriad of other details to take care of. None of which are exceptionally exciting." He sighed and leaned back in his chair. "If you have any ideas of how to increase subscribers or advertisers, or bring in boat loads of money, I'm all ears."

Optimism had never been his forte.

Stephanie crinkled her nose in the cutesy way she'd always done. "Right. And I'm Santa Claus."

Jason chuckled. "Speaking of Santa Claus…" He leaned sideways and strained to pick up a partial stack of files he'd moved from Stephanie's seat to the floor beside his desk. He pulled a thick purple folder from the pile and replaced the rest. "My news editor had been doing something with these. Christmas decorations are missing from some public displays and private residences. With a town sold out to Christmas, people are upset. Police have been notified of the incidences. That pretty much sums it up. Initial thoughts?"

Jason held out the folder, conscious of the barren office. The only Christmas decoration they had around here was the floral arrangement in the break room, thanks to Emily. Since when had the office become a reflection of his heart?

Stephanie crossed the room in a few steps and took the folder from his outstretched hand and sat back down, nose buried in the printed papers. Her accidental touch left an irritating path of fire he couldn't extinguish, the same one she'd left at the vending machine with the peanut episode. He clenched his teeth together and inhaled through his nose. The guard around his heart cracked with one whiff of her cucumber melon soap.

He could not let her get to him again.

Jason tugged at the collar of his dress shirt and focused on the scramble of words on his screen. Anything was safer than the woman sitting in his office.

Stephanie's presence was intoxicating. Even when she said nothing.

He chanced a look her way and let his eyes linger only for a second. With her nose stuck in the pages of the file, he could still see glimpses of the eager journalism student he'd fallen in love with buried beneath the veneer of her current professional aspirations. D.C. may be a different setting and politics a different subject, but she was still the same Stephanie deep down inside. He questioned the past that had defined their future.

If he'd made a mistake, it was in pursuing the story the day after Stephanie fell ill. That particular story would have given him a solid reputation and perhaps the same Pulitzer she thought he still craved.

Never had he realized the collateral damage just pursuing the story would cause.

He'd never printed it.

And he'd still lost Stephanie.

"Did you read these?"

His fingers paused above the keyboard, and he glanced at the folder she held. "No. Emily summarized them for me sometime last week. Why?"

Her nail danced against the thick file. An irritating tapping habit she still had.

"The missing Christmas decorations are completely random and don't make sense." The lines in her forehead deepened as she waved one printed page.

Inwardly, Jason groaned. He knew that look and what it would cost him if he opposed her. He rested his hands next to the computer and waited.

"Mrs. Johnson says she had twelve drummer ornaments in her yard, and when she'd looked outside a few days ago, she'd counted only eleven." The gleam in her eye was likely to burst like a Christmas cracker if he let her continue with the train of thought he was sure she was on. Likely the same one Emily had ridden.

"Maybe the wind knocked one over. We've had a few windy days this month." The logical explanation was not appreciated if that nasty frown was any indication.

Her shoulders straightened, and she pulled another paper from the file. His mouth twitched in amusement as she summarized the document. Her confidence might be premature, but that was one thing he'd always admired in her.

"Mr. Roberts put Christmas bows along their white picket fence, lampposts, and garage door. They all disappeared." She lifted the page closer to her face. "He found a note with '*I O U twenty four bows. Merry Christmas*' tied to a sprig of winterberry." She pursed her lips. "It was left in his mailbox."

Jason chuckled. "Well at least it's an honest thief."

Stephanie's lips turned down as she shot him an indifferent stare. "This file is full of similar incidences. Christmas wreaths, strands of lights, a baby Jesus." Stephanie shook her head. "Who would want to steal a baby Jesus?"

Jason laughed. "Now that I hear you summarizing it, I agree with my initial assessment of what I had told Emily. The story is a waste of time. If you want something to do while you're stuck out here, I'm sure I can find something else. I've got a whole Christmas festival to cover in addition to regular news." Not to mention a gazillion other things. Jason turned back to his computer. The irritating *tap-tap-tap* of her nail against the file nearly drove Jason to insanity. He clasped his hands and rested his forehead against them while silently counting, eyes closed. At the count of ten, he opened them.

"If you think it's a waste of time, why did you want me to look at it?" She frowned.

Good question.

"Emily thought there was something there, and I wanted a second opinion. She was usually right about these kinds of things." Jason unbuttoned the cuffs of his sleeves and rolled them up, his movements jerky. Why did Emily have to leave? Couldn't she just elope and then come back after the snow was done falling outside?

"You're wrong. I happen to agree with Emily. There's something fishy about it, and I want to find out what it is." Stephanie slapped the file down on his desk, sending a wash of loose papers across his already messy desk. She pinned him with her stare. "That is... someone should check this Christmas Caper."

Jason buzzed an exaggerated exhale, flexed his fingers, and resumed typing the rest of the week's assignments for the festival. "I still say it's a waste of time."

He resisted the urge to stop typing and capture the memory of her sitting across from him, in his heart. His neck heated.

She slid her chair closer to the edge of his desk, and he stared at the letters on his screen, his movements stilled. He had important work to do and it didn't include observing a beautiful woman sorting through pages from a file he had no intention of following up on.

He needed to focus on something other than her.

"You said your news editor is gone." The pages stopped shuffling. "What are you going to do?"

Jason shrugged and steeled himself against the concern chipping away at his carefully constructed wall. It hurt too much to care about anyone or anything anymore, but the responsibility to run the family business was his. Duty and honor would take precedence over emotions and compassion any day. They had to.

"Whatever I need to do to survive." His voice quieted, his focus directed to the monitor in front of him. Two more reporters were needed for Thursday's events, and he should really send an email to everyone to work from home tomorrow. The forecast was abysmal. It wasn't supposed to stop snowing until sometime around five in the morning. That was another five hours of accumulating precipitation. He sighed. "If you come up with any bright ideas for the paper, I'm willing to bite if it's going to keep us alive."

He didn't want to feel anything for this woman. Let her think him cold and heartless. He needed to throw away the key to his heart before he fell, otherwise he'd have to beg her for mercy, and God knew he didn't deserve another chance.

Even if she did forgive, he wasn't sure he'd have the strength to let her go again.

The Independent was his life now and less complicated than a woman and her family. The only family he had to deal with was his own. He was happy to keep it that way.

"The least I can do is look at the file and investigate as a way of saying thanks. With this weather, I'm not going anywhere." She gestured toward the window, and he turned in that direction. The window rattled, and the wind whistled outside. Nothing but black beyond their reflections in the glass. With the midnight hour approaching, it looked like they'd have to wait it out here until he could find help in the morning. Snow was probably halfway up the sides of his SUV by now, so any chance of driving anywhere was next to nil. At least for the moment.

"Jason, let me make myself useful." She gathered three other folders from his desk and the papers she'd sent flying, straightening them into a neat stack before setting them down on the tidied corner. Jason stretched out his hand and stilled her wrist. His desk may be a mess, but she didn't need to clean up after him. He preferred his organized chaos to color-coded files and over-the-top organizational systems.

She looked at him with a warm gaze, ever the helpful friend. He could miss deadlines because of those eyes, and he'd be hard-pressed to keep his promise to Senator Clark, her father.

He released her hand and pinched the bridge of his nose. Wasn't that what he'd asked for?

"All right."

She grinned, picked up the folder again, and clutched it to her chest. "You won't regret it. I'm going to find the biggest Christmas story your paper has ever published."

Jason smiled. "And if you don't?"

Stephanie smirked and shook her head, her confidence oozing from her crooked grin. "That's not going to happen." Her eyes twinkled, daring him to contradict her.

Jason's chest rumbled with laughter. "There's no way there's anything newsworthy in these silly high school pranks. Wasting time working on that story when I'm down a reporter. For the record, you'll owe me for going on a wild goose chase when you could be making yourself useful."

Stephanie waved her hand as she turned to leave, the file tucked beneath her arm.

"What is it that I would owe you if I'm wrong?" She paused in the doorway and raised a perfectly shaped eyebrow. "Not that that's going to happen."

Jason chuckled, enjoying the banter a little too much. "Oh, don't you worry about that. I'm thinking something along the lines of writing me a *real* story." He smirked. "Like, how does Santa deliver all those presents in one night?"

FOUR

Stephanie capped the syringe and stuck the used needle in the plastic jar she'd confiscated from the unclaimed plastic containers cupboard.

She rolled her shoulders and kneaded a knot out of her neck from the few hours of sleep she'd managed on the uncomfortable break room sofa. Her muscles still ached with a dull throb from the lingering effects of her snowstorm adventure yesterday, enough discomfort to merit another painkiller this morning. Brushing the sleep from her eyes, she yawned and pulled the bottle of ibuprofen from her purse. Stephanie slid one tablet out and downed it with cool water from the tap. She hadn't seen Jason since she left with the file from his office around midnight. Sleep had called her name. Stephanie looked across the room. The file still lay on the floor beside the couch where she'd left it before she'd succumbed to slumber.

The coffee maker belched while she selected a mug from the cupboard.

What a bizarre feeling waking up in a strange break room. She hadn't done that since her early reporting days. All-nighters were the norm back then. But now, by 7:30 on a normal Tuesday morning, she'd have already showered, eaten breakfast, and walked to the coffee shop at the corner of her street in D.C., in her desk chair by 7:45 ready to tackle stories of the political life in the capital. None of those stories thrilled her half as much as the file Jason had handed her last night.

Stephanie strained her ear. A faint *tap-tap-tap* filtered through the building. It sounded like Jason was busy at his computer again. Did the man never stop? Whether he had stayed up working or fallen asleep in his office, he would likely be ready for a fresh cup by now. She took out another mug from the cupboard.

She looked out the window over the sink. The snow was still falling like a heavy lace curtain against a gray sky. The trees that haunted her night-time trek bent under the weight of snow, looking like an army of abominable snowmen. Her car was probably buried by now considering the rolling mounds of snow out there. It was overly optimistic to think her vehicle could be fixed even if it was dug out and towed to the nearest garage, wherever that was. Still, a girl could hope at Christmas.

She pressed her lips together, forcing the uneasiness back to where it came from. Old Red had to be salvageable.

She had to make it home in time for Christmas.

Stephanie drew her fingers through her hair as she squinted through the fat drops of snow. She should call a tow truck and inform her insurance company at some point. It wasn't likely anyone was coming or going today, so the tow truck could wait. Thank goodness Jason had thought of his staff yesterday and sent them home early. No one was getting in or out of the office today. And thank the good Lord above, she wouldn't starve with all the snacks in the fridge and vending machine—ones she could eat at any rate.

She pursed her lips and laughed inwardly. How quickly plans changed. She shouldn't be surprised though. God's plans had a way of derailing her own. Her three week vacation had barely begun. The skiing part of her first weekend was okay, but after a few cross country trails by herself, it wasn't as fun as she'd thought it would be, and her mind had been more focused on Daniel's job offer than on the sport. A full body massage and spa treatment at the resort had been the highlight, but she was a doer and without anything else to do, she'd grown antsy. Long drives alone were therapeutic for her and often, she'd solved her biggest problems while driving.

She shook her head. Well, this was a problem she hadn't seen coming. Crashing into that sign last night hadn't helped her figure anything out. At least Jason was willing to give her a place to wait out the storm and a project to keep her mind occupied. A Christmas one at that.

Stephanie enjoyed this time of year. Family time, beautiful trees decked out in the colors of the season, music and candlelight services celebrating Christ's birth. Those were the best things the season had to offer in her opinion. She hummed Christmas tunes, her hands busy readying the coffees.

Someone living in this Christmas-giddy town was overly obsessed with decorations to the point of theft. Her gut told her there was more to the story than what appeared on the surface. Real criminals didn't leave "IOUs" at the crime scene. If there were enough victims, this one piece had the potential to morph into a series, a running story. The possibilities were endless. Writing about a Christmas mystery could be enough to lessen the sting of landing in a town that reminded her of the most difficult time in her life so far.

Stephanie paused her song, certainty gripping her heart. The story was just the kind of distraction she needed from the pressure of making a life-changing decision she wasn't sure she was ready to make yet. Yes. God saw her here this morning and was providing her a reprieve.

"Thank you." The simple prayer brought another melody to life, and her body moved in time as the notes lifted higher.

Jason's conclusion to the thefts was logical, but her investigative instincts were telling her to dig deeper. She was anxious to get started this morning before it was time for her to leave, though with the snow still piling up there was no telling when that would be.

The song she'd been singing left her lips, a drawn out sigh replacing the refrain.

What would Christmas be like if she stayed?

Stephanie pulled the carafe from the burner and filled the two mugs on the counter. The cutlery rattled as she fished another spoon out the drawer. One scoop of sugar or two for Jason? It had been so long that she'd forgotten his preference. Then again, he'd always had a sweet tooth. Two it was.

Being stranded here forever was definitely out of the question. Vermont was a great place to visit, but she lived in D.C. and worked there, too, both currently and in the future. Daniel was handing her an opportunity of a lifetime by working for him. She enjoyed his friendship and had never turned him down for the casual dinner out or the occasional date night. More than once he'd hinted at wanting more, and she hadn't really considered it until he shared with her his vision of the future a couple of months ago.

If only she felt a fraction of the sparks she'd experienced last night over a package of peanuts, she'd take the plunge and see where a relationship went with Daniel. It wasn't fair to give him her heart when a piece of it had been left behind in Winterberry Falls the last time she was here. But the professional advantages he was offering…Was she crazy by taking her time to answer him?

Stephanie laid the spoon in the sink and wiped down the counter. Whether she took the job with Daniel or not, he needed an answer by Christmas. With the holiday two weeks away, she was running out of time.

The piercing ring of the telephone from somewhere in the newsroom interrupted the comfortable silence of the early morning hours. Inhaling the rich aroma of coffee one more time, she gathered the cups and made her way to Jason's office. Stephanie adjusted her grip to hold both mug handles in one hand and knocked on his open office door.

Jason turned from his spot at the window and motioned her inside with a nod, a handset pressed against his ear. "Thanks, Doc Hudson. She just walked in so if there is any change, I'll let you know." He gave her a thumbs up as she placed the coffee next to his computer. "Yeah, I think so. I'll be sure to tell her."

Jason disconnected his call, moved toward his desk, and took a sip of the still steaming brew. He gestured toward the empty seat she'd used the night before, and Stephanie sat. "How are you feeling?"

"Better," she answered into her cup, the heat from the coffee warming her nose. The liquid soothed her throat like a warm fuzzy blanket on a cold winter's night. She leaned her head against the smooth wood on the wall, tucking a clump of hair behind her ear. She watched the muscles in Jason's right arm press against the fabric of his shirt as he lifted the mug to his mouth. He had filled out since their school days, and he likely had a string of women vying for his attention.

She bristled at the very idea and slurped from her cup in defiance.

They can have him!

"Doc Hudson will come to check on you as soon as she can find a way to get here. But with the snow as deep as it is and still falling despite the original forecast, she might not get here today. It'll be sometime until the roads can be cleared this far out of town." Jason set the mug down on his desk, dragged his chair closer to Stephanie, and sat. "I'll have to shovel out a path to the doors at some point today, too. Best to be ready for the doc when she gets here to check your sugars and make sure you didn't do damage to yourself with that crash. She wants you to take it easy until she gets here."

Stephanie frowned. She was fine and didn't need the doctor to risk her safety in coming. Jason, on the other hand, should be the one ordered to rest. The dark circles under his eyes looked more like a nasty bruise rather than purely lack of sleep. Based on the creases in his cheeks, it looked like he'd slept the night away on the cuff of his sleeve. If he kept up this pace and didn't get proper rest, he'd have a heart attack before his next birthday.

Jason cocked an eyebrow. "She's coming whether you like it or not."

Stephanie's neck grew warm as she clamped her lips together. There was nothing she'd rather do than slap that know-it-all grin from off his annoyingly inviting lips and erase the twinkle from his eye.

Jason rubbed his face with both hands and yawned. "We'll have to tough it out here for a bit, just the two of us. I had already emailed my staff to work from home today. There's no use risking their lives trying to get to the office. Besides, if I know the town as well as I think I do, there'll be plenty of news to report from there for Saturday's edition. They keep the festival going at all costs, and I'm sure the organizers will be creative with this dump we've gotten."

Stephanie peered outside. Wise call, keeping everyone away. She shifted the mug in her hands and tugged at the hem of her red sweater. "I need to report my crash and call the garage."

"Already done. I left a message last night at the police station, and I called Roger this morning. Once the storm lets up and the road is cleared, Roger said he'll send his guy to check things out."

Her hands gripped the mug tighter. Jason was making it too easy for her. It should be a good thing, but her emotions were quickly spinning out of control. "Thanks."

Jason's stare held… friendship. Guilt rushed at her like a team of flying reindeer.

"No problem." He stood and crossed to the stack of file boxes on the opposite side of the room. He squatted, lifted off a lid, and rummaged through the box.

Why did you have to make him so attentive, God? Can't he at least be arrogant and self-serving? That'd make it easier to stay mad.

Stephanie's cheeks heated with shades of embarrassment. Thank goodness he couldn't read her mind and kept his back turned. She couldn't quite explain it herself, and for the moment, a gingerbread man had more sense than she.

Stephanie averted her eyes from his backside and admired the photo wall instead.

She rose, coffee cup in hand, and stepped closer to examine the photos. Glorious landscapes and scenes from town events covered the wall and captured moments of people enjoying life. Stephanie smiled. No doubt Jason's work.

Did he still shoot?

Her breath caught as her focus narrowed in at the bottom right corner.

That decade-old photo stirred the memory to life.

A last-minute decision brought her here. She'd gone home for a visit to rest before the last week of classes and finals started. There were too many distractions living in residence, and she'd wanted to end her year well. Graduation was just around the corner, and she missed spending time on campus with her best friend. When Jason told her he had news he wanted to tell her in person, no other persuasion was needed to get her to Winterberry Falls. They'd gone on a hike, camera in hand, to the foot of Bread Loaf Mountain. It had been a magical visit. The sun was setting, he snapped her photo, and then everything had gone terribly wrong.

She closed her eyes against the piercing pain in her heart as she reached out and placed her fingertips against the cold glass covering the picture.

She'd woken up in the hospital in Montpelier, after being airlifted from the medical center in town, and never saw Jason again.

"If I'd had my way, things would have turned out differently."

Stephanie jumped at the whisper of Jason's assertion in her ear, liquid sloshing inside her mug. Shivers slid across her skin. It seemed they both had things to regret.

She turned her head and studied his face, now inches away from her. The years had deepened the lines around his eyes, and his forehead bore the weight of his worry. Trails of anxiety left their indelible mark behind, but the face was still the same. It still belonged to Jason.

She backed away from the picture and flattened her free hand against her chest, taming the erratic beating of her heart. "God always knows best."

His eyes flashed wildly. She turned back to the photo, afraid of what she might read in his stare. She gripped the mug with both hands and stared blindly at the picture in front of her, too aware of his presence nearby.

"Yeah, well…" He took a step backward. "Even so, it's the best picture I ever took."

Stephanie wrapped her arm around her middle, her stomach twisting. This trip down memory lane would end in disaster, just like it had the first time. How had it gone so horribly wrong?

Her mouth filled with the bitter taste of regret.

Something had radically shifted in Jason over time. He used to talk nonstop about the goodness of God. It was because of his vibrant faith and the guidance of other Christians that she'd come to know Christ.

An unsettling feeling took root in her spirit, an urgency to pray for him.

SNOWBOUND IN WINTERBERRY FALLS

Perhaps that's why God had brought her to his office door.

She forced her thoughts in another direction. "When do you think the roads will be plowed?"

Jason shrugged. "Hard to say. I checked the satellite images earlier. It was supposed to stop around five this morning, but there's more coming. Predictions are at least another twelve hours of the stuff. The town's plow will have to work around the clock to clear the main roads, but based on how fast it's falling, I'm not sure the plow will make much headway." He breathed a wistful sigh. "Today's edition has been printed, but readers will have to wait for their favorite Tuesday paper to arrive on their doorsteps."

"Why is Tuesday's edition their favorite?" Stephanie shot him a glance.

"Because it's the only paper they get on Tuesdays." He smiled, and Stephanie laughed. "Us Vermonters don't let a little snow stop us from getting around. It won't take long for things to start moving again. Until then, you're stuck with me." Jason winked and returned to the boxes on the floor.

Stephanie turned back to the pictures and sipped the rest of her coffee. A blanket of fatigue wrapped around her. Climbing a mountain while avoiding the dangerous cracks of their shared past was enough to suck the energy from anyone.

In your weakness, I am made strong…

65

"Emily… computer if you need one."

Stephanie blinked and turned. Since when had he been talking?

"Pardon?"

Jason sat behind his desk now, bleak eyes peering at her above his laptop.

"You can use Emily's computer." He dropped his gaze, and his fingers tapped across the keys.

He was overwhelmed and exhausted. It was written in the creases of his forehead and in the downward twist of his bottom lip. His shoulders sagged, and the pressure was snuffing out the light that used to be Jason.

She prayed for his relief.

"And her computer is…?"

Stephanie's heart beat in empathy as he massaged his face. He dropped his hands and turned red-rimmed baby blues her way. "Next office." His head nodded to the right before he rummaged through a drawer. He held out a single paper, and it trembled midair.

She took the paper from him and scanned the handwritten note. A list of passwords and user names. She looked back at Jason. "You're working too hard. You need help."

A weak smile. Glassy eyes.

Stephanie pressed her lips together, fighting the urge to offer what she shouldn't. She should just respond to the call of prayer.

"Let me help you." The offer felt right. He'd given her one article to write, but she could do more than that. He was surrounded by file boxes, stacks of unopened mail, and piles of files, not to mention a calendar full of his handwritten notes. She ran her own department at the magazine and understood only too well the pressure of managing a team. She could handle Emily's files and help Jason with the interviews until he found someone else, or by some miracle, she left for home. She would help Jason whether he wanted her to or not.

A cloud of gray and blue stared at her for so long she could have sworn he'd fallen asleep with his eyes open.

"Just until your car is fixed." His expression softened as the storm faded from his eyes. "And Steph?" Jason's lips pulled taut, and he rested his elbows on his desk.

"What?" She hugged the mug to her chest.

"Nothing. It's…" His voice trailed off, and the room seemed instantly too small and too warm. "I'm glad you're here." The comment was heavy with the sentiment. He held her gaze, a look that sent shivers down her spine.

Stephanie offered a smile and left a weary Jason alone, pulling the door closed behind her.

Leaning her head against the scratched wood, she willed her pounding chest to steady. The truth surely showed on his tired, but handsome face. He wasn't the only one who had lost someone special all those years ago.

Her eyes stung, grief casting a shadow across her heart.

Please God. Help us both.

FIVE

The more correspondence she read, the more Stephanie was convinced something strange was going on in Winterberry Falls. Not only were the items random, but every time a piece went missing, a sprig of holly with a receipt of sorts was left at the scene.

She tapped the end of a pen against her forehead and bent over the contents of the file she'd spread across Emily's desk. Every incident had been reported to the police, yet nothing had come of the investigation.

She tossed the pen on the desk and groaned.

"There's no way this is a prank by kids. Too organized. Too considerate of the thief." Stephanie grabbed a fistful of hair and twisted it into a knot at the nape of her neck, shoving the discarded pen into the mass to hold it together.

But why would someone do this?

With a frustrated sigh, she swept the papers back into the file folder.

"I need to think of something else." Switching tasks when she couldn't think any more usually worked. Her best ideas typically popped up during a mundane task, like washing the dishes or folding laundry.

Was there a cell signal today? There were probably a few texts in the queue. Stephanie pulled her phone from her sweater pocket and checked the display. Still no signal. She clicked on the photos icon and scrolled absently through the pictures she'd taken at the ski resort. Other skiers had been happy to snap her image while strapping on their skis to take to the trails. She paused at a photo of her first evening there. The sunset had been stunning so she'd stopped at the entrance of the resort to capture the moment on her phone. Stephanie pursed her lips.

Something should be done about the welcome sign that had butchered her car. She'd feel better about the whole ordeal if she replaced the sign instead of waiting for someone to demand it. She scribbled a note to ask Jason about it later and slid her phone to the corner of the tidy desk.

A sense of familiarity suffused her spirit. Stephanie was at home here in Emily's office. The organized room resembled her own at the magazine. Not a spec of paper was out of place, and strategically placed file trays held a variety of colored folders. Pinned above a filing cabinet was a corkboard organized into rows with notes and lists, most notably a list of twenty names with emails and extension numbers divided into departments, Jason's name at the top. A staff directory. Next to the bulletin board mounted on the wall was a futures calendar and white board. Both were covered in the same neat feminine script labeling the folders on Jason's desk, marking deadlines, stories and appointments for the next month. There was no white space left.

It was an ambitious workload for one person.

The hair on the back of her neck stood on end.

Foreboding lumped like figgy pudding in her stomach.

Jason was in trouble.

There was no way he could meet all these deadlines, especially while juggling his own extensive duties. Judging by his hurricane-strewn office, the bags under his eyes, and the collection of coffee cups left in the break room sink, he didn't have time to eat, let alone interview and train someone to replace Emily any time soon. If she was reading between the lines correctly, the paper was struggling and under-staffed. No wonder he looked overwhelmed and ready to drop.

She moved closer to the calendar and studied the content. The highlights and colored text with dates and descriptions were enough to make her want to bury her head in the snowbank until the New Year.

There was never a good time to leave a newspaper job, but leaving at this time of year was a bit extreme. With the winter festival in full swing, she was sure it was all hands on deck, even in the middle of a snowstorm and working from home, for a small paper like *The Independent*. While she couldn't fault Emily for running away to get married, the woman could have timed it better.

Stephanie sat on the edge of Emily's clean desk and stared at the calendar. Jason could be difficult to work with when he was under a tight deadline, something a trainee would find distressing if an error was made. He preferred uplifting stories rather than the depressing ones that peppered newspapers everywhere. Then why was he so against Emily's Christmas caper story? No. Now was not the time to train someone new. He needed someone who understood how he worked. Someone who would help carry the workload, not add to it.

"Okay, God, You put me here so I'm going to help while I can. Make Jason accept my offer, stubborn man that he is."

She probably could have done without the last part, but God would know what she was thinking anyway.

If Emily was as organized with her electronic files as she was with the paper ones, Stephanie would have no problem picking up where Emily left off. She retrieved the paper Jason had given her earlier from the purple caper folder and placed the list of usernames and passwords next to the monitor. She'd have to remember to return the list to him.

As the computer came to life, she smiled.

It felt good to be working on something other than politics. Jason had also requested Stephanie's ideas to help the paper financially. Okay. He hadn't specifically requested she *look* at the financials, but it would help to know where things stood if she had to think big in terms of gaining new subscribers and advertising dollars. She wasn't an expert by any stretch of the imagination, but she had enough experience running her own department to know where to look for savings. And she had taken one accounting class in college. Maybe Emily had a copy of the latest financials or expense reports on her computer.

Two hours later, the alarm on her wristwatch bleeped and pulled Stephanie's attention from the newspaper's latest set of financial statements. Her hunch had been right. Emily's electronic files were immaculate, a girl after her own heart. It hadn't taken long to find the email from the paper's bookkeeper with a downloadable file.

Anxiety twisted her insides. Jason might not be happy that she reviewed the numbers in as much detail as she had, but he did want financial suggestions if she had them. He'd left out the tiny detail whether or not she could look at the files, but she needed to know where the paper stood before submitting ideas willy-nilly. The bottom line wasn't great, but not entirely hopeless.

Working with her father had taught her a thing or two about finances, first in his insurance business and then while he was a state senator. And with her position at the magazine, she'd discovered what worked and didn't when it came to subscribers. She had plenty of ideas for Jason to consider. It was just a matter of finding the right time to tell him.

She rolled her shoulders back and moved her head from side to side before standing. Stephanie had been at the desk longer than planned, and the night spent on an ancient couch hadn't helped much. Maybe they'd have to toss a coin for it tonight. Lord willing, the storm would stop by noon so someone could come rescue them from having to make that decision. They'd have to go easy with the food in the fridge. It would dwindle fast if they weren't careful.

Her stomach growled. Speaking of food…

A cool shiver crawled up her arms, and Stephanie hugged herself as she headed to the break room. Not long after the fateful hike with Jason, doctors had confirmed her diagnosis: Type 1 Diabetes. Insulin-dependent, she was meticulous with her eating and exercise schedule and checking her glucose levels. She never missed her twice daily shot of insulin.

As long as she stuck to a healthy lifestyle and didn't over-exert herself, she was fine.

Her long drive from northern Vermont had been pushing it long before the storm and crashing into town. She wasn't eager to repeat the exercise.

Newsrooms could be equally stressful, except she thrived on the energy. She bit back a smile. Even with empty desks and silent printers, her nerves tingled with excitement, and her heart played to the fast paced rhythm of the reporter's domain.

Nothing was impossible when she was working on a story.

"Thank You, God. You knew just what I needed." As she skirted past empty cubicles, she sang. God had been so good to her.

A snore interrupted her music, and Stephanie paused in the doorway to the break room. Jason lay sprawled on the couch, one leg stretched across the arm of the sofa while the other heel rested on the floor. An arm covered most of his face, and his chest rose and fell in a slow, deep rhythm. He would have a terrible ache in his back if he stayed like that.

Stephanie flipped off the lights and tiptoed to his side.

Even tough newspaper guys needed rest.

She crouched, careful not to disturb his much-needed nap with noise, and braced her hands under his lower leg. With gentle, slow motions, she hefted it up to the arm of couch next to his other leg.

Poor guy, he was exhausted. There wasn't even a pause in his snores. It was all the more reason for Stephanie to help and take matters into her own hands.

She stood and looked around the room. This place could do with a good cleaning. The mugs and dishes they'd used were piling up and surfaces were in need of scrubbing. Crumbs and dried coffee stains littered the counter and table. And the floor was coated with salt and dirt. Puddles of melting slush accumulated by the door next to a shovel, leaning against the wall. Jason must have shoveled out the path he mentioned earlier and succumbed to the fatigue afterward. But the cleanup would have to wait for now.

Stephanie moved to the counter and prepared her glucometer for testing. She glanced outside. Th snow was still coming down, and the mounds looked higher than earlier this morning, if that was possible, So much for hoping this snow would stop. It appeared as if that coin toss would indeed happen later today. If she lost, she'd have to be creative with Emily's office and use her clothing from her bags to make a soft enough place to rest.

She pursed her lips and checked her sugars. Perfect.

Stephanie discarded the used lancet in the same container she'd found this morning and poked through the fridge looking for an apple.

"Steph?"

She turned at the breathless moan of her name.

The couch squeaked and huffed as Jason turned, eyes still shut.

Dreaming.

A heavy cloak of sadness draped itself around her heart as she held the handle of the refrigerator.

They had been such good friends in college and had clicked professionally. They complemented each other in every way, and at one time, they'd dreamt of winning a Pulitzer together. When she came to Winterberry Falls that day, she'd been hopeful and ready to confess her love for him. The last time she'd seen Jason was at the top of the mountain when she collapsed. And then, nothing. He hadn't tried to visit her in the hospital or at home, and he hadn't return her calls. He'd disappeared off the grid and left her flailing. It hadn't made sense.

At least she'd kept her feelings to herself and hadn't embarrassed herself in front of someone who hadn't felt the same way about her.

Stephanie watched him sleep.

It didn't make sense even now.

She bit into the apple and wished back their last day together, before her diagnosis and before a decade of rebuilding her life.

Stephanie swallowed back the pain with the juicy bite.

Reliving the past was not part of her plan for however long she was stuck here.

She needed to rest and sweep away the unsettling questions for now.

And maybe, if she was lucky, Jason would come clean.

But if not, she would go home without any more thought to her past and enjoy the rest of her well-deserved time off with family and friends. Two and a half glorious weeks of vacation still waited for her, and she planned on enjoying as many Christmas events she could. Seven years had been too long to wait to take time for herself, and if she took the job with Daniel, it might be just as long before she could relax again. As soon as she had wheels to go on passable roads, Stephanie would head straight for D.C. and join her parents as they made their annual rounds to charitable, political, and social appearances this season.

She would lock away the mental pictures of one dark-haired, blue-eyed editor and leave him far behind in Winterberry Falls.

SIX

Stupid. Stupid. Stupid.

Jason's thoughts scattered like a shattered glass ornament beneath a decorated tree as he stared at the emails Stephanie had sent him while he'd been busy sleeping the rest of Tuesday away and sorting through more archive boxes this morning. He rolled his shoulders back and worked out the crick in his neck. That lumpy couch really needed to be replaced if he were to continue sleeping at the office. A pillow and a throw blanket would be a nice added bonus. His neck and shoulders would thank him. Or, he could hire a news editor and some additional staff so he could actually go home to sleep.

Thinking of news editors, he hadn't seen Stephanie since yesterday. She must have holed up in Emily's office for the night. The last he remembered was a chat with her in his office, shoveling fifty gazillion pounds of snow, and sitting on the couch for a minute. His watch alarm had woken him at six this morning.

He rubbed his face.

Did he open up the floor for suggestions and ideas? He remembered saying something about increasing subscribers and sponsors, but he hadn't given her carte blanche to stick her nose into the paper's bank and financial statements. Nor into the expense reports. After all, it was still his dad's business. Jason huffed. Stephanie was being kind, and he was an idiot.

Jason couldn't keep his promise, let alone think straight, with her around. Quite honestly, he was tired of the lies he had buried in order to save those closest to him. Stephanie, as far as he knew, never found out what happened in her dad's office when he was a member of the Vermont Senate. Senator Clark had made it pretty clear to Jason that his daughter was to be left alone.

The senator would have his head if he knew Stephanie was here.

This craziness had to stop. It was bad enough letting her run with the—what had she called it?—Christmas Caper story Emily had started, but now she was poking her nose into his family's business. And if she dug far enough, she might not like what she found.

Never make someone else's family business your business. That wasn't a lesson he was going to repeat.

Jason glared at the screen in front of him and clenched his teeth. He knew better, but he had given Stephanie the password to Emily's computer anyway. The woman was meticulous with her files, and it wouldn't have taken Steph long to find anything she wanted to find. The two women were like clones of each other. And now, not one but five documents had been compiled since yesterday. The woman had certainly been busy. All that work done by, he glanced at the clock at the bottom of his screen, 8:30 a.m. Wednesday.

It seemed Stephanie thought she could fix his financial problems.

No way was anyone with the last name Clark *helping* him. The last time that happened, these walls were filled with IRS agents.

Jason sighed and looked closer at the email subject headings Stephanie had sent. Yes, it appeared she had dug around the financials, but she'd uncovered more of Emily's unfinished projects and completed them. As much as he hated having her know about his money woes, she was just the person to fill in the gap and carry a load that was getting too heavy to carry alone. Give him a month with Stephanie around, he could start working normal hours again and bring home a paycheck. If only…

The rumble of a distant motor drew his attention to the frosted window. The sky was finally blue, and the snow had stopped falling. The weather alerts had been cancelled for this region in the middle of the night according to an online report he'd seen earlier. Efforts would have started last night to clear town, which meant rescue from this bizarre situation may soon be theirs. An engine gunned. Must be nice to take advantage of the freshly fallen snow.

Jason snapped to attention. Of course. He could call in a favor or two and get someone out here on a snowmobile. This was the perfect weather to lay some freshies, leaving trails for others to enjoy. His cousin owned a B&B in town, and she would likely take Stephanie without a reservation.

Stephanie's voice bled through the thin fibers of the wall next to his desk. She was probably pursuing leads and doing all the things she once had loved doing, obsessing over details. With her persuasive manner and friendly personality, people opened up to her. If she hadn't lost her touch, she'd be finished with her story by day's end, and he could get her out of his building.

Jason frowned. Despite his desire to keep her at a distance, to keep his promise intact, he still needed her. Professionally. She'd already proven invaluable during the storm with her work ethic and efficiency. He could really do with her sticking around longer. The paper would survive with her taking over Emily's job if only she didn't have bigger and more exciting plans in the nation's capital. The Dynamic Duo, their nickname in college, worked well together at the college's campus newspaper. It could work again.

Or not. He had no right to expect she'd want to stay here after what he'd done.

Jason fired off a quick email to his cousin, seized the mug on his desk, and sighed.

Empty.

Just like him. There wasn't anything anyone could do to make the pain of past mistakes go away and fill the void in his heart except maybe God.

God. When was the last time he'd really thought about God? Rapid, whispered prayers for help didn't exactly count.

Ashamed, his fingers absently rubbed the length of the worn desk top where Stephanie had tidied the other night. His grandfather had purchased this desk when he bought the building for the paper and had sat here every day for fifty years, writing stories and reading scripture. It was a different time then, but Granddad consulted God on a regular basis. And Dad had followed in his footsteps.

His hand stilled, and his fingers curled into a fist. *He* needed God. And it wouldn't hurt to talk to God about his current predicament. But to give God a laundry list of wants? It wasn't right, especially when Jason had blamed Him for ripping Stephanie from his life in the first place.

Jason's throat constricted. This wasn't him. He didn't get emotional. Maybe he was just overwhelmed with the paper. The lack of sleep. Stephanie's presence. His secret. Life.

There is a way that seems right to a man... The verse was one Granddad had drilled into him as a boy. He cleared his throat and pushed the rest of the passage out of his head. He didn't need a reminder how messed up things were.

Stephanie meant well. He could see it in every fleck of gold in her eyes, with every glance she'd tossed his way when she'd first sat in his office catching up on their professional lives. And when she'd expressed her enthusiasm for following up Emily's story, her face had glowed like the light displays lining every window, fence, and railing along Main Street. He'd barely had time to think before he'd heard himself agreeing to her help.

How was Jason to keep his promise to her father if she insisted on staying?

Jason jumped to his feet and sent the chair flying, stopped only by the mound of paper and files he'd left on the floor Monday night.

He needed to refocus.

And his coffee cup was still empty.

Stephanie's dampened laughter pierced the relative quiet of the office.

"God..." he whispered, and the mug in his hand quivered.

84

God knew his heart and how hard Jason tried. It had to be enough for the moment.

Jason moved from behind his desk, determined to put space between himself and the laughter reminding him of dreams lost.

He zigzagged through the newsroom, empty mug in hand. Duty had called him home, and this was where he belonged. He needed to leave the past alone and say goodbye to his youthful dreams. He couldn't change what had happened, but he could look to the future.

The distant motor drew closer.

For now, his future was to figure out a way to keep this newspaper running so his dad had a job to come back to. And even if the ideas she'd emailed him worked, he had to stop wondering what it could be like with Stephanie by his side again. The senator would surely have something to say about that.

Jason placed the cup in the overflowing sink, adding to the sad testimony of the gallons of coffee consumed during the storm. He readied the sink with soap and water. Nothing like a little elbow grease to take his mind off troubling thoughts.

A purring engine cut off outside the office building, and Jason glanced at the door, arms and hands deep in bubbles. Two people chatted, their conversation muffled as something scraped along the bottom of the outside porch. Jason dried off his hands and rushed to unlock the entrance. He gripped the handle and opened the door, allowing the rescuers to stumble inside, arms loaded with shopping bags and helmets.

A young man dressed from head to toe in blue and silver striped snow gear entered first, a silly grin plastered on his face. His Social Media Manager and IT guru was a snowmobile riding fiend. He thrived on the thrill of the ride, and Jason should have guessed the guy would have come to his aid following the area's big dump of snow.

"Mark!" Hallelujah, they were rescued.

Mark stomped his feet on the indoor rubber mat.

"Hey boss! Brought the doc with me and thought you might be hungry. That, and I need to check Anna's computer. She was complaining about it being too slow on Monday." Mark's cheeks were reddened by the wind, and he flicked clumps of snow from his sleeve. A woman clad in purple stomped her boots against the bottom of the door frame outside and crossed into the warmth of the building.

"Hi, Doc." As he reached for the door, Jason spotted Mark's newer looking snowmobile model, sitting in the snow-covered parking lot next to his half-buried SUV. The pathway to the door he'd shoveled out yesterday looked to have been redone. Jason frowned. Stephanie must have had something to do with that, completely disregarding the order to take it easy. She must have snuck past him when he was sleeping.

"Nice ride." He slammed the door, shutting out the cold, and turned.

Mark beamed. "The only way to get around. Don't know why you haven't got one yourself." Mark set down the grocery bag on the table, slipped his backpack off, and slid his arms from his jacket. He looped the hood on an empty hook on the wall.

"Someone's got to run this paper." Jason took the other grocery bag and a backpack from the overburdened doctor, placing them both on the break room table. "Thanks for coming, Doc."

She smiled warmly and unwound her scarf. "How's our patient? You haven't put her to work I hope." The twinkle in her eyes contradicted her disapproving frown.

Jason shook his head. "I haven't put her up to anything, but even I can't keep her from doing what she loves. She's in Emily's office." Jason nodded toward the general direction of the news editor's office, and the doctor left the room. Let Stephanie admit to the doc she'd been overdoing it since that shot of glucagon.

"The doc is some lady." Mark pulled packages of vegetables and fruits from the grocery bag he'd deposited on the table.

Jason raised an eyebrow and followed Mark's lead in putting away the food they'd brought. "Don't even think about it. She's at least a decade older than you." Jason stowed the last of the groceries in the cupboard, except for a box of rice crackers and applesauce cups. Thinking better of it, he grabbed a block of cheese from the fridge and left it on the counter. He could use something to eat right about now. Coffee and a granola bar two hours ago were a poor substitute for breakfast.

Mark turned on the water and washed his hands at the sink.

"I don't need another key player running off to get married and leaving me hanging." Jason's stomach growled. "Especially one who brings me all kinds of food."

Mark laughed as Jason pulled a cutting board and knife from a drawer. He slid the knife along the seam of the sealed cheese and cut off a few slices. Jason moved easily around the kitchen gathering cutlery and dishes for one, finally settling into his favorite spot at the end of the break-room table.

"Doc Hudson made sure it was all healthy stuff, but I snuck you some contraband in my backpack." Mark winked as he ripped open the top of a package of baby carrots, pulled one out, and snapped it between his teeth.

"May I?" Jason pointed at the backpack where Mark had left it sitting on the couch.

"Front zip pocket." Mark popped the last of the carrot in his mouth and pointed with his chin at the bag. Jason leaned over, his chair inches from the couch, and freed two chocolate bars. Excellent. One of his favorites.

"How're things in town?" Jason righted himself and then layered his cracker with cheese. "I imagine the storm caught everyone by surprise. Weather station reported this morning thirty-four inches in thirty-two hours. Almost as bad as the storm of 2010."

Mark blew a long breath and lifted both eyebrows. "Not great. Seems the town plow broke down after clearing out the police station and fire hall. Couple folks have cleared what they can, but the plow might take some time getting up and running. Only business that seems to be able to function is the grocery store. Jim said he had a staff member strictly on shovel duty since Monday night. Diner was trying to dig out when we left, but it's going to be awhile before anyone else can open up today." Mark reached for the coffee pot. "I'll take the doc back to town when she's ready, and I'll come back for you later. You really should consider getting a snowmobile. Keep it here for days like this."

Days like this. One of his granddad's catch phrases.

Mark was right though. He should keep a snowmobile here in the winter, even if it was just an excuse for a break in the middle of the day to clear his head and enjoy the nature surrounding his grandfather's building. Jason slipped the cracker and cheese into his mouth, enjoying the sharp zing of the cheddar. If he'd had one, he wouldn't have spent the last two nights avoiding Stephanie or being reminded of a decade old promise he never should have made.

Then again, it wasn't an expense he could afford—especially for fun.

Mark slurped from his mug and eyed Jason. "You okay? You're awfully quiet this morning."

Jason shrugged. "I've just got a lot on my mind. Not in the mood for talking, I guess." He shoved the rest of the cracker into his mouth.

"I'll be in Anna's office until someone needs me." Mark topped off his mug and grabbed the rest of the carrots before leaving Jason alone.

Jason leaned back in the chair and closed his eyes.

There will always be hard days like this. We can't control circumstances, but we can control how we react to them. We can change our attitude, make choices that will either better or worsen the situation. What are your priorities, Jason? If God's for you, who can be against you? His grandfather's voice was clear in his mind as if he were seated across the table. Jason winced. He had locked away his deceased Granddad's counsel long ago. Maybe it was time to admit he'd made poor choices and his priorities were in all the wrong places. Life had defeated him, and he wasn't half the kind of man his grandfather had taught him to be. The kind of man God intended him to be.

Jason opened his eyes and fiddled with the empty plate in front of him.

Perhaps he needed to start looking at Stephanie's surprise arrival from a different angle, not just a stopover for her to rest and receive medical attention.

Maybe it was time for both of them to finally let go of their past.

And for Jason to let God run his future.

#

Stephanie felt silly resting with her feet up in the break room while Jason worked away in his office. Except, even though the accident was over a day ago and her glucose levels had been mostly normal ever since, Dr. Hudson had insisted she rest for at least an hour this afternoon. She was forbidden to touch anything work-related for the whole hour. It was a good thing she hadn't admitted to shoveling out the pathway earlier or she'd be side-lined for the rest of the day. Granted, she had paced herself, taking twice the amount of time she normally would have, being careful to rest a full thirty minutes between shoveling stints until a decent patch had been cleared. Jason hadn't stirred once from his spot on the couch as she'd tiptoed past him and pulled the door closed with barely a click of the lock set.

Stephanie pursed her lips together and released the pent-up air from her lungs. Stephanie hated being sick. She'd had enough of it the last year of college and had spent every year since then avoiding catching anything. She was still a bit stiff from the accident, and maybe from the spontaneous decision to shovel the office walkway, but it wasn't anything she was worried about. Dr. Hudson was a good doctor, Stephanie could tell just by talking with her, and she had been to a lot of medical appointments in her lifetime. She was thoughtful, too. Before she left, she slipped a new vial of glucagon into Stephanie's kit for "just in case." The doctor was being extra cautious with Stephanie's medical history and her recent run-in with the town's sign.

The common ceiling tiles overhead tempted her to count their brown spots. It was better to count something than allow her mind to slip down an icy slope to her college days in northern Vermont.

"Sleeping on the job?" Heavy footsteps entered the room, and Stephanie turned her head. Her lips curled up at Jason's rumpled appearance.

So much for good intentions.

The shirt he wore was new, though terribly creased, and its deep hue brought out the blue in his eyes, not that she'd noticed. Old habits died hard. He must still keep a second change of clothes folded in his desk like he did back in the day. The scruffy start of a beard wasn't half bad. It made him look older. Quite the difference from the skinny kid he used to be.

"No, just following the doctor's orders."

Stephanie turned back to the ceiling tiles and listened to Jason's lively, though slightly off-key, whistling of Christmas tunes. Cupboards opened and closed and dishes rattled. She winced at a sour note.

"Did you tell Santa what you wanted for Christmas yet?"

The whistling stopped, replaced by a low chuckle. "Can't say that I have." Jason's response was somewhat contemplative, sending a surprising pang of melancholy into her gut. She strained her neck and studied the slow movement of his hands as he prepared himself a sandwich. She returned her focus to the tiles.

Fourteen days until Christmas and this year was far from her normal routine. Usually, she spent the weeks leading up to the holidays writing year-in-review articles for the magazine's New Year issue, baking cookies, and volunteering to pack Christmas shoeboxes before heading to her parents' place for food and presents.

With taking vacation time two weeks before the holidays, she was bound to notice the change in routine anyway, but she hadn't quite caught the excitement of the season. She should be elbow-deep in Christmas preparations right about now and have attended several high-profile holiday events for the magazine already.

But rather than think of where she ought to be, she'd rather focus on the work she'd started yesterday and continued this morning. She shifted her attention to where Jason stood at the counter. "Did you get a chance to review the documents I sent to you? I really think there's something there." Stephanie's blood pumped with excitement.

A dish clattered in the sink, and Jason's shoulders stiffened. Her pulse skittered to a stop as she stared at his rigid form.

Apparently he didn't want her help even though he agreed to listen to her suggestions.

"I know you said you were open to suggestions, but I'm sure you have a million other ideas that will work just as well, or even better." The words tumbled from her mouth, and she turned her attention back to a fading brown splotch above her face.

She was messing up everything before she even got started.

Stephanie counted dots in the ceiling and tried to ignore the chair legs scraping the floor next to her. Except her senses exploded. Looking from the corner of her eye, Jason was too close with those rippled arms hidden beneath the blue fabric of his shirt.

He leaned forward, elbows firmly planted on his knees, close enough to feel the warmth of his breath.

She laced her fingers together across her stomach. The messy locks of his hair were in need of a good shampooing, and her hands were more than willing to do the job. She bit her lip and closed her eyes, scorning the hint of spearmint tickling her nose.

Come on, Steph. Get a grip.

Jason had left her once, and he'd do it again if given half the chance.

And what about Daniel? She could have something pretty special with him if she wanted.

Her breath hitched.

Didn't she want something more than casual dates with Daniel?

"You're right. I asked." His tone was distant, almost disconnected. And she could understand where he was coming from. No one wanted to be in the position he was. Financial problems. Staffing issues. A sick parent. A dream job put on hold. And now an old friendship materializing that hadn't exactly ended well. "Feeling better, Steph?"

Her eyes snapped open. "I wish everyone would stop asking me that question. I'm fine." She unlocked her fingers and flexed them. "Yes, I crashed my car. Yes, I walked through snow. Yes, I'm diabetic, but I know how to take care of myself."

Jason locked gazes with her, his expression unreadable. Her nerves buzzed, and her temper flared, but the stubborn streak she'd been born with held his eyes prisoner.

"I made arrangements for you to stay with my cousin Tilly tonight. She runs a local B&B. You'll sleep better there, and investigating those disappearances will be easier from town."

Jason appeared as if he wanted to put distance between them. Whatever happened to their truce?

Well, if he wanted space, she would give it to him. And if that meant going to a place with a real bed, a hot shower, and a continental breakfast, then she'd gladly go. She wouldn't fight his insistence. He could have this lumpy couch back.

Jason pushed back from his chair and checked the clock on the wall.

"Let me know when you want to get out of here. We can take Mark's snowmobile whenever you're ready." He tapped her shoulder and swiped his plate from the counter before his footsteps faded away.

Stephanie squeezed her fingers tighter across her stomach and lifted her chin.

She wasn't ready.

She wasn't sure she'd ever be.

SEVEN

Jason's cousin tilly leaned close and whispered, "She's not who I think she is, is she?"

Jason watched Stephanie retreat up the stairs, dodging potted poinsettias and avoiding the garland strung stair railing. Almost as soon as they arrived in town where the cell signals were strong, her phone dinged with what seemed like a thousand messages. Always the self-sufficient woman, she refused his help with her bags after checking in with Tilly. She then waved a quick goodbye and took the call from Daniel, who had an uncanny sense of timing. With the phone pressed against her ear and bags slung from each shoulder, she disappeared down the decorated hallway to her room on the left at Champlain House B&B.

He shoved his fingers into his tangle of hair and scratched behind his ear. "I wish I could say she isn't." He shifted his weight and looked at Tilly.

She clucked her tongue and twisted a strand of dark hair around her finger as she stared at the empty staircase.

From above, Stephanie's muted burst of laughter hit a bull's-eye right in his gut. The swift flare of jealousy was completely unpleasant. If only he could turn back time—about a decade and a half—his spirits would improve.

He caught a whiff of cinnamon as he turned to Tilly. She must be baking her famous Christmas cookies for the festival again.

"I've got coffee on and shortbread baking in the oven. Looks like you could use some." She nudged Jason's arm and led him to the kitchen.

The floorboards creaked as Jason followed her through the grand entrance where evenly spaced Christmas plants, wreaths, and twinkle lights gave the area a seasonal glow that spilled into the long hallway leading to the kitchen and other rooms for guest use. Greenery threaded with white and red holly hanging from sconces, wooden fixtures and tabletops. Candles and even more twinkle lights filled the blank spaces. Tilly had a magical touch with all things Christmas. He could use her touch around the office to brighten things up, after all it was the season to be jolly and all that jazz.

The bright afternoon sun pierced through the heritage lace curtains of the kitchen, casting its rays on the center island where rows of Christmas cookies covered the dark granite countertop.

Tilly pulled a bar stool from under the island and motioned for Jason to sit while she slid her hands into mitts and opened the oven door.

"So, you gonna tell me how she got here?" The rush of heat from the oven spilled into the room. "And what in the world you're thinking by helping her?" Tilly pulled out the cookies and placed the hot baking sheet on the glass stove top with a *clunk*. She removed her gloves before turning around and leaned against the counter, her dark eyebrows forming a perfect set of arches.

Jason frowned. "She showed up at the paper and needed help." He rested his cheek in his fisted hand and returned his cousin's stare.

"You gonna tell me more?"

"You said you had coffee and cookies." Jason pouted, batting his eyelashes.

Tilly laughed and threw an oven mitt at him. "Yes, I did."

He caught the glove and chuckled, happy for the close relationship he had with his slightly younger cousin.

A few minutes later, Tilly pulled a second stool from under the counter and sat next to Jason, two cups of steaming coffee and a plate of shortbread between them. He snatched a cookie from the plate and savored the melting treat, just like their Grandma Miller's baking.

"Steph crashed her car into the town's sign on Monday night and somehow she managed to hike to *The Independent* before collapsing on the break room floor. Thank goodness she was wearing one of those medical alerts on a necklace. I was able to get Doc on the phone, and she talked me through what to do." Jason looked at his cousin and sighed. "I couldn't very well turn a sick woman back out into the storm. I gave Steph a place to stay until the snow stopped, and Mark brought out Doc Hudson on his snowmobile this morning so she could check her. And now I'm bringing Steph to you." Jason bit into his shortbread and swept the crumbs from his shirt.

Tilly frowned and handed him a Santa napkin. "Isn't she the senator's daughter?"

Jason pursed his lips, finding the Santa napkin more interesting than his cousin's question.

"Wasn't he the reason the IRS showed up at *The Independent* all those years ago?"

Jason shoved another bite of cookie into his mouth, forgetting the crumbs, and stared at the coil of steam lifting from his mug.

"Didn't he force your hand to stay away from Stephanie?" Tilly's question was quiet as Jason wrestled against the resurfacing emotions, the unwelcome interruption to his carefully controlled life. He glanced at her.

"So, what are you doing, Jason?" Tilly's eyes were round, filled with compassion and an understanding that only came from hardship and lost dreams.

Jason's eyes misted, and his nose tingled. He sniffed and shoved the rest of the cookie into his mouth. He averted his gaze and surveyed the cluttered counter instead. Grains of spices sprinkled the cutting board next to the empty cracked eggshells and wooden spoon. A mixing bowl sat beside an empty baking sheet. A reflection of his empty life. What was that about? Was he really hoping Stephanie would forgive him, they'd pick up where they'd left off in college, and the senator would be happy about it?

"She's got someone and is living in D.C." Jason chewed faster. "That was her 'friend' calling her. There's nothing to worry about, Til."

"I might believe you if you weren't my cousin." Tilly stood and cleared the empty plate. It landed with a thud in the sink, and a gush of water from the faucet ended that topic of conversation. "You might as well take a few back to the office. There are plastic bags next to the plates. Help yourself." Tilly pivoted and nodded toward the rows of cookies while her hands disappeared beneath the sudsy water.

Jason filled two medium-sized bags, one for himself and the other for the staff. Her cookies were always a hit at the office. "Thanks."

"No problem." She smiled. Jason watched her work. It was a shame his cousin hadn't been snatched up by now. He loved her dearly and would be thrilled to see her have her happily ever after.

"And Jason…" She rinsed a plate and set it in the drying rack before turning, dishtowel in hand. "Be careful."

He smiled what he hoped was an assuring smile before he turned on his heel to leave.

Be careful.

As he slid his arms into his winter jacket and grabbed the borrowed helmets from their spot on the floor, Jason let the words swirl through his head.

And wondered how in the world Tilly knew him so well.

#

"Bye, Daniel." Stephanie tossed her phone on the plush down duvet, tugged off her boots, and sank into the mattress with a tired sigh. The smooth cotton of the floral cover cradled her arms as she stretched across the full length of the double bed.

She stared at the rustic glass light fixture above her bed, snippets of her conversation with Daniel buzzing through her tired brain. It seemed every other question consisted of her ETA in D.C. in some form or another. He was anxious to launch his campaign and obsessed with Stephanie leading his PR team. Daniel's steady stream of words left barely any room for her to say something and convinced her he already considered her a permanent part of his life.

Her hand clutched her stomach where a tight ball snarled in the middle.

While she'd been out of town, plans for Daniel's campaign continued to progress. Technically, she wasn't due back home until today or sometime tomorrow, so she wasn't sure why Daniel had been so worked up. It wasn't like she'd been able to ask him anyway. Stephanie's head spun with the details he'd hurled at her, but she couldn't fault him for being excited about his new—though secret—endeavor.

He had shown an enthusiasm she'd rarely seen, and he wanted to come up with a PR plan as soon as her feet touched D.C. soil. So much for waiting for her job offer decision. She might as well say farewell to the much-needed break her editor had practically forced her to take. At least *he* understood the benefits of getting away. Daniel, however, seemed to think she was made of tougher stuff and could handle whatever he threw at her. While he recognized her abilities and what she could do for his campaign, not once had he asked after her health, though it shouldn't surprise her. She'd lost track of the number of times she reminded him of her diabetes when attending various dinners and social events together. Was he really into her? It didn't matter how much he promised doing this campaign together would be fun and worth her while, she dreaded long days and late nights of endless work.

The knot in her gut twisted tighter.

It seemed as if her decision had already been made for her.

Stephanie nestled deeper in the duvet and crossed her ankles on the bed. She closed her eyes and pressed a hand to her forehead, the cold fingertips soothing her heated brow. Where was the peace she'd been seeking over this decision? *D.C. Affairs* was a good and steady job with a wonderful boss while the elections campaign would give her the one up she needed to start her own public relations firm. Especially if Daniel won. Yet neither option inspired the spark of creativity she'd had in the past two days working on a small town Christmas mystery. She thrived on the atmosphere of the newsroom. Would she thrive with the energy of an election?

"God, why does it have to be so complicated?" Her voice wavered as the whispered prayer slid from her uneasy soul.

If only she could erase the past few days and those eight glorious school semesters from her mind...

Stephanie blinked and sat upright. There was no way she was going to even entertain the idea. Small towns weren't for her. She'd only be setting herself up for another broken heart, ending up back home anyway. Winterberry Falls, Vermont was no Washington, D.C.

She noticed the room for the first time since her arrival, and she took in the little details of the creams and subtle pinks pulling the room together. Her bags with her clothing and her purse sat on the floor next to the bureau where she'd dumped them while talking to Daniel. The glittering pine needles and sprays of white holly from the Christmas arrangement resting on top of the bureau brightened her room with holiday cheer. Jason's cousin had done a wonderful job of bringing a little bit of Christmas into her guest room.

Her mother had offered Stephanie her professional decorator's name again this year. She seemed to think Stephanie's efforts at outfitting her two bedroom apartment for Christmas was abysmal. This year, her mother might be right. She hadn't decorated before she left for her skiing weekend, but had planned a decorating party for one with a cup of hot apple cider and her Christmas playlist for when she returned. Stephanie enjoyed the process and wandering through memories of Christmases from her childhood when she pulled each piece out of the lone plastic bin containing everything she had for the holiday. Her favorite piece was the little crèche her dad had bought her the first year she moved into her apartment on the southeast waterfront in D.C.

"Why does Daniel's offer feel forced? Is my timing off? What is it?" She huffed and pushed to her feet. There were only two options. And neither was particularly appealing. Tracing a finger along the smooth edge of the bureau, Stephanie touched the plastic snowflakes peeking through the needles of the arrangement.

Glitter fluttered from her fingers.

Her parents would be thrilled if she left *DC Affairs* and joined forces with Daniel, her dad's protégé.

Politics was her family's thing.

Stephanie flicked her fingers and shook the stubborn shiny squares from her hand.

The constant tension in her gut and suffering in the spotlight would be worth it if it meant being her own boss later. As Daniel's PR Director, she would gain the credentials to branch off on her own. She'd be free to choose her high profile clientele and then get to write when and what she wanted.

She only needed to make it through the election until next November.

The chirp of her phone pulled her from the dresser, a trail of glitter following her hand across the bed as she picked it up. This far into town, the cell signal filled all the bars, and her phone had started pinging as soon as Jason dropped her off at the B&B. The deluge of beeping had mostly stopped since then. It hadn't taken long to get used to the solace of being unplugged, and she was tempted to stay disconnected.

Jason: PICK YOU UP AT 8. SLEEP WELL. J

A smile made its way to her lips.

Of course he would be by. She had no way to get to the newspaper office and no way of getting around until her car was extracted and fixed.

He didn't mean anything by it. He was her temporary boss, and she was working for him.

An engine revved outside. Stephanie moved toward the window and pulled back the heavy rose-patterned curtains. The snowmobile she'd ridden in on glided through the snow the same way they'd come. She watched Jason's back until he turned the corner, swallowed up by a tall row of evergreens. Her smile faded as she dropped the curtains back into place and sagged onto the mattress.

Jason had had his chance during their graduating year to prove he cared about her. There was no mistaking their friendship was turning to something more serious. Her cheeks heated. She and Jason had shared a passionate kiss or two—okay, way more than two—but they'd never made it official and never talked about those intimate moments at their senior end-of-year party. They'd had big plans of traveling the world together chasing the big one. The story that would win them a Pulitzer. They professional dreams together that she imagined meshed into romantic dreams, too. Or so she thought. Obviously, she'd misread the entire situation.

Stephanie tightened her grip around her phone. Jason had disappeared while she was laid up in the hospital, leaving her at her worst. Once he'd gotten his story, he left her. He'd duped her. And how she hated the humiliation.

She swiped at a rogue tear in mid descent and gritted her teeth. She'd been so angry when she found out about his betrayal. She wouldn't even read the story and had demanded that anything he wrote be destroyed. Her parents convinced her that seeking out Jason Miller to demand answers would only hurt her in the end. They had been right.

Stephanie tapped her phone against her knee and hardened her resolve.

Jason had used her once, and she wouldn't let him do it again. She would occupy herself with the running story of Christmas articles as a thank you for shelter in the storm and for saving her life and then write her resignation letter to the magazine. She would work for Daniel and see where their relationship led. Anything—even the frantic pace of D.C. politics—was better than falling for the handsome-but-backstabbing newspaper man again.

As soon as she had a set of functional wheels, she would drive away as fast as she could, leaving Jason Miller and Winterberry Falls behind forever.

EIGHT

Thursday's midmorning sun brightened Jason's office as he gnawed on the yellow pencil, the numbers bouncing around on the paper in front of him. Surely Anna, the paper's bookkeeper, had missed something. The figures couldn't be right.

He dropped the pencil next to the financials and rested his head in his hands, fingers combing through his unkempt hair. He scanned the columns as his brain kicked into overtime working through the math.

Anna had been doing the books forever and warned Jason months ago that changes were needed.

His fingers tightened around the strands of hair.

He couldn't fail at this, too. The paper employed so many families, and his parents, far from retirement, depended on the support from the business. His sister, Megan, needed money to finish school so she would have the training to eventually take over the leadership of *The Independent*. His dad was collecting his salary while he was ill, and Jason had taken some cuts in pay up to the point of not taking a paycheck for the past two months. Yet, still the bottom line was suffering.

There was only one other time in his life he'd felt this trapped.

And he didn't like it any more now than he had twelve years ago.

"I prefer you with hair."

Jason looked up from his desk and loosened his grip. Stephanie stood in the doorway, a vision in red, alluring dark tendrils escaping her makeshift bun. She was stunning and captivating as she beamed at him. If life had been different, perhaps he'd know every freckle that sprinkled her nose by now and would have learned to focus on something other than those luscious lips currently turned up for his benefit.

He dropped his hands from his head and straightened the spreadsheets of numbers on his desk. He cleared his throat. "I'm afraid if this keeps up, I'll prematurely go gray or, worse, lose my hair."

Stephanie held up her fingers, matching the tips of her index and thumb to frame his face in her hands. She squinted as if holding a camera to her eye from across the room.

"Hmm…" She pulled her lips to one side.

Jason waggled his eyebrows.

"Nope. Can't see you without hair, but going gray isn't all that bad. In fact, it'd make you more respectable."

Jason laughed, and she dropped her hands.

"Well, in that case, I'll be happy to go gray." Jason picked up the pencil and rolled it between his fingers. "I'm assuming you're still good with numbers." He focused on the bottom line of his page, the one with only three digits instead of four. Of course she was, she'd already sent something of a financial nature to him, which he hadn't opened yet.

"I try. I dabbled a bit in keeping records for some work placements and again when I started at the magazine. Dad made sure I took some finance courses in college in case one day I wanted to work for him. Remember how much I hated those classes?" She crossed the room, pulled up the chair Jason had left empty of files, and sat.

Did he ever. The first year they'd met she couldn't stop complaining about them and someday working for her dad in insurance if he remembered correctly. However, she'd neglected to tell him one tiny detail about her father later on in their friendship. That he'd become a state senator and was running for U.S. Senate. Jason gritted his teeth. Indignation heated his blood at the mere mention of the senator.

Stephanie's fragrance tempered his anger as she leaned over the stack of pages he studied. He breathed her in, while silently begging God for... anything.

"What's this? I didn't see these the other day. I saw the month end, bank statement, and expense reports for last month. Those numbers on your page look promising, especially if you can boost your subscriptions and advertising dollars. Did you get a chance to review what I sent you on Tuesday?" She tucked a stray strand of hair behind her ear.

Jason rubbed his face, eager to wipe away the pulsating desire to pull that pencil from the bun and tunnel his fingers through the silky softness of her hair. "Which one? You sent at least five. Two relating to finances and the others relating to assignments and approvals."

Stephanie's sigh swept the back of his neck, pushing him to his feet and across the room.

This was impossible. No good could come from having her this close to him. He'd forgotten how pretty she was and how easily he could fall under her spell. He paced the length of the office and back again, dodging file boxes and stacks of old newspapers.

"From what I can tell at first glance in this newest statement, your situation is not entirely hopeless." Her expression grew pensive as she leaned over the paper on his desk.

"But?" He raised his eyebrows.

"It's not great either."

Jason guffawed. "Gee, thanks for stating the obvious."

Stephanie laughed. "I already came up with a few scenarios with new advertising and subscription rates that I think will do wonders for your bottom line. And there are also some cost savings I found from the expense reports and department budgets. I summarized everything for you in each document I sent." The confidence in her ideas was enough to grate a nerve. She had implied as much in the emails accompanying each document.

All five electronic documents were labeled so as to leave no question about the content of each one. Except he'd been so frustrated with her meddling and then Mark and the doc arrived, he'd neglected to even open one of the five emails. Just as soon as she left him alone in his office, he would take the time to look over each one. Maybe there was something there he could use. Jason stopped pacing next to the window. Hope flickered with her assessment of the paper's situation. If he was reading his bookkeeper's report from this morning correctly, there was every reason to have hope. *God?*

He scanned the sweeping mounds of snow surrounding the office and covering the branches of evergreens outdoors. One of the staffers had cleared out the lane and parking lot with his truck plow, freeing Jason's vehicle from of the bank of snow that had trapped him here for another night. He appreciated Mark's help with transportation, but he didn't want to take advantage of his generosity. With

113

the parking lot cleared and volunteer crews working around the clock to clear the roads in and out of town, his staff were able to return to work today. And Jason had been able to bring Stephanie back to the office.

Thank goodness the storm had passed, but Christmas would be here before he knew it, and it would turn out badly for many if he didn't get the company finances straightened out.

"I never wanted this job of running the entire paper. I was living my dream taking photos and telling the stories no one ever hears about. A new place every few weeks. New cultures. Worlds away from Winterberry Falls and small town living." He kept his back to her, his tone low, and watched a cardinal leave its nest. How liberating it would be to switch places.

Quiet footfalls stopped next to him. She brushed his arm, her touch soft enough to shake his illusion of a well-ordered life and the appearance of having everything under control. Her silence was soothing, and he was reluctant to interrupt the moment. She understood him.

The nerve in his temple twitched. One look her way and he would come undone.

"But now, if I can't increase revenue with subscribers and advertisers while keeping the pages filled with stories... This is the busiest reporting time of the year for us, Steph. I'm down one major player, and I need at least one, maybe two more to handle the load we currently have. Then there's the town's anniversary edition to print for January. If I can't get things on track, my family's legacy will be gone." He could hear the pain in his own voice. "If the paper fails, my family loses everything."

The urge to pack his things and run as far away as possible tempted him, but the faces of those he was responsible for flashed through his mind. He couldn't be the means of destroying his family or anyone else connected to *The Independent*. He wasn't a coward and would never give anyone a chance to accuse him of being one.

If only Stephanie were to stay...

"Jason."

Her whisper should have been a balm, but it drove his fear deeper, reminding him he'd already crashed and burned.

"You are not going to fail." The firm command resounded in the grip she placed around his wrist. Sparks shot from her touch and scorched his arm, yet he refused to look at her.

"You are capable. You are smart. You are good at what you do." Stephanie's voice grew stronger, striking blows to each fallacy taunting him. "Your dad would not have trusted you to lead if he didn't think you were competent."

She huffed. "Besides, you're forgetting two things you have guaranteeing this paper will succeed." Her tone lightened as she released his wrist.

"What's that?" He finally turned to look at her, thankful for her presence and ability to pull him from his funk.

She placed her hands on her hips and shot him a half grin. "God."

His chest tightened.

She was certain he and God were still close.

What would she think if he admitted the truth? As soon as he divulged the ugly secret that drove him away in the past, she would think less of him. And he was pretty sure she'd disapprove of his beef with God, might even call it running away like Jonah.

Jason cleared his throat. "And the second thing?"

Her smile grew wider, and a snap of fire lit her eyes. What this woman could do to him.

God, she's so confident. Why does she believe in me after what I've done?

"Me."

He didn't breathe.

Stephanie's smile held in place, illuminating a beauty that went beyond her skin and begged to be noticed. Oh, how he'd missed her. These past few days he'd been walking in a fog, not truly understanding how she could be here. He loved her banter. Her competence as a reporter. Her ability to see the truth of the matter. Her heart was even more beautiful than he'd remembered.

Jason's feet turned and touched the tip of her toes. A spark ignited every nerve in his body. He watched through heavy lids as her smile slipped, and her chest began moving in a perfect dance with his, her raspy breaths drowning out the creaks of the old building.

He leaned closer, the heat from her body melding into him.

Another inch, another sigh and he'd be close enough to kiss those sweet lips. The mouth that spoke to his aching heart. His nerves hummed with the memory of their first kiss under the atrium in the campus library, begging him to recapture the moment. The beautiful innocence of first love. Her eyes fluttered before her lashes brushed her cheeks, inviting him closer.

Jason reached for the pencil in her hair and stopped.

What was he doing? He had no right to kiss her, and her father wouldn't think twice about destroying his family's business again. Only now that he was a U.S. Senator, he'd crush Jason this time.

Jason cleared his throat and dropped his hand to his side.

"You? Yeah, well. Gotta give me more than that. Especially since I only have you until your car is fixed so you can be on your way back home where you belong."

Her eyes flew open, her cheeks wearing a flattering shade of pink. She offered him a tight smile and stepped back.

Jason's thundering heart slowed as he pivoted and took a step sideways. He watched the cardinal go back to his perch outside.

"I'll take a closer look at those documents you sent and see how I can use them. I'm sure there are some ideas you've come up with that'll increase our revenues and save us money somewhere."

The evergreens waved with a flash of red, and snow tumbled to the ground. Jason observed the band of red until it disappeared into the surrounding forest, taking his envy with it. He glanced at her, and his spirits sank. He'd hurt her again judging by her clenched jaw and crossed arms. Could he get nothing right with her?

"Thanks, Steph for trying to help." He hoped she understood how grateful he was. For believing in him. Jason turned back to the window, searching for anything to distract him from yet another mistake.

"You're welcome." Her response was soft and decisive. "We'll figure it out. With God's help."

She inhaled a noisy breath. "With God, all things are possible." Stephanie squeezed his shoulder and left him alone.

Jason leaned against the wall, her absence and words weighing down on him like a cookie press.

With God, all things are possible.

Jason flinched.

When had he stopped believing that?

#

Stephanie couldn't escape Jason's office fast enough. She headed straight for the break room, needing something to calm her frazzled nerves. She pulled a bag of grapes from the fridge, broke off a stem, and closed the door. Tea. Tea was like a warm blanket that took the chill away. She occupied her hands with the tea preparations and then rinsed the fruit under the tap. She stared outside and popped a grape into her mouth. She should have kept going to the break room in the first place, but passing by his office and seeing Jason hunched over and his classic hair pulling quirk when he was under stress pulled at her sympathy. The questions swirled in Stephanie's head like the tufts of snow playing a whirling game of tag with the wind from her vantage point at the sink window.

What just happened? Was Jason going to kiss her?

That was not good. Being in close proximity to Jason Miller was creating havoc. And the fact that she nearly let him kiss her did not bode well. For either of them. At least he had enough sense and stopped before they crossed that line.

She snapped another grape off the vine, popped it into her mouth, and chewed faster this time, pushing the thought of Jason aside.

"Hey, Stephanie. Feeling better?" Mark entered the break room and lifted the coffee pot from the burner, filling his cup with fresh brew.

"I am, thank you. Tilly's taking good care of me." Stephanie took a single serving milkette from the fridge and emptied it into her mug. She squeezed out the paper tea bag and tossed it in the trash.

"Tilly's food is to die for." Mark grunted his approval, and it made Stephanie laugh.

"I've only had one breakfast, but I'd have to agree with you on that one."

She stared at Mark as he added a heaping spoonful of sugar into his mug and stirred. He took a drink of the sludge, and Stephanie shuddered. He smacked his lips, smiled, and raised his mug to her. "Sugar makes it better." Mark swiped two treats from the plate of Tilly's baking Jason and Stephanie had brought from the B&B this morning, and whistled on the way back to his desk while Stephanie trailed behind him, tea in hand.

Some people and their sweet tooth. By God's grace she managed to limit the sweets, though this time of year proved challenging.

She returned to Emily's desk and set her mug down next to the printed article she'd been proofreading before her detour to Jason's office. She rolled the office chair from under the desk and sat.

A deep voice droned from next door.

Jason.

Something didn't make sense.

He had always been fiercely loyal. She saw that even now when it came to the burden of the newspaper's support of his family and employees. And he hadn't pushed her away when she needed help on Monday night. He didn't have it in his heart to abandon anyone who needed him. So something was off.

What was she missing?

She pressed the balls of her feet into the tiled floor and swiveled from side to side. The relaxing lilt of his voice conjured vivid memories of the worst time in her life. The last time she'd found herself in Jason's town.

Stephanie hadn't planned on waking up in a Montpelier hospital, or to a world without Jason, and she had been merciless with her questions about him. Until her mother finally cracked.

"You want to know what happened to that boy, Stephanie?" The words spat disgust across the room.

"His name is Jason, Mom. Not 'that boy'." Stephanie's tone held an edge she'd never used with either of her parents before.

"Only boys play games they know nothing about. And little boys use little girls to get what they want." Her mother's eyes narrowed as the heat burned Stephanie's face.

"If you're implying that Jason and I…"

"I am not implying anything of the kind. I am simply telling you what that boy wanted was a sensational news story. Something to boost his career, and when he discovered how easily a future senator's daughter could be played, he played. You were merely a puppet to be tossed

aside when he got what he wanted. He was only after a story, Stephanie. Well, he got a story all right. And now he's done with you." The ice in her mother's voice chilled her, though the idea of being a means to find a story chilled her even more.

Her eyelids sank closed, moisture dampening her lashes.

"Why God? Why did You bring me here only to remember?" Her nose stung and teardrops splattered her shirt. "Have I been wrong about everything?" She sighed, resting her head against the chair back.

Jason had never given her any reason to think badly of him before her hospitalization, but her mother had no reason to lie to her either. She swiped a trembling hand across her face. The Jason she was getting to know again didn't fit her mother's painting. The resolve so firmly planted to protect his family's business didn't connect with the actions of someone who would use people.

Stephanie's tongue drew across her dried lips.

Someone was lying.

Or Jason had drastically changed since college. If that was the case, what really happened between the time she passed out in Winterberry Falls and woke up in Montpelier?

Stephanie downed the rest of her tea. Forget betrayals and history that left her spinning like a dreidel.

She had a life in D.C. and a story to write.

And write a story she would. *Where Did Baby Jesus Go?* A running story with at least four articles following the missing decorations, exclusive interviews with victims of theft, and the cold hard facts that there was a caper afoot in Winterberry Falls and *The Independent* was on the trail. The photos would be sensational. A row of eleven drummers drumming instead of twelve. The mysterious I.O.U.s left behind and the splash of red holly berry adding an ominous feel. Jason could place the story where he wanted it, but she'd write a spectacular piece that readers would be begging him to print on the first page. Her story would be the ticket to launch the paper into a new realm of reporting, and the good folk of this out-of-the-way mountain town would clamor for more. It would be the best Christmas Caper story she was capable of writing.

Christmas in Winterberry Falls.

NINE

"You've got to try this. You've never had a cup of cocoa like The Cocoa Cabin's." Jason raised a large Christmas takeaway cup toppled over with a mess of whipped cream, chocolate shavings, drizzled sauce, and sprinkles. His eyes sparkled above the rim of the cup as he took another sip.

Stephanie stared, slack-jawed at the diabetic-coma-inducing-drink. "I'm sure it's amazing, but that my friend, sends my pancreas into panic mode." She wiggled her index finger at the trail of melting whipped cream left behind on the outside of his cup.

Jason's eyes darkened for a moment before he shot her a dazzling smile. "Well, then, I guess I'll just have to take a hit for the team." His nose emerged from the cup smeared at the tip with a dollop of whipped cream and swirls of chocolate.

She grabbed a few napkins from a stack sitting on the protruding counter, handed the pile to Jason, and laughed. "I think you'll need those."

Jason grinned and swiped at his nose, missing a smudge of chocolate. Stephanie pointed to the spot on her own nose.

"So, it really is Christmas here." Stephanie's eyes scanned the transformed downtown area where The Cocoa Cabin's temporary kiosk sat proudly in the middle of town square. No surface lacked Christmas lighting or a splash of holiday decor. Rows of roughly constructed snowmen with floppy hats and Christmas attire peppered the open expanse around the Cabin, an impromptu festival contest event, and the banks of snow edging the square and the sidewalks added to the winter wonderland feel of town. The surrounding shop windows were decked out in magnificent displays surrounded by twinkling lights, garland and more holly than was fathomable. Stephanie was convinced Winterberry Falls held the record for most holly on exhibit of all New England.

"Yup. It has been since December first." Jason chucked his napkin in the garbage pail.

From somewhere above their heads, Christmas carols played through speakers as they strolled the busy sidewalk and dodged mounds of what remained of the storm. The volunteer clean-up crew had done an amazing job clearing the road and pathways since they'd started three days ago, and there didn't seem to be a thing the festival organizers hadn't thought of for the Saturday schedule of festivities. And judging by the bouncing children and laughing adults, people were happy to be out of doors once again, despite the nip in the air.

Stephanie adjusted the strap around her shoulder and felt the bulge of her purse pocket. She'd made sure to grab her notebook and pen before meeting Jason in town. Emily and Jason's names had been marked in bold on the calendar on the news editor's office wall next to tonight's festival event. And with Emily gone, the obligation to fill her shoes seemed inevitable.

"So where is this gingerbread house contest taking place?" Stephanie stuffed her hands into her coat pockets and shivered. The mid December evening was lovely, but crisp.

"At the Art Gallery." Jason took another slurp from his cup, weaving through festival attendees. People meandered along the main thoroughfare, nodding greetings, while others stopped to admire store window displays. Couples huddled close together, engrossed in conversations, while shoppers loaded with packages sidestepped them. Stephanie hadn't seen this many people roaming the festival since she'd checked into Tilly's B&B.

A bell-ringing Santa hollered his Christmas greeting next to the grocery store and nodded his thanks as Stephanie dropped coins into his bucket.

She smiled. This must be what the songwriter meant by the feeling of Christmas.

A sprout of red and green in a shop window stopped Stephanie in her tracks. A shiver of excitement tickled her scalp. Stepping closer, she focused her attention on the tiny, obscure detail nestled between a set of matching Christmas tea lights and hand painted wineglasses.

She tugged Jason's elbow. "That's it! That's what all those reports were about." Stephanie pointed to the holly inside the display and resisted the giggle bubbling inside.

"Every person who has contacted the paper about some Christmas item or another gone missing have all said a sprig of holly with a note attached was left." Her grin widened. Another lead to add to her growing list of missing items. The response to part one of *Where Did Baby Jesus Go?* was over the top. Emily's inbox had been flooded with correspondence resulting from this morning's Saturday edition. It seemed everyone either had something taken or had a theory about the thefts. Not surprisingly, items hadn't been reported missing for the duration of the storm. "Do you have your camera?" She bounced on her toes, avoiding the impulse to dance.

Jason glanced around. "Here, hold this." He handed Stephanie his cup before pulling his camera from the bag secured to his back. He flung the neck strap around his head, fiddled with dials, and aimed the lens in her direction, the subtle *click* confirming his intention. She covered her face, and Jason chuckled.

"Jay, stop!"

Her squeals were no match for his boisterous laugh, and the camera still followed her the more she protested.

If you can't beat 'em, join 'em.

She stuck out her tongue and laughed. Crooking her arm behind her head, she jutted out her hip. "How's this?" Her lashes fluttered, and she lifted his takeaway cup to her mouth. Pretending as if she were about to take a drink, she almost pressed her lips where his had been.

Holding her position, she watched Jason's finger still above the shutter. The camera eased from his face, his confused gaze fastening to hers. A shiver brushed her skin, and her pulse pumped at an impossible rate.

"Perfect. Except, you can't drink that."

His concern set her heart on fire. He cared about her and watched out for her health. With a man like that, she'd always be safe. Stephanie had buried any desire or hope of a life with Jason the day her mother spoke of his betrayal.

The thrill of the moment thundered to a stop.

She shot a professional, but cool smile at him, chiding herself for being ridiculous. Stephanie lowered her arm, still clutching the cocoa, and nodded once toward the window.

"If you got a picture of the holly already, shall we go in?"

Jason nodded curtly and capped the lens. "Got it. Thanks." He took the cup from Stephanie's outstretched hand, chugged the rest down, and tossed the cup in the receptacle next to the entrance to the store. His lips pressed together, and his body was stiff.

Good. He felt it, too, and maybe now, he'd get the message and stop flirting with her. Stephanie was here on business, stranded but working all the same. They both were. Nothing more.

Sleigh bells crashed against the window pane of the door as it eased shut behind them. Scents of cedar and cranberry welcomed them to the overcrowded shop. Crafts and gift-ware occupied every available space with larger items taking up floor space.

Stephanie wandered toward the back of the store, leaving Jason to explore on his own. A small woman behind the cash register finished a sale and called out a holiday greeting to the next customer in line.

Stephanie admired the lovely glass ornaments, pot lid snowmen, upside down wine glass candle holders, and other handcrafted items. She paused midway down the aisle and examined items on a shelf. The pieces were made from recycled materials and showed a remarkable talent and artistic eye.

"Merry Christmas and welcome to Second Chance Sally's. Is there anything in particular you're looking for?" The woman behind the counter aimed a pleasant smile at Stephanie. A pair of spectacles sat on the tip of her nose. A green and red chain dangled from the glasses and wrapped behind her neck.

Stephanie held out her hand and moved to the counter. "I'm Stephanie Clark, and I'm writing an article for *The Independent*."

The woman's face brightened, and the glasses slipped off her nose, bounced on her chest, and finally rested against the ugly Christmas pullover. Her arm bobbed with enthusiasm as she gripped Stephanie's hand. "Welcome, Stephanie! I'm Sally Fitzgerald. You're that reporter doing the story on all those decorations gone missing. Catchy title, *Where Did Baby Jesus Go?* I read your article this morning. Strange business going on around here and bit unnerving. I hope you figure it out and keep us informed. Will you be staying in Winterberry Falls long?" The whites of her eyes expanded in curiosity.

"I'm only here temporarily."

Warmth radiated from Sally's face, matching the temperature of the air blasting from the overhead vents. Stephanie unzipped the top of her jacket and adjusted her scarf. She scanned the store for Jason and spotted him partway down the middle aisle, flipping price tags and frowning.

"Actually, something in your window caught my eye, and I wanted to ask you about it." She gestured to the front window display.

"What's that, dear?" Her red and green fingernails clicked along the edge of the counter as she skirted around it and stopped next to Stephanie.

"It was the sprig of holly." Stephanie watched her closely.

Sally started, brows raising in a perfect arch. Her red, glossy lips tamped into a thin line. "Now that is a mystery. And I'm not surprised it caught your eye with all the research you must be doing."

Stephanie followed the shopkeeper to the front of the store. Stopping beside the large window, Sally leaned across the display and picked up the sprig.

"Had me some log reindeer outside the shop door, cute little family I'd made last year. Loved it so much I couldn't part with it, so I decided it'd be a nice display to invite customers in." Sally pressed the sprig into Stephanie's hand. A corner of a note peeked out from its spot behind a cluster of red berries.

"Happened a week ago Friday. I said 'goodbye' to my reindeer after closing shop and next morning, they were gone. This here sprig of holly was sitting on the windowsill outside next to the place where the display had sat." Sally sighed, her breath scattering chunks of confetti snowflakes across the fake snow and garland behind the glass.

"At first, I thought it was a prank, but like you wrote in your article this morning, a lot of that is happening, and I wonder why." Sally placed a hand on her hip as Stephanie opened the folded paper.

"What do you make of the note?"

Sally shrugged. "Beats me. Says, 'I.O.U. four reindeer' so I'm waiting to either get paid or find my little guys back in their spot sometime soon." Sally waved to onlookers outside in the cold who returned the gesture.

"Thing is, I'm happy to spread Christmas cheer, but it's a puzzle as to why someone would have a reason to do this. After all, this is the center of New England Christmas, good will and peace toward men. No other town does Christmas better than Winterberry Falls. I don't know of many who would begrudge helping another find a little bit of Christmas." Sally's eyes dimmed.

Stephanie frowned. The woman's statement made a lot of sense, but it brought up more questions than answers.

"It's likely no one from town." Sally nodded to the holly Stephanie still held in her hand. "You can borrow that for your story. However, I would like it back, though, when you're through in case our mystery thief wants to collect their I.O.U.s."

Stephanie thanked her and unzipped her purse. She carefully placed the holly inside and pulled a business card from her wallet.

"If you think of anything else, I'm staying at the Champlain House B&B, and my cell number works in town. You can also reach me at *The Independent*."

Sally glanced at the card before tucking it in her sweater pocket. "Will do, Stephanie. I hope you solve this mystery. It would make a lot of people rest easier." Sally tapped Stephanie's arm before heading to the back of the store and to the shoppers waiting at the cash register.

"Find what you were looking for?" The heat from Jason's breath skimmed across her neck.

Stephanie closed her eyes and swallowed hard, frustrated by the effect he had on her.

Focus, Stephanie, focus.

"I think so." She forced her words to steady. A fire lit by the gentle touch of his hand on her shoulder burned a pathway down to her toes.

With the determination to resist the handsome photographer, she slipped from his grasp and dodged a display of low-hanging wind chimes on her way toward the front of the store. Bamboo and metal tubes rang together as she brushed past them.

"Let's go see some gingerbread houses." Stephanie squeaked as Jason caught up to her and stopped. She ignored his quizzical look, fixing her eyes instead on the wooden display cabinet draped in red cloth behind his shoulder.

Jason opened the door and held it for her. Sweeping aside the mushy feeling his gesture inspired, she adjusted the strap of her purse and zipped up her coat. A flash of the gold bracelet tucked in the cuff of her jacket reminded her exactly why she had to resist Jason Miller.

And exactly why she'd been asking God for direction.

#

The soft lighting in the art gallery was as perfect as the creations made from sugar, spice and everything nice. The details, right down to door knobs and hanging icicles from frosted rooftops were easily captured with the change in aperture.

Why am I running a desk instead of this? I've missed being behind the camera, but it's nice not having to live out of my suitcase.

Jason's finger became one with the shutter release. He squinted through the view finder. He craved finding stories through the lens of his old friend. His camera had traveled thousands of miles with him and never let him down. Jason almost felt guilty for having left his trusty camera in its padded bag since he moved back to Winterberry Falls to a job he never really wanted anyway. Maybe one day he could live that dream again. And even stay in one place this time. Time and circumstances dictated he drop his youthful dream, but feeling the cold plastic against his nose and cheeks again stirred the embers of a passion that had never really died.

Along with the dream of being worthy of the woman he loved.

Jason pulled his face back from the camera.

Where had that come from?

Yes, he enjoyed Steph's company, and they worked well together, but love? After all this time?

Stephanie laughed and stepped into his sight line as she spoke with one of the organizers of the event, her ever present notebook and pen in hand. She'd always liked going old school. His breath caught somewhere in the center of his chest. He moved the camera closer and watched her through the lens, animated and in full color.

He had cared for Steph a great deal. She had captured his attention all throughout their college semesters together and near the end, he found himself falling hard for the dark eyed beauty. Maybe he even fancied himself 'in love' with her. But when presented with an ultimatum from her father, whatever Jason had felt for her hadn't been enough.

His brow furrowed at the unfairness of the situation.

He adjusted the zoom. Now *this* he could do. It was his happy place, and he would shoot until the glowing wick of unwelcome emotions were snuffed out. And if he did well enough at keeping the paper going and leaving Megan something to run someday, then he could resume his first love of journalism and do this for the rest of his career.

Jason scanned the room through the viewer and paused again at the vision of loveliness. Stephanie stood behind an empty pedestal talking to patrons and pointing to various pieces of gingerbread art. She was more beautiful than he'd remembered, but her confidence and friendliness toward all people was even more attractive.

Any guy would be blessed to have her in his life.

Jason's finger hovered as he stared ahead.

This memory was all he'd ever have of her.

They lived worlds apart. He couldn't give her the kind of luxury she was used to. He couldn't even afford to buy her one of the glass ornaments he'd seen her admire in Sally's store, a thank you gift he'd like to give her for helping him out. There was enough in his bank account to buy food and pay minimal rent on his loft apartment to his parents, but that was it. Stephanie deserved better than that.

He blinked and narrowed the camera's lens on a display of dancing gingerbread men. He snapped a photo. If only he could dance away his troubles like these sugarcoated edible men. Their biggest problem was avoiding hungry mouths.

And Jason's problem? Senator Clark. He didn't approve of Jason in college and had made it abundantly clear Jason had no business associating with his daughter after the senator had made the connection. It wasn't likely her father would think anything different now.

"How's our patient doing?"

Jason glanced at Doc Hudson who'd stopped beside him. "Appears to be fully recovered I'd say.

She's looking for a story and she's found one." Jason's gaze followed Stephanie even as Doc Hudson laughed.

"Good to hear. As long as she's not working too hard."

Jason tore his gaze from the subject of conversation. "I'll tell her that, but she's not likely to listen."

Doc Hudson smiled. "I'll remember that when I see her next time." She patted his arm and moved to chat with other guests.

Noticing an empty table, Jason sidestepped his way through the crowd and set his camera bag down. He released a weary sigh and settled into one of the vacant plastic chairs. He'd grown soft sitting behind a desk and leaving exercise to others. His fingers worked the fabric strips of his camera bag apart, exposing a pile of SD cards in the pocket. He popped out the card from his camera and placed it in the little plastic cover he reserved for full cards.

A chair scraped against the newly polished floor, and Stephanie laid her notebook and pen next to his camera. She flipped her hair behind her shoulders as she sat.

"This is the strangest story." Her forehead scrunched. "Who steals a gingerbread house and leaves a polite note? This time, the donor—" Her fingers flicked twice in an air quote. "—is thanked for their donation and assured their creation will bring

137

much joy this holiday season. Told that the piece will be returned when it has fulfilled its purpose." Her lips pursed into a frown.

Jason's gaze journeyed across her face. Gone were the sleep-filled eyes, strained lines around her mouth, and defeated spirit. Her eyes sparked like a flashbulb, her energy cranked to high and her excitement contagious. She was unstoppable when it came to digging for her story. The job fit her well, and she'd wither under the pressure of a fast-paced elections campaign in D.C. Her editor had been right. She'd needed to get away for a while. Away from the pressures of accepting a job that would squash the beautiful woman she was right now.

"What do you think?" Her eyes widened.

He stared at her and cringed inside. She'd probably slap him if she knew he wasn't listening and would be horrified at what he was really thinking.

Besides, he didn't deserve a second chance with her, the hard-headed young reporter he'd been.

Jason cleared his throat and focused on the cards in the camera bag instead. His fingers slid across the tops of the empty cards before selecting one. He slid the square disc into place and clicked the camera shut, buying himself time, disturbed by the truth of his thoughts. A truth he needed to ignore.

"I think." Jason paused, lifted the camera to his eye, and adjusted the lens to focus on the soft curves of her cheeks. "I trust your judgement."

"You have enough photos of me already!" She shrieked and covered her face.

Jason lowered the camera. How this woman was able to capture his attention was beyond him. He'd met a lot of women in his career and photography adventures, but not one had held his interest longer than the time it took to unwrap presents on Christmas morning. With Stephanie, it would be Christmas all year long.

He breathed in the gingerbread aroma that permeated the small gallery.

He'd made the right choice in college to protect his family, but knowing that didn't lessen the pain or move the mountain of regret for leaving Stephanie behind.

If only he could turn back the years.

Jason blinked.

He hadn't let God lead him then.

But if he were wise, he'd let God lead him now.

TEN

Stephanie wrapped the fuzzy bathrobe tighter around her waist, relaxed from a solid night's sleep and a hot morning shower. She slid a brush through her wet hair.

The relative stillness of the house was a reprieve from the crowded Art Gallery of last night. Big events were not her cup of tea, despite the years spent with her parents working the social gatherings of the political elite. Large functions usually zapped her energy for days. But last night's event felt different. Fun even. Maybe it was the friendliness of the crowd, or she'd finally caught the spirit of the season.

Stephanie drew the brush down the length of her hair one last time and placed it on the bureau. She wiggled her bare feet into a pair of fuzzy slippers and stepped across the room to the covered window. The sun was shining and it looked to be clear skies today.

Perfect turtleneck weather. Good thing Stephanie had a tendency to over-pack and that Tilly gave her use of her washer and dryer yesterday morning. Her clothes had been beginning to smell, and not in the good way they did today. She slid the patterned velvet tapestry through her fingers and examined the snow-covered grounds below. The property boasted several winterberry bushes and evergreen trees backing onto a creek that slithered into the neighboring acreage and bordered the road to Main Street.

Her notes were detailed from last night's event. She had enough facts from the gingerbread house contest to write a summary of the event for the next edition, but with yesterday's encounters she'd found another two missing items to add to her series of articles.

Jason had run the first part of her story yesterday, what she'd managed to piece together from Emily's folder. The feedback to the first article surprised her. It seemed those who responded were just as convinced as her that it was more than just a prank. If she wrote fast enough, she could have a copy ready for proofing tomorrow, and Jason could run it for Tuesday's paper. After writing her summary of the gingerbread event, of course.

However, the Christmas Caper had her stumped.

Why the police weren't pursuing the thefts was suspicious at best. A visit to the police station was in order. And soon. She would have more time to mull things over after church today.

Who was she kidding?

She didn't want to head into the office any time soon, not that she had transportation any way, but because of Jason. The way he'd looked at her last night unraveled the tightly woven pieces of her heart. Maybe she could write at the B&B later instead.

The chemistry between them was broiling, and if she wasn't careful, she was bound to leave another piece of herself here in Winterberry Falls. It'd be best to hurry back home.

Stephanie pinched the bridge of her nose.

She wanted to take up Daniel on his offer, if only for the professional challenge it presented.

Her stomach clenched.

Daniel was a good man, honest and trustworthy. He'd make a great boss.

Guilt pricked her conscience. Daniel cared a great deal for her and wanted more with her down the road. If she took the job, wouldn't she be doing the same thing Jason had done to her in college? Using someone to get ahead professionally?

Stephanie blew a hot breath on the window and doodled snowflakes and miniature hearts with her finger. She pressed her forehead against the glass.

She was a hypocrite and a horrible person.

"God, what's wrong with me?" The heavy fabric bunched in her fist, and her muscles tensed.

SNOWBOUND IN WINTERBERRY FALLS

Frustration cranked her core temperature. "Why is this not working?!"

With an exasperated huff, she lowered herself to the floor and pulled her knees to her face. She clasped her hands around her legs and sorted through the facts, like any good reporter would do.

Fact—She lived in D.C. and had a great job at a magazine.

Fact—Daniel Walker was offering her a golden opportunity to lead a Public Relations team in the upcoming election.

Fact—She wanted a change.

Fact—Daniel's offer was key to establishing contact with high profile clients for her own firm someday.

Fact—Her stomach wrenched every time she thought about working for Daniel.

Fact—Jason Miller had used her for a story.

Stephanie squeezed her eyes shut and hugged her knees tighter.

She couldn't cause Daniel similar pain. He didn't deserve that.

"I'm sorry, God. I just don't know what to do." Her throat constricted as she stared across the room.

A lopsided pile of personal items sat next to her open overnight bag on the floor. The inside mesh pocket bulged with the only gift Jason had ever given her. She'd never had the heart to get rid of it.

Stephanie moved to her knees and fumbled with the luggage pocket. The well-worn leather of the Bible was cool against her fingertips as she lifted the cherished gift from her bag. She traced the embossed letters, their sheen lost years ago. The spine cracked and pages crinkled as she flipped the thin paper to the one spot she hadn't read since Jason disappeared twelve years ago.

To Steph, You can find what you're looking for, if you look hard enough. God is never far away, and He will answer if you ask. You are loved. Your friend, Jay

Stephanie could almost hear his youthful voice again, insisting she come to the college campus meetings with him knowing full well she'd refuse. Religion had no place in her life at the beginning of their friendship. Her parents didn't go to church, and she followed their example. It wasn't until he gifted her this Bible that her heart began to change and their friendship took a different turn. She read passages and asked questions. Jason answered without fail. His strong faith in God was the reason she *could* count on him.

But something had changed since then. Doubt now shadowed his eyes at the mention of God.

She slid a finger across the inscription, tracing the scrawled message. Her new faith had floundered with Jason's disappearance, and it was a very different young man who helped her grow in her relationship with Christ. Daniel's patient guidance and faithful example had launched her onto a path of dependency on the Lord. They grew up together in the political arena of their fathers and understood the pressures that came with it. Friendship had been a given, but mostly Daniel's quiet faith and companionship was the constant reminder of the friend she'd lost.

A tear fell to the ink below and left a bleeding blue *Jay*. She watched the veins of ink extend its fingers through the salty mess. She pulled a tissue from her bathrobe pocket and dabbed at the lone tear.

Stephanie flipped through the ancient words, opening to a worn section.

"Trust in the LORD..."

She swallowed hard, poised against the guilt, frustration and hurt wrapping a tight ribbon around her heart. She should close the book and ignore what she long suspected to be true.

Stephanie sighed and looked at the Bible again.

You'll find what you're looking for...

Yes. It was about time she did.

\#

"Roger, how's it going?" Jason smiled at the tall, lanky mechanic who entered his office on Monday morning.

"Not too bad now that the roads are all clear and we've been able to dig some folks out." He removed his hat and drew a grease-stained hand through his messy hair.

145

"Can I offer you a coffee? Not the best in town, but at least it'll warm your insides."

Roger shrugged. "I could go for a cup of tea if you've got any."

Jason patted him on the back and led him to the break room. He filled the electric kettle, placed it on the base, and flicked the switch on while Roger made himself comfortable.

"Help yourself." Jason placed a box of tea on the table along with an empty mug. He opened a new batch of goodies Tilly had sent back with him when he dropped off Stephanie on Saturday and arranged a small selection on a plate.

The water in the kettle boiled, and the switch flipped off on its own. Jason brought the kettle to the table, poured the boiled water over Roger's tea bag, and replaced it on its stand before settling into a chair across from his visitor.

"So, what brings you our way?"

Roger brushed cookie crumbs from his jacket. "Finally dug out Ms. Clark's car this morning." He brought the steaming mug of tea to his mouth.

"Is it fixable?" Maybe it wasn't as bad as he'd envisioned it could be considering the condition Stephanie had been in when she arrived.

Roger's thick eyebrows lifted. "At this point, it's not looking good. You can see for yourself. Got it hitched to the back of my truck." Roger paused and scanned the plate.

"Town'll need new posts for the sign. Doesn't look like the plaque survived the crash too well either. Cracks in the frame and letters falling off. Found the sign making itself home in the front seat of her car." He shoved another cookie in his mouth and reached for a napkin.

"That bad?" Jason's stomach dropped, a vision of Stephanie's ordeal flashing through his mind. The woman must have been positively terrified. Thank God she wasn't hurt more than she had been.

The mechanic nodded. "Is Ms. Clark here?"

"No, not yet." She'd texted earlier not to pick her up this morning. She wanted to verify something in town and would find a way in to the office on her own. He'd missed her company this morning on the ride in more than he cared to admit.

Roger wiped his hands on a napkin and rose. "Will you tell her I stopped by? I'll let you know what I find out once I get Ms. Clark's car in the shop. Not sure I'd want to fix a car as old as that one anyhow if she were mine." Roger's brow furrowed. "Probably better to find a car sooner than later what with the holidays coming."

Jason frowned and rubbed the back of his neck. He thought for sure Daddy would have suited her up with the latest model luxury sports car or some such thing. Either way, Stephanie would not be happy with that news.

"All right. Will you let me know as soon as possible what can be done with her car?" Jason pushed back the chair and stood.

Roger lifted stained fingers to his chin and rubbed the scruff along the ridge of his jaw. "Shop's full at the moment, but I'll see what I can do for Ms. Clark. Even if I could repair it, I might not get to it before Christmas. Had a backlog going on before we got hit with all this snow."

Small towns operated at their own pace, so the news wasn't surprising. It fell like Santa's sleigh after a long night of deliveries though. And if she wanted her car fixed—if it was even possible—then it wasn't likely Steph would find a way out of town for Christmas. The only place around here to purchase new or previously owned vehicles didn't have a huge selection, and those weren't exactly the kinds of cars the Clark family drove. Jason shoved a hand into his pocket and massaged the back of his neck. The thought of Stephanie being stranded here for Christmas made him feel... what? She loved family time at Christmas and made it pretty clear she needed to be there this year. He wanted her to be happy, but he wanted her to be with him.

Whoa. He was losing a grip.

"Sorry I didn't have better news for Ms. Clark." Roger put on his hat as they moved to the front entrance of *The Independent*.

148

"It's okay. We'll figure something out. Thanks for stopping by." Jason grabbed Roger's hand and shook it.

The town's mechanic stepped outside and pulled on heavy gloves while trudging across the parking lot.

Jason crossed his arms and examined the wreck chained to Roger's truck. Was that the same car she'd driven in college? She'd been so proud about that car. From the looks of things, Roger could probably use it for parts. It wouldn't be worth Stephanie's money to fix up the ancient red beast. He watched the red lights of the blue tow truck pause at the entrance of the parking lot and then disappear down the highway, pulling what was left of Stephanie's car behind. Maybe she hadn't changed all that much after all.

If there was a blessing in learning Stephanie was now stranded by the lack of transportation, Jason couldn't see it. He was thankful for her help and appreciated the glimpse of what it would be like to work with her again, but he hated the memories her presence stirred. The ultimatum from her senator father had already driven a wedge between them and would continue to tear them apart. Every time he saw Steph and breathed in the scent of her, the pain of chasing a story he'd never published stole any shred of peace he had left.

A gust of wind rattled the windowpane of the door in front of him.

He needed to get Stephanie to D.C. one way or another so he could bury the past for good.

The longer she hung around, the more likely he was to break his agreement with her father.

A promise that would surely tear Stephanie—his best friend—apart.

ELEVEN

Stephanie stomped the snow from her boots, loosened her scarf, and waved bye to Tilly. She'd been kind enough to drop off Stephanie after running some errands in town this morning. Mondays apparently were Tilly's designated errand day.

"Jason said he wanted to see you as soon as you arrived." The young woman behind the desk kept her eyes glued to the monitor. It looked like the girl who ran the classifieds and obits got moved to front desk duty today. So Jason was already trying to implement the staff changes she'd suggested, and streamline duties.

"Merry Christmas to you, too." Stephanie was sure the muttered greeting was lost on the girl. Her fingers didn't skip a beat as Stephanie wriggled free from her cumbersome winter coat. She slung it over her arm and started for the break room. It was nearly midmorning snack time, so a glass of juice would tide her over until she finished with Jason.

Five minutes, and several greetings to staffers later, she rapped on the battered door. It had seen better days.

She strained her ear. Muffled conversation filtered through the crack of the door, and the hum of Jason's tenor drew closer. She waited to be invited in.

"Great. You're here." Jason swung open the door, and his eyes were wide with... Was that relief or desperation? His jaw was set and his lips pulled back into a forced smile. What was going on, and what was with the death grip on that piece of paper in his hand?

Stephanie narrowed her gaze. "Yes."

She peered over his shoulder. A pair of long, slender legs encased in black nylon crossed at the knees and bounced the cutest ankle boots Stephanie had seen since arriving in Vermont. There was no reasonable explanation for the band cinching her stomach tight.

The door opened wider, and Jason stepped aside. "Kimberley, this is Stephanie Clark. She'll be joining us."

Yes, his smile was definitely forced, and the little twitch in the corner of his eye fired rapidly.

Stephanie stepped into the office and froze.

The owner of those long legs looked like a model fresh off the cover of a fashion magazine. Red hair, blue eyes, and the trendiest power suit, a pencil skirt ending at the knee with a stunning fitted jacket, likely from a high end boutique. This girl screamed high maintenance. What in the world was she doing here in the out-of-the-way town of Winterberry Falls? Did she crash her car, too?

"Ms. Clark, pleased to meet you." The woman floated from her chair and held out long slender fingers, her nails painted a fiery red. Stephanie took her hand and shook it. Not the delicate handshake she had imagined.

"So, Kimberley…" Stephanie glanced at Jason and back again. "What brings you to *The Independent*?"

Kimberley grinned, reached into her designer handbag, and pulled out an envelope. "Well, I saw the ad in the weekend edition, and I'm here about the news editor job. Here's another copy of my resume."

Stephanie's pulse skittered to a stop.

Jason couldn't seriously be considering hiring this woman to work with him. She didn't look a day older than twenty, and Winterberry Falls couldn't support her fashion addiction. She must have mixed up the job advertisement with another paper. After all, *The Independent* was a common enough name. It was likely her lines got crossed. The fumes from nail polish could confuse a person sometimes.

Stephanie snatched the envelope from Kimberley and tugged at the hem of her red sweater. The woman was serious. She was here for a job interview, though

Jason had neglected to inform her he was expecting someone.

The hot press of Jason's hand on Stephanie's back spurred her forward. Her head spun with his dizzying touch, and her nose stung with the bold scent of lilac. Stephanie teetered and leaned against the corner of the desk while Jason hid behind it. Coward.

"Why do you want to work here?" Stephanie infused a tone of professionalism into the question and laced it with a bit of frost. "It's a long way from New York City or any fashionable place." As evidenced by Stephanie's current attire. Jeans and a sweater—her vacation outfit of choice—was the normal dress code around here. Stephanie would be out of place if she wore half the items in her closet back in D.C.

Jason cleared his throat from behind his desk, and Stephanie shifted her position, feeling the glare he shot in her back. The man needed someone to watch out for his interests and for the moment, Stephanie was it.

An image of a cartoon mouse crossed Stephanie's mind as Kimberley laughed. "Yes, it is." She eased into the chair. "When I saw the ad on Saturday, I knew I had to come. I know I'll do well here. I graduated from a University in New York and have been working at various papers for the past two years. I also interned for one of the big New York papers. I realize I don't have the experience your ideal candidate would have, but everybody needs to start somewhere. I'm willing to work hard and believe *The Independent* can benefit from the skillsets I have. It's all right there in my resume and cover letter." Her kitten heel clapped the floor as Stephanie cast a look at Jason and frowned. With his nose buried in his copy of the woman's resume, he had no idea how ridiculous he looked. She should really lift his chin from the ground and give him a cloth to wipe off that gobsmacked expression.

"Thank you for stopping in, Kimberley. I hadn't realized we had a candidate lined up so soon." Jason cleared his throat behind her, and Stephanie slid to the center of his desk, blocking his view of Kimberley. "I didn't have a chance to review this in more detail prior to your arrival. I'll take a look at your resume when I have a moment. Is there anything else you'd like to add? Something we should know about you perhaps?" Stephanie clutched the envelope and studied the young woman, not wanting to even glance at the paper inside. Kimberley was put together and spoke like an educated woman. There was no earthly reason why Jason shouldn't consider her, especially if her resume was as professionally put together as the woman herself. Yet, Stephanie's stomach jolted at the very thought of Jason spending long hours working next to the red-headed beauty.

"I took the liberty of including a list of contacts, and I put together a portfolio of my work. It's all right here." She smiled sweetly. Leaning over the side of the chair, Kimberley pulled out another file from her over-sized designer bag. She rose and placed an inch thick folder on the desk. Close to Jason's elbow.

Stephanie watched Jason from her perch in the middle of his desk as he flipped through the woman's file—article clippings, magazine copy and papers testifying to the truth of the women's qualifications. Stephanie tugged at the collar of her sweater. Had someone turned up the heat in the building?

Let him deal with another file. Stephanie would rather focus on other things.

Like getting home and as far away as possible from Kimberley. And the disturbing sense of jealousy the woman's presence inspired. Stephanie should be happy Jason would have qualified help to ease his burdens. With a news editor in place, Stephanie had no reason to hang around the paper. Once she had wheels, she could be home in time for Christmas. Like she wanted.

"You're thorough," Jason said, admiration in the compliment. "I like that."

Stephanie averted her eyes, too slowly to miss the knowing look on his face.

"If you work here, there will be long hours. We can't pay what other papers in bigger cities do, but it's enough to make a living." Jason's statement confirmed what he was thinking. The woman was practically hired. One word from her and it was a done deal.

Kimberley shifted in her seat.

Good. She didn't want to be there.

"I'm okay with that." The young woman's small smile widened, revealing model-perfect teeth.

Stephanie drew a long breath. The woman had no idea what she would be in for working here. Stephanie used her nails to sharpen the fold of the envelope Kimberley had handed to her. "It's so refreshing to meet someone who is eager to jump right in." Stephanie pulled her lips into a tight smile. "If someone had told me I'd be working until all hours of the morning without overtime in an itty bitty town of no consequence, and little compensation for my passion and work ethic, I'm not sure I would be handling it as well as you."

Jason moved behind her, and Stephanie rushed ahead with her train of thought.

"But look at you, Kimberley." Stephanie gestured to the girl. "You know what you want and you go after it. It's an admirable trait."

Kimberley's body stiffened in the chair, adding fuel to Stephanie's rant.

"Winterberry Falls would be lucky to have someone like you heading the news department. I'm sure you've had lots of offers with better pay and better hours. Likely even some with benefits." Stephanie pressed her palms on Jason's desk, the envelope still clutched between her fingers. "By the way, where are you from?"

Jason cleared his throat.

The impulse to spin the negatives in positive light was irresistible and totally beneath her. She hated who she'd become in the throes of jealousy.

Kimberley smoothed down her charcoal pencil skirt. "New York City."

"Ahh." Stephanie shifted her weight on Jason's work space and crossed her ankles. "The Big Apple. The City of Dreams. The City that Never Sleeps."

Kimberley released a nervous laugh. Her eyes darted from Stephanie's face to something behind Stephanie's shoulder, the young woman's features pulled tight. Jason's office chair creaked. He must be ready to wrap things up. Stephanie uncrossed her ankles and slid her feet to the floor, her weight still supported by the frame of the desk.

"Well, I can tell you that this town definitely sleeps. Everything closes after five when it's not festival season. Everything but the diner and *The Independent*. News never sleeps you know."

A hand clamped on her shoulder, jolting Stephanie from her monologue. Stephanie looked up at Jason and swallowed the lump in her throat.

"Stephanie has a way with words, doesn't she?" The ice in his eyes matched the coldness of his tone as he glared down at her. She dropped her gaze from his marked expression, finding a spot on her boot more interesting.

Kimberley's laugh was enough to make Stephanie cringe. "No worries, Jason."

Her skin crawled at the syrupy pronunciation of *Jason*.

"I worked hard in University and learned to live on few hours of sleep. Some of my best pieces came from those days, and I included them in my portfolio."

Jason's grip on her shoulder was like iron. Stephanie winced. Now was probably a good time to keep her mouth shut. Warning heeded.

"Thanks for stopping by, Kimberley. I'll take some time to review your portfolio, and I'll get back to you." His tone was all politeness. Maybe he wasn't as upset with her as she thought.

Kimberley rose and nodded. She wore a charming smile, probably meant only for Jason. "Thank you for your time." She bent gracefully and threaded her slender arm through the handles of her purse where it still sat on the floor.

"Just one more question, Kimberley, if you don't mind."

Stephanie bristled, and Jason squeezed her shoulder tighter.

She frowned. She might as well be invisible for all the attention she was getting now. The young woman's eyes focused on Jason. If Stephanie wasn't mistaken, those runway gorgeous eyes twinkled ever so slightly.

"We're looking to fill the position right away. When would you be available to start if we were to offer you the position?" His delivery was calm and curious. He really was considering hiring her. Well, good for him.

Kimberley's tone was coated in chocolate sprinkles. "I'd need some time to arrange things." One perfectly shaped eyebrow arched. "Day after Christmas? A week from Thursday?"

Jason chuckled. "Is that a question?"

Kimberley's laugh grated Stephanie's frayed nerves. "No, it's not. I can start a week from Thursday."

Jason guided Kimberley to the office door and out through the newsroom where staff were busy working away.

Stephanie rubbed her shoulder and waited for their chatter to die away before opening the girl's resume. She moved to the seat Kimberley had vacated and sat. Scanning the page, her chest thundered with the erratic rhythm of her heart.

The young woman was impeccably qualified and looked like she knew what she was doing. Stephanie flipped to the last page and blew a wisp of hair from her face. Kimberley included glowing letters of reference and heavy endorsements from previous positions.

Stephanie was such an idiot.

"What was that all about?" Jason's voice thundered, and the door slammed behind him when he returned. The collection of wall photos shook with the vibration and pages from files near the door flew to the ground.

Tread carefully, Stephanie...

If looks could kill, Stephanie would already be roadkill.

She offered the sweetest smile she could muster. "What was what all about?"

Jason jammed his fingers in his hair and shot her a cold look, sending a shiver of sleet through her veins.

She'd crossed the line for a brief moment of green insanity. Which was ridiculous. She was not jealous, even if she clearly acted that way. *God, what's wrong with me?*

"I needed your support, Steph." He nearly growled. "Not some crazy woman with poisonous darts spewing from her mouth."

The comment drove a knife deep into her gut, shame stinging her eyes with unwanted tears. Her chin quivered. But she would not cave. "And I thought you needed a news editor, not some red-headed, blue-eyed..." The words stuck in her mouth as her chest heaved. She couldn't be mean to a woman who was qualified for the position.

Jason's eyes sparked and then softened, his hands dropping to his sides.

The smile tugging at his lips exposed the slightest hint of a dimple on his left side. Stephanie lowered her gaze and fiddled with a piece of lint on her pant leg. His footsteps treaded lightly across the floor, stopping next to her chair. The man didn't have enough sense to stay on his side of the room, but there was no bossing this guy around. Her eyelids sank closed. His closeness overpowered her.

She needed to leave Winterberry Falls before she hit rock bottom. There wasn't enough chocolate or diet soda in the world to nurse a broken heart the second time around.

"Is there something you want to tell me?" The low pitch teased her, and she trembled beneath his spell.

If he only knew…

Stephanie opened her eyes, inhaled a noisy breath, and ignored the fervor in his stare. Time for a subject change. "Do you know a Mrs. Sweeney?"

He stepped back. His eyes seemed to study her, worry crossing his features. "My really old third-grade teacher?"

Stephanie shrugged. "I got a request to meet her at the retirement center this afternoon, something about the *Baby Jesus* story that ran on Saturday. I thought I might borrow your vehicle if that's okay. I finished my report of the gingerbread house contest this morning and sent it to the copy desk. I'm almost done with the second installment for the caper series. I'll have it in by deadline. I'm just curious as to what Mrs. Sweeney has to say. Where are your keys?"

Jason's eyes narrowed, and he held her gaze. He fished his keys out of his pocket and handed them to her. She took them from his hand and offered a polite smile. Stephanie rose, tossed Kimberley's resume on the desk, and tried to brush past him. Her breath caught when he blocked her with a gentle, but firm hand on her wrist. The tender touch of his thumb all but stole her composure. Her gaze focused on the fingers wrapped around her wrist and journeyed up his arm until she met eyes pooled with concern.

She swallowed hard, wishing strength into her weak petition. "Please let me go." Tears pricked her eyes as she stared at him.

A nerve pulsed in his cheek, and Stephanie's breaths grew raspy.

One minute more and she wouldn't have the strength to leave.

"Please." Her voice cracked, her eyes pleading with him.

Jason nodded, and his shoulders heaved as he exhaled.

Not a moment too soon, he released his grip, his touch still burning a memory into her skin. Stephanie raced from his office, her cheeks hot as her resolve to resist his charms weakened.

Why, oh why was she here?

For the thousandth time since crashing into town, Stephanie wished she'd crashed someplace else.

\#

The Fallsview Retirement and Assisted Living Center, nestled at the bottom of Bread Loaf Mountain, struck Stephanie as welcoming and warm despite the lack of Christmas decorations that the rest of the town held in spades.

When Stephanie cared to mention that fact, Mrs. Sweeney, a long-term resident and retired elementary teacher, scowled. Apparently it was a sore spot in the otherwise contented life she lived at the home.

Mrs. Sweeney sipped from her fine China floral teacup while she swayed in her wooden rocker in the corner of her bedroom suite. She turned the bluest of eyes toward Stephanie. "Thank you, Ms. Clark, for coming to see me. It's not often I have such a distinguished visitor to host." A kind and sincere smile turned up the corners of her pale, thin lips.

Stephanie savored the minty warmth of the tea and replaced her own delicate cup on the table, careful to keep the beverage from jostling. It was just the balm she needed.

She pushed back her bracelet and tucked it beneath her sleeve. "Thank you for having me here, Mrs. Sweeney."

Mrs. Sweeney dabbed at her mouth with a lace-edged linen napkin and swept it across her lap where it stayed. "That's such a lovely bracelet, dear. He must love you very much." Mrs. Sweeney pushed her glasses down to the front of her nose as she leaned forward, withered finger pointing to Stephanie's wrist.

Stephanie's cheeks heated. Why was she still wearing the gift from Daniel? If a stranger could tell it was a gift of love, then maybe Stephanie had led the poor man on without realizing it.

"Oh, dear. I fear I've made you uncomfortable." She clicked her tongue and patted the back of Stephanie's hand.

The older woman reclined in her rocking chair, the rhythmic sway of the chair squeaking with every push of her feet. A walking cane clattered to the floor nearby, and Stephanie righted it again, earning a beaming smile.

"Like you, dear, I love a good story." Her mouth relaxed, her clear blue eyes seeming to focus on a distant memory. "Do you know I was in love with a newspaper man once?" Her eyes twinkled. She rested her gray head against the back of the chair.

"Of course, Mother didn't approve. He was a nosy busybody who made it his business to report on every Tom, Dick, and Harry's escapades and then charged people to read it." The girlish laugh brought an image to Stephanie's mind of a much younger woman.

"What happened?" Stephanie shifted on the edge of the bed where she sat.

"I listened to Mother. I didn't marry Charlie. I married Matthias." Her expression softened at the mention of her husband's name. "Matthias was a good and kind man. He owned the bank, so Mother was pleased with the match." Her face moved through a series of emotions Stephanie couldn't quite decipher.

Mrs. Sweeney inhaled and brought a wrinkled hand to her chest. "We had a good life together." She picked up her cane and used it to point to a photo on the bureau. "That's my Matthias on his seventy-fifth birthday. We had a humdinger of a celebration. He helped a lot of people in this town during troubling times, so it was only fitting we throw him a big birthday bash." She laughed. "Ever see a seventy-five-year-old man swing dance? Boy, could he ever!" She shuffled her feet and hummed a lively melody. Stephanie giggled as Mrs. Sweeney moved her shoulders up and down in time with her dancing eyebrows, her song growing louder.

"Matthias and I had some good times together, but sometimes I wondered what my life would have been if I'd married Charlie." Tenderness infused her voice at the mention of her long-gone newspaper man, and Stephanie's heart filled with empathy. It seemed like Mrs. Sweeney's story was a future telling of Stephanie's own if she chose the "safe" way. The woman had loved two men and married the one who made the most sense, yet there was still a longing in her elderly heart…

"Ach. Look at me. I'm such a ninny when it comes to sappy romance. Charlie could woo a pig." Mrs. Sweeney paused her rocking and sipped from her cup once more. "God's plan was for me to marry Matthias, not Charlie. God gave us such a beautiful life."

She replaced her tea things on the small, round table next to her and leaned on her cane, wobbling to her feet. Stephanie stood and braced the older woman's feeble arms and waited for her to steady. Mrs. Sweeney squeezed Stephanie's arm and hobbled to the door. She shut it, clicked the lock, and stood with her back to Stephanie for a moment before shuffling around on her heel. Stephanie raised an eyebrow and focused on the curious woman.

"I've read your article, Ms. Clark, and there are some details missing that are essential to getting your story right." Her face grew stern, the picture of a school Marm. "I have a confession to make, but you must promise to help me achieve my ends and to not print a word of truth until after Christmas Day."

Stephanie narrowed her eyes, studying the determined woman before her. She would listen to her confession and then convince the old woman to change her mind, because Stephanie planned to be long gone before then.

She pulled her pad and pen from her purse and looked up at the woman, indicating nothing.

"Good." Mrs. Sweeney waddled to the bureau standing against the wall at the foot of her bed. She tapped her cane on the floor and rummaged through the top drawer, heavy breathing filling the quiet room.

"This is my James. He's police chief and is wise beyond his years." She turned and winked. "He has to be with a mother like me."

Stephanie smiled and took the photo from Mrs. Sweeney's outstretched hand. A young, distinguished-looking man in a police uniform smiled at the camera, the resemblance to his mother evident.

"What I'm about to tell you is no secret to Winterberry Falls' men in blue, but it is to the rest of the town. And this is a secret that must be kept at all costs." Mrs. Sweeney's gaze swept over Stephanie from head to toe and back up again. "At least until Christmas Day."

Stephanie rolled her eyes inwardly and poised her pen over her pad of paper. Nothing could be *that* imperative a secret when it came to an elderly retired teacher living in a retirement community on the edge of town.

"Now, dear, about that secret…"

TWELVE

"You're not going to get the interview if you don't at least wait your turn."

Stephanie shot Jason a slanted look. "If you think for one minute I'm going to stand in that line and—"

"You've got to stand in line if you want to get the story. No one's going to take too kindly to you butting ahead to see Santa." Jason's hand swept across the line of eager participants and restless children. It looked like a sea of people from her vantage point at the entrance of the large tent.

She crossed her arms. She needed this interview to verify Mrs. Sweeney's admission. And once that was done, she was so out of here. Stephanie had hinted enough to Jason without breaking her noncommittal promise to Mrs. Sweeney, or breaking trust with her source, that the police of Winterberry

Falls knew exactly what was going on, but weren't doing their job. Stephanie huffed. Enough of this town, secrets, and the blue-eyed newspaper man who threw her composure into mush and her senses into spin cycle.

"Like I said, if you want the interview, you have to follow the rules." Jason's left eyebrow rose, something akin to irritation written across his face.

She knew she shouldn't have asked Jason to come with her to interview the chief of police. He was still upset with her performance yesterday morning and would make this tough on her. Part of her wanted him at the interview to prove her hunch was right. And that his was wrong. If waiting in line was the way to get what she wanted…

Fine. She could be tough, too.

"I've never been great at following rules." Stephanie tossed her hair behind her shoulders and relaxed her arms.

Jason's guffaw carried above the crowded room. "Says Miss-Never-Break-The-Rules. Nice try." His eyes narrowed. "You're in my town now. And I say, if you want the interview, you gotta wait in line."

Stephanie clenched her teeth and scrambled for some reason Jason would accept. "I'm a member of the press. I should be able to jump the queue."

The quip did nothing to sway his stoic stance.

Heat throbbed in the tips of her ears. He likely saw right through her. His hardened expression, frozen into place, sent a nervous tingle down her spine. She bit the inside of her cheek and forced order to her scattered thoughts. Hopefully, she had just one last caper article to write, and then she could leave the rest of Emily's deadlines to Jason. Or to *Kimberley*. No ridiculously attractive man with strong arms, a chiseled chin sporting a five o'clock shadow, who was a brilliant photographer and a good temporary editor-in-chief was going to stop her. His concern about the safety of his staff through a storm, his care for her, and his loyalty to his family's well-being was admirable. So what? He worked hard and ran the paper as if it was his own, but it didn't mean he could boss her around. Even if he did have power to veto her story.

"Not gonna happen. And I'm here to make sure you follow the rules." The slight shake of Jason's head and the turn of his lips into a knowing smile caused an aggravating flutter in her stomach.

"Okay, fine." Stephanie huffed again, unzipped her jacket, and joined the line.

This would not do.

Nearby, the freestanding mounted speakers piped songs of Christmas into the crowd, pushing her patience level over the limit. No Christmas spirit from this reporter today. Stephanie had a solid theory about the missing decorations, but the secret Mrs. Sweeney had shared left it full of holes. An interview with the chief of police could put the story to rest, giving her time to focus on other things. Like how to get home for Christmas.

Scanning the long line ahead of her, Stephanie related to the little boy jumping from one foot to another. The boy and his mother stood ten people and one turn ahead in the winding queue, about four turns before Stephanie's intended target.

Heat permeated her upper body despite the nip in the makeshift tent outside the general store. She shrugged off her jacket.

A movement at her side pulled her focus from people watching. Jason grunted as he slid beneath the barrier to stand next to her.

"You don't have to check up on me, you know. I can be a good girl and follow the rules. If you want to go back to the office, I'll be fine on my own. I'll walk back to the B&B. It's not far from here." Stephanie draped her jacket across her arm and held it against her stomach. He was smart enough to pick up the hint, so why was he staying? Right. Because she'd been silly enough to ask him to join her.

Heady scents filled her senses as Jason stretched to his full height next to her. Stephanie would never look the same way at soap again. And chocolate—another of Cocoa Cabin's specials if she were to guess. Now that was just plain cruel, even to a diabetic. How could she hate chocolate?

"You did ask me to come so the least I can do is keep you company."

Stephanie wrinkled her nose and kicked herself for that one. "I just want to wrap this story up." And escape home to D.C.

Jason nodded. A flash of emotion crossed his face and disappeared as quickly as it had come. "I know. And then, you can be home in time for Christmas."

Christmas in D.C. That's what she wanted, wasn't it? To be home with her parents and to officially step into the role Daniel offered her, paving the way to her own public relations firm. To go back to a fast-paced life where appearances mattered and the selfless acts of friendship were only found in novels or those feel good holiday movies. To dress in the latest fashions and purchase the latest gadgets. To be invited to private dinner parties with the Washington elite while wearing a plastic smile and telling everyone she was "fine" and to "hold the sweets."

Stephanie slid a hand across her throat to still her racing pulse. The sudden intensity in the whirlpool depths of Jason's eyes ripped the seams she'd sewn around her heart.

Her carefully constructed professional façade crumbled, and she swallowed hard as the weight of her future sucked the breath from her.

"Am I making a mistake?"

\#

She was making a mistake. Taking the job with Daniel and going back to D.C. when Jason needed her here had to be the wrong choice. He watched the deep chocolate of Steph's eyes swirl with questions he was ill qualified to answer. She held his gaze, his own fears and uncertainty reflected there. How could he let her go again when she was the light that filled the dark spaces of his life? She was needed here, not in D.C. where she would wither into a faded flower left in the overcrowded field. Winterberry Falls was good for her. In the week she'd been here, she'd blossomed into the vibrant reporter and compassionate friend he'd known in college. But how could he ask her to stay, when it would violate his promise to protect her always? Or how could he let her go again when his heart had never recovered the first time?

The protective side of him wanted to pull her close and solve all her problems. All it would take was one word from him.

Jason held back from caressing her cheek to assure her everything would work out.

But whatever brought on the question was something she needed to figure out for herself.

Her query didn't mean he couldn't persuade her on another topic though.

Something less painful than breaking their hearts all over again.

Stephanie had returned from her interview with Mrs. Sweeney convinced the police were up to no good. She hadn't relayed anything from her visit, other than the need to talk to Chief Sweeney. But reading between the lines, Jason had a hypothesis about Stephanie's agenda today. "If you mean to rat out an upstanding citizen of our town, then yes, you are making a mistake."

A flash of lightning blazed across eyes. She pulled her shoulders back, her body stiff with defiance. "I'm not a rat." She stepped closer, her nose inches from his chin.

Jason shook his head. "I didn't say you were."

"I'm following a lead I believe has merit. And if it turns out to be what I think, the truth has to be reported. If the police chief knows about the thefts and isn't doing anything about it, then he's not doing his job. The community deserves to know." The fury in her eyes wasn't enough to melt the ice in the accusation. At least she had the wisdom to keep her voice low enough for only Jason to hear in this crowded tent.

Truth was a worthy pursuit, but in this case, she was out for blood. He wasn't about to let Senator Clark's daughter desecrate one of Winterberry Falls' most dedicated and trustworthy citizens for the sake of the twenty-five inches he'd allotted for each article. A running story she'd write, three or four articles at most, leaving a mess for him to clean up when she was gone.

The irony struck him squarely in the face.

For the first time in twelve years, he understood the senator's position.

"Is it really about finding the truth, Steph? Or are you just following your emotions? From where I'm standing, this is not a fact-finding interview." Jason's chest hammered with the echo of years gone by. The arguments she used now were the same ones the young reporter in him used against her father.

Stephanie's face flushed a deep red. Fire couldn't be hotter than a determined woman. Or in this case, a determined woman he'd just offended.

Jason pressed cold fingers against her parted lips, the heat from her breath searing his skin. He breathed a prayer for words she'd understand.

"You're willing to sacrifice a man's reputation, his job, his family, and the safety of this town for the sake of a story that has nothing to do with what you're supposed to be writing about." A nerve pulsed in his cheek, and his heart hammered. Jason stuffed the anger back inside and reminded himself he'd been on the other side of this argument before. He could extend her a bit of grace mixed with understanding, even if she was out to bury the chief.

A cold and clammy hand wrapped around his fingers and yanked his arm away with surprising force. "And what am I supposed to be writing about, if not the truth?" She nearly spat the words.

Jason sucked in a steady draw of stale winter air. "The story I assigned you is about Christmas decorations gone missing and the people who want them back."

He watched the fury fade from behind dark lashes. The crowd moved forward, and the music track changed to a pleasant up-tempo carol, but her feet didn't budge.

Something stirred his heart as he watched the silent struggle on her face, his own pain constricting his chest. *God, help her to let this go.* An assurance filled his soul. How he'd missed praying all these years.

Somehow, he knew God was in control, and this conversation where his past decision collided with the present, as painful and strange as it was, was part of God's plan.

Stephanie spun on her heel and stepped ahead with the others. She fiddled with her jacket, and Jason waited for her to look at him.

A hearty "ho, ho, ho" riddled the electrified atmosphere as another satisfied child skipped from Santa's chair, candy cane in hand.

Stephanie nearly whispered when she finally spoke. "I have a source who not only told me what's going on, but heavily indicated that even the chief of police already knows and is doing nothing about it."

Jason studied her profile, her eyes focused ahead. "An eighty-seven-year-old woman living on the outskirts of town in a retirement home and who is a known storyteller."

She glanced up, the fire gone from her eyes. "His mother."

Jason shook his head and shoved his hands into his pocket. "Still not a reliable source. And if she's your only source, you'll need more than that."

Stephanie's lips inched into a smug smile. "Which is why I'm standing in line waiting to interview—"

"Santa Claus." Jason smirked.

"…my lead." Her smile slipped, and he chuckled.

Holding in a sigh, Jason focused on the back of the head of the mother in front of him, her little boy tugging on the yellow rope of the queue.

It was no use trying to convince Stephanie to lay off pursuing this lead. He knew her too well and knew she would get the details she wanted. However, as the editor-in-chief, he had final say in what was printed and could wait until she handed in her assignment to challenge her again, if needed. Perhaps he should trust her enough to write a compelling story, but to leave allegations and accusations alone.

"Look, the truth is out there, and I want to find it. Anyone who is entrusted to a public office is accountable for their actions." Her sigh filled with resignation, and Jason's gut knotted with her statement. Her words were a reflection of a belief he'd held tightly to, but understood too well how devastating the truth could turn out to be.

If only she knew how many times truth slipped through the cracks.

"The constituency deserves the truth and to know what kind of person has been put in a position of trust.

If the chief is hiding something, the people of Winterberry Falls have the right to know about it." Her gaze softened as she swept her hand across the crowded room, over the children who rocked on feet, jumped, and tugged on hands of indulgent parents, eagerly anticipating Santa's fulfillment of their deepest wishes.

"Like that dad over there with his kid. Doesn't he have the right to know if the police are keeping his family safe?"

Jason looked in the direction she was pointing and watched the pair interact. The little boy's mouth moved at a rapid pace, and the dad nodded along as if hanging on to every word.

If he were a dad, wouldn't he want the same assurance for his family? To celebrate Christmas in a community that was protected by honest people?

Jason sighed in retreat.

Christmas was hard enough for some families. He didn't want to be responsible for making it worse by printing a story that could divide the community. It had the potential to invite bigger trouble than just some random Christmas decorations going missing.

She ambled ahead with the others in line, but Jason stayed next to the dividing rope.

He thanked God for the woman she'd become, a defender of justice and one who sought to keep leaders accountable. An idealist in the middle of a political production.

Thank God he hadn't destroyed her life back then. If he hadn't agreed to her father's ultimatum, her family would have shattered, leaving Stephanie fatherless.

He moved ahead, filling the gap his woolgathering had caused and offered an apologetic smile to the frazzled mother behind them.

He leaned over, his breath stirring wisps of Stephanie's hair at her temple. "I agree with you."

She turned her head, eyes wide.

A stray eyelash sat on her cheek, and Jason held back the urge to brush it away. Why was she the only woman to make him wish for things he could never have? He closed his eyes. This persistent attraction to the senator's daughter had to stop.

"Which part?" Her whisper swept across his troubled soul.

"That truth must prevail." Lifting heavy lids, he willed a steadiness in his tone. A strange, but not wholly unwelcome, feeling tightened his stomach. "Still, you have to ask yourself something first."

Stephanie's boots scuffed the ground as she angled her body closer to his. A little too close. "What's that?"

The intonation of her voice, smooth as silk, chipped away at the ice around his heart. If not for the same question he'd had to ask himself a million times over, the trust in her eyes would melt it completely.

"Are you prepared to live with the responsibility of destroying another man's family, for the sake of your story?"

Sadness masked her expression as she stepped back. Stephanie stared at him so long he wondered if she'd finally figured it out. If he didn't need to break his promised silence because of the intuitive woman she was.

A child nearby screamed for candy, and Stephanie's gaze flicked to stare at the scene. Jason backed away and ducked beneath the barrier. With the fussy child appeased and Stephanie still watching the family, he turned and strode toward the open flap of the tent, leaving the mayhem of Christmas behind him. He prayed with all his might Stephanie would do the right thing.

And leave Chief Sweeney alone.

THIRTEEN

After what seemed like an entire afternoon wasted waiting in line for her turn to tell Santa all she wanted for Christmas was the police department's response to the Christmas Caper articles she was writing, Stephanie had spent another hour waiting at the police station for Santa to grant her request. She finally settled into a seat in the chief of police's office and pulled her notebook and pen from her purse.

"What can you tell me about the missing items around town?" She held her pen poised above the paper like a kitten ready to pounce on a mouse. The still-costumed man sat on the corner of his desk facing her, but said nothing. Who would want to put Santa Claus behind bars at Christmas?

Apparently, she did.

Jason's words had softened her resolve and edited her accusation about sweeping petty crime under the rug. But it was still unsettling, the man who gawked at her beneath his fake white eyebrows.

The chief pulled off his floppy red hat and white curly wig, revealing a full head of matted graying hair. He folded the costume pieces and placed them next to his spot on the desk.

"I've read your articles. Your writing is impressive, and your investigative skills are to be commended, but Ms. Clark, my mother is the one you should interview. She has a much better story to tell than I do." He removed the impeccable white gloves one finger at a time. He seemed to study Stephanie for a moment and offered a kind smile.

"Whenever hard times fell here in town, my mother was a guardian angel to more than one family. A child would come to school in the middle of winter without gloves and Mom would have a pair for them the next day. She'd place the items on the child's hook and never say a word." He gestured to a framed picture of Agnes Sweeney on the wall behind his office chair. "When the recession hit, Mom single-handedly started the soup kitchen from the community church's basement at the ripe age of seventy-five, and when the boys, some of my family members included, didn't come home from 'Nam…" His voice caught, a shimmer of emotion in his eyes. "It was Mom who held this community together."

Stephanie recalled the kind old women she'd met and could see the truth in what Chief Sweeney was telling her. She doodled at the top of her page. But if everything she had confided in Stephanie was true and there was a greater purpose in what was going on, what would it do to the woman's heart to see her son in jail for helping her? Or what officer would arrest a sweet old lady who'd done so much good for the community?

The chief shrugged out of his red coat, stood, and then reached for the over-sized hanger dangling from the back of his office door. He paused the commentary and drew the faux fur-lined sleeves of his Santa coat across the wired frame, swept a hand down the front of his costume, and replaced the hanger over the hook.

"Candy?" He held out a glass jar filled with candy canes.

Stephanie waved her hand in front of her face. "No thanks. Diabetic."

He set the jar back down and settled into his modest, but comfortable-looking chair. He pressed the tips of his fingers together, his brow creasing.

"Where are you from, Ms. Clark?"

What does that have to do with my question? Stephanie gripped her pen tighter.

"Most recently, Washington, D.C."

His fingers danced together. "And before that?"

Stephanie's eyebrow arched. "Montpelier." What did the capital of Vermont have to do with anything?

So far, his line of questioning was going nowhere except to establish she wasn't from Winterberry Falls.

The chief puckered his lips.

"Ever live in a town like ours, Ms. Clark?" His voice boomed across the room. Stephanie cringed inwardly at the thought of being interrogated by him as a criminal.

"No, sir."

The glued-on eyebrows formed a deep V as they touched together. "Then, Ms. Clark, there's something you need to understand before you start stirring the pot with the story you seem to be implying here."

Stephanie straightened in her chair, smoothed down the page of her notebook, and clicked open her pen.

"I'm the chief of police in this town, and people trust me to keep them safe. I grew up here. They all know me and elected me to head their law enforcement."

Stephanie's pen hovered above the blank page.

Chief Sweeney dropped his hands and ran them across the worn arms of his chair. "Believe me when I say this, Ms. Clark, the citizens of Winterberry Falls are in no danger. Christmas decorations have gone missing, and we will pursue the matter." He lifted his foot still in a shiny black boot and rested it across his red-clad knee. He tugged at the heel of the gold-buckled boot and set it on the floor. He switched feet and worked off the other boot.

"When?" Her voice was firm and sounded every bit the professional she was.

"When, what?" He narrowed his eyes.

"People deserve to know if their chief is sweeping petty crime under the rug because it would otherwise implicate his own mother. Where I'm from, that's called nepotism. When will you pursue the matter?" Stephanie's neck heated as her pen scribbled gibberish across her page, an attempt to avoid the piercing gaze directed at her.

"Is that a threat, Ms. Clark?" His voice deepened, and Stephanie looked up.

"It's a fact, Chief Sweeney."

The older man dropped his sock-clad foot to the floor, his face unreadable, an excellent trait for a policeman. "Well, here's another fact for you. The WFPD takes threats seriously, veiled or otherwise." The stare held very little of the warmth she'd witnessed while Santa Sweeney had entertained children and listened to Christmas wishes.

Stephanie bristled, but clamped her mouth together. She should have listened to Jason and left the chief alone.

The seconds dragged into hours before the chief's features softened.

"Tell you what." He peeled back the fake eyebrows, and Stephanie winced.

"I promise you'll have a story—maybe not the one you want—but you'll have your Christmas story that will explain… the matter clearly." A hint of a smile tugged at his lips. "You just have to be a bit more patient. When the festival slows down a bit, I'll give you your interview. After all, Christmas decorations have been reported missing."

He moved both boots to a shoe tray next to his filing cabinet where a pair of black shoes sat.

"Now, if you'll excuse me, Ms. Clark, duty calls me to shed the rest of this getup and don my blues." His stood and extended his hand to Stephanie.

Be kind, Stephanie. He promised you a story and that's the reason why you came. You'll just have to wait a bit longer for it. Meanwhile, this new development gave her time to verify whether Mrs. Sweeney's secret was fact. Or fiction.

She gathered her things and shook the chief's hand.

"I suggest that instead of working so hard that you take time to enjoy the full extent of the remaining festivities in our merry month of mistletoe. A young gal like you needs to have some fun once in a while, and there's no better place than Winterberry Falls in December to do just that."

#

Jason snatched a piece of paper with lists of gibberish on it, scrunched it up, and tossed it toward the garbage can next to his filing cabinet across the room. He missed. His temples ached from clenching his teeth nonstop since he left Stephanie in line at Santa's Village.

Stephanie was going to bury the police chief's career with her hard line against him. Whatever the old schoolteacher had said to Stephanie, it was enough to send her after the chief of police. And there wasn't anything anyone could do to change the determined woman's mind.

Jason grunted.

The apple didn't fall far from the tree. Senator Clark had gotten his way, and it appeared Stephanie was following his footsteps. He hoped she'd been smart enough to keep things private instead of launching into her questions while other children waited to sit on Santa's lap. Politics was in her blood, and it was no wonder the PR job was something she was considering. Daniel would no doubt win his campaign with Stephanie by his side, and likely her heart as well.

Jason shuffled his feet across the fading carpet, picked up the wad of paper, and chucked it into the can this time. He leaned an elbow on top of the cabinet and stared aimlessly at the wall.

Why did he care about Daniel's campaign anyway? He was hundreds of miles away and whether he won the Attorney General seat or not had nothing to do with Jason.

Unless Stephanie joined him there.

He jammed a hand through his matted hair and rubbed his face.

He was in charge of *The Winterberry Falls' Independent* and had warned her she was pursuing the wrong story for her next article in the running series. He shouldn't worry about what to do until she turned it in. And even if he refused to print it, facing her anger was better than letting her do to the chief the one thing Jason had refused to do to her and her family. He'd killed his article; he could kill hers, too.

His stomach knotted. History tended to repeat itself in some way or another.

Senator Clark's U.S. Senate election campaign had had all the makings of a cover-up that a much younger Jason Miller had been eager to reveal. Had he chosen to actually write what he knew...

Jason shook his head. How quickly he forgot God. God was bigger than the senator and could do the impossible. After all, Christ left Heaven to become a little baby. The Christmas season, or his personal troubles, shouldn't have to remind him that God could take care of Jason's paper and the community of Winterberry Falls.

And Stephanie. No matter where she was, or what she decided to do, God would take care of her, too.

"Mr. Miller, may I have a moment?" Anna's voice pulled him from his musing. Jason dropped his elbow from the cabinet and looked at the middle-aged bookkeeper, standing in the doorway with a stack of papers cradled in her arm. Her dark eyes carried a hint of excitement.

"It depends. Do you have good or bad news?" A nerve in his cheek twitched.

"I think you'll be pleased." She grinned as she settled into the vacant chair. He rolled his office chair from behind his desk and sat in it next to her. She rearranged papers and held out a thin clipped bundle for Jason.

"You've done well, Mr. Miller, and will continue to do so if you follow the plan you outlined in your email to me last week. After reviewing the summary of where we can be more efficient and with the proposed steps to acquire new subscribers and advertisers, I'm happy with the projected numbers. Ms. Clark's ideas implemented with your own will have an impact on the bottom line for next quarter." Her voice was firm, but motherly.

Jason leaned back and slid off the paper clip, pulling the bundle apart. He studied the columns of numbers and text summarizing the information.

His eyes grew wide as he skimmed the projections on the last sheet Anna handed him. "Are you serious? We'll be in the black again?"

Anna nodded.

"Yes, Mr. Miller. With your juggling of staffing responsibilities and the proposed plans for marketing, subscriptions, and online presence, the numbers show

The Independent could be... well, independent once again."

Anna explained the details, and Jason caught her enthusiasm. The longer Anna spoke, the lighter the burden of running the paper became. The tightness in his chest had eased by the time she finished.

"So, it will be a Merry Christmas after all." Jason's nervous laugh brought a larger-than-life smile to her matronly face.

"Yes, it will." She patted his shoulder.

Jason rose, placed the updated files on his desk, and thanked Anna as she left.

He watched the snowflakes cascade outside. The tails of the red bows hanging from the lantern in front of the aging building swayed in the late afternoon breeze, reminding him of how close Christmas was. One of the staffers must have noticed the lack of décor around here and dug out the box of Christmas decorations in the basement. Jason should have decorated weeks ago since the holiday was around the corner.

One week away.

He leaned against the wall, and the tension melted with visions of happy times around the Christmas tree and holiday gatherings with family. His wish this year was for his brother and sister to come home with their significant others, and a healthier version of his dad while his mom fussed over every detail of the celebration.

Family. That's what this time was about.

However, a round of laughter from the newsroom reminded him there was still work to do before he could sit with his family again. Maybe he'd go to the Christmas candlelight service this year. His mom would be thrilled.

But until then, there was another week of around-the-clock-reporting on the Merry Month of Mistletoe festival.

The Character Breakfast, Shortbread Bake-Off, and Carol Karaoke would be the highlights of the rest of the week before the Community Live Nativity next week on Christmas Eve night. He had two reporters ready to cover the events, but he could only think of one he'd like to attend with him, despite her determination to vilify their town's Man in Red.

Would she still be here then? Or would she have left him with a mess to clean up in the community?

Jason sagged into his chair.

Less than a week until Stephanie shook the snow of their little town from her boots for good.

This past week had shown him what it was like to have a good woman by his side. Stephanie challenged him in ways only she could. And he was better for it.

Jason was planning on attending church services this coming Sunday, and he was already talking to God again because of her.

The Independent would keep running because Steph gave him a kick in the pants.

How could he let her go?

Jason's eyes grew hot as he imagined the rest of his life without her. He could survive again if he knew she was happy. But this time, it would be different. This time he would trust God to see him through.

Jason wriggled his nose.

One more week of keeping his word to guard her father's secret.

A promise he never should have made in the first place.

FOURTEEN

Stephanie scowled as she threw her notebook onto Jason's desk, scattering papers and pens across the crowded space. She had stewed all night about her interview with the chief of police and blamed her lack of story progress on her temporary boss.

Jason looked up from his place behind the computer, the lines in his face deepened, a mixture of annoyance and curiosity. "Should I even ask how it went yesterday?"

If she could scowl more, she would. Stephanie huffed and crossed her arms while her fingers drummed against her sweater. The steady tap of her boot-clad toes did nothing to release the pent-up energy she'd built since leaving the police station yesterday.

"He's definitely hiding something, but he's not willing to talk." Yet. Stephanie couldn't help the whine from creeping into her voice. The urge to stomp her foot and pout until Christmas was next to impossible to ignore.

The chief gave her nothing... and yet, everything. But the fact she had zilch to quote made her regret the time spent in line at Santa's Village and waiting at the station for Santa to finish his shift with all the little kids.

She tugged at the collar of her turtleneck. Someone should really turn down the heat in this building.

Maybe her sugars were low. Low sugar made her irritable. Sometimes.

Jason pushed back from the desk and gestured to the vacant chair nearby.

Stephanie bit her cheek and shook her head at his outstretched arm.

His brows lifted.

Why was she being so stubborn? He was willing to listen, but for some inexplicable reason, she wanted to refuse and prove she was right. The chief *was* hiding something and if she were to be believed, his saintly mother seemed to be orchestrating things.

"Sit." The sheer volume of the command startled her feet into action.

She flopped onto the seat and sank her face into her hands.

A gentle, soothing touch of Jason's hand warmed her shoulder. Just the reassurance she needed.

How could he be so kind to her after the way she behaved yesterday?

She dropped her hands onto her knees and contemplated their renewed friendship.

"Have I always been this way?" Stephanie swallowed hard, the whispered question hanging between them.

A warm, steady gaze fused to hers, understanding reflected in a pool of blue. "You've always done what you believe is right." He dropped his hand from her shoulder and sat back in his chair.

"Then why is everything going against me?" The thread of pain laced her hoarse response, a cloak of sadness covering her heart.

Scenes from the past days since crashing into Winterberry Falls threatened to release an avalanche of snow over her. A rash decision to speed through town in a snowstorm set her on a crash course of History Repeats Itself, and she hated the rut she was in.

Muffled voices and the hum of news on the other side of the door calmed Stephanie's distraught emotions.

"If God is for us, who, or what, can be against us?" He recited the passage with a contemplative tone. Maybe her prayers were working.

The verse from the New Testament chipped away at the despair swelling inside. How easy it was to forget God in the middle of circumstances. Sadly, circumstances didn't have to be good or bad to forget about God. Too many politicians pursuing power had taught her that.

"I didn't have aspirations to be a political correspondent or work for a political anything." She cupped her knees with her hands. "It's like it keeps sucking me in. Like, I'm destined to spend my entire career breathing politics."

"So why are you even considering working for an election campaign?" Jason swiveled from side to side, fixing a stare at her.

Stephanie eyed her boots, uncomfortable with the question she had avoided asking herself. Then, she lifted her chin. "It's the best way to start my own PR company. If Daniel wins the election, I can have my pick of clients and do what I want to do." She drew her tongue across dried lips. "It will give me the credentials I need to be marketable."

Jason snorted. "Sounds like a bunch of hooey to me."

Stephanie huffed. "You have no idea what it takes—"

Jason held up his hand. "You don't need Washington or a successful political win to launch your own PR firm. Not if that's what you really want, Steph." He pinned her with an intense stare.

197

She rolled back her shoulders. He had no idea what it would take for her to make a name for herself not attached to her senator father.

"PR Firms are a dime a dozen in D.C."

Her cheeks burned with the insolence, and her lips parted, ready to blast his arguments to smithereens.

"If you really want to start your own PR firm, start someplace where they need you. Someplace where life centers on the everyday and where small business can use your services." He scratched his chin. "If high profile is what you want, those clients aren't limited to D.C. They're everywhere."

"Like here?" Her laugh was thick with sarcasm.

Jason frowned. "Anywhere."

Stephanie held his gaze. She feared if she let this line of conversation continue, his argument might convince her to rethink her plans. But those eyes also showed the weariness of a burden carried for far too long.

"What happened to you, Jay?" Stephanie clasped her hands together as a shadow crossed his face.

"Life happened, Steph. Like life is happening to you now."

Stephanie sighed and looked around the room. Life. Her eyes rested on the wall of photos, snippets Jason had captured from the lives of others. She pushed up from her chair and moved to the wall. She touched the photo of her twenty-year-old self, resigned to how the years had affected them both. How much they'd changed. If only they could recapture those moments in a bottle, Stephanie would do some things differently. Beginning with Jason's disappearance.

"You used to talk about God all the time." She could still hear his youthful voice. "You used to be on fire for God, Jay."

She scanned the other photos on the wall, a wash of tenderness filling her as she examined the beauty Jason had captured through the years. She turned her attention back to him, and her breath hitched at the pained expression he wore.

God, what happened to him?

"Whoever she was really did a number on you." Stephanie crossed her arms. She fingered the simple chain and medical ID pendant she wore around her neck and gazed out the window behind him. A black truck sped past the office, whipping up drifts of snow in its wake.

"What makes you think it was a woman?" Jay's tone challenged her.

She released the chain and peered at him.

"Because the Jason Miller I know was solid in his faith." She lifted an eyebrow. "All it took was a woman or two to pull Samson down and a whole slew of them to turn Solomon from God." Stephanie dropped her hand and smirked. "You're no Samson, and you're definitely not Solomon."

Jason snickered. "Definitely not."

Stephanie laughed. She sauntered across the room and picked up her notebook and pen from his desk, a thought niggling at her heart. God had planted the notion to pray for him, and seeing him now, she could only imagine what he'd been through since that fateful hike with her.

She paused next to his chair. His jaw notched up, shadows heavy beneath his eyes.

Her pulse skipped, and a longing to sweep her hand across the dark stubble and cradle his cheek tugged at her heart. "Don't wait to settle things with God, Jay."

He averted his gaze, his fingers gripping the arms of his chair.

"To everything there is a season." Stephanie strolled to the door and stopped, her nerves pulsating to the tips of her toes.

Keeping her back to Jason, she squared her shoulders and prayed God would get through to him. She glanced over her shoulder.

"Isn't it about time to heal?"

#

Stephanie snuggled into the comfy chair at the Champlain B&B later that evening and adjusted the decorative pillow behind her back. The fire in the grand room snapped and hissed as ash rose through the flue, and the yellow flames danced around the logs. With her eyes fixed on the flames, she reviewed the events of the past week and a half and let the blaze slow the speed of her overwhelming thoughts.

Stephanie had spent the last two hours on the phone up in her guest room with Daniel's personal assistant reviewing details for the Christmas party he was hosting. Several times, Becka had mentioned Stephanie's transition to his campaign, and Stephanie had redirected. It didn't matter that she hadn't committed yet, plans were still clearly underway for her to join the team.

The resignation letter to *DC Affairs* hung over her head like an overstuffed stocking. She'd left it upstairs, composed in her laptop's draft folder unsent, a sure sign of indecision. However, if her boss heard the campaign rumors before Stephanie made an official decision, she'd have a lot of explaining to do when she got back from holidays.

There wasn't much she wanted to deal with in her life right now.

Stephanie sighed and sank deeper into the cushions. It appeared Daniel thought it was a done deal despite his promise to wait for her answer. His plans were to be revealed to the selected guests invited to the Walker family home the evening of the 24th at their annual Christmas Eve bash.

Come to think of it, why was Stephanie expected to come up with party favors for the guests? Wasn't that his assistant's job? But since she'd already given her word, she'd have to take care of it first thing tomorrow.

A log crackled and spit glowing cinders from the fire, drawing Stephanie back to her beautiful surroundings.

Her gaze traveled across the carved mantle and oval-shaped mirror above it. Crown moulding bordered the top of the wall, the curved lines matching those of the fireplace. Tilly had used her magic, making this space welcoming and full of Christmas cheer.

Stephanie was at peace in this room and wished that feeling would follow her to D.C.

After that marathon phone call had pushed her stress level up, she'd brought her Bible downstairs with her hoping—and still praying—for clarity about her story after the heated discussion with Jason and the interview with Chief Sweeney. But nothing helped. She smoothed down the pages of her Bible.

"You've got to give me some sort of clue, God. Things are moving so fast with Daniel. I wonder if it's Your hand moving them along." The whispered prayer slid through the grand room as a sigh of bewilderment.

Daniel's offer was what she wanted if only as a step toward becoming her own boss. When things happened in God's timing, they happened quickly. Didn't they?

She rested her elbows on her knees, the Bible spread open on her lap.

"I've got a pot of tea steeping in the kitchen. Can I bring you a cup?" The soft cadence of Tilly's voice was a soothing interruption to her muddled thoughts.

"I'd love a cup." She smiled at her hostess, and Tilly disappeared through the door.

You promised if anyone lacks wisdom to ask, so I'm asking, God.

Stephanie studied the text she'd been trying to focus on since taking up space in the wingback chair. A man plans, but God directs. Give your work to God, and your plans will be established. Wasn't that what she was doing? But why was it so hard to make a decision? Question followed question until her brain hurt. After several minutes she gave up.

She rubbed her eyes.

Perhaps she was over thinking everything.

"Here we are. Thought you might like a fresh cookie to go with your tea, too." Tilly placed a small silver serving tray on the coffee table next to Stephanie's wingback chair. The delicious smell of ginger from the single cookie wafted from the tray. It was a blessing to have such an attentive hostess. Stephanie had mentioned her diabetes the first morning at breakfast, and Tilly had shown such care for her dietary needs since then.

Tilly passed her the teacup and inclined her head to the book on Stephanie's lap. "What are you reading?"

Stephanie ran her fingers across the page she'd stopped reading and trying to figure out. "Proverbs."

Tilly smiled. "The book of wisdom."

Stephanie blew steam across the delicate china in her hands and watched the vapors fade. "If only I knew which verse would apply, I might have a chance at making one of those wise decisions."

Tilly sunk into the overstuffed chair across from where Stephanie sat. Her petite legs stretched under the coffee table. "It's surprising what you find when you ask the right questions." Tilly glanced at the fire and turned twinkling eyes to Stephanie. "But then, you already know that being a reporter."

Stephanie grinned. "It's easier getting answers from people rather than God sometimes."

The fire hissed as Stephanie sipped her tea. Its warmth soothed her throat and calmed her restless thoughts.

Tilly pointed to the Bible. "Sometimes what we perceive as God not listening, is an answer in itself." Her smile was warm. The yellow flames highlighted Tilly's face, and Stephanie could see the family resemblance to Jason from this angle.

"Expect the unexpected." Stephanie moved her opened Bible to the coffee table. She vaguely remembered a pastor saying that in a sermon once about praying to God.

A log crashed, falling from the grate. Tilly grasped the fire poker, rearranged the burning logs, and added wood to the fire. Yellow and blue flames roared to life.

"Tilly, what happened to Jason?" Stephanie picked up the cookie from the plate as Tilly's back straightened. "He used to be so strong in his faith."

The fire poker scraped against the stand and Tilly turned. "It's not my story to tell, Stephanie." Her hostess' eyes filled with sadness.

From somewhere farther back in the house, a buzzer sounded.

"The last batch is done." Tilly's face brightened before she retreated down the hall.

Stephanie stared at the fire, listened to the movement coming from the kitchen, and bit into the soft cookie.

The peppery taste of ginger bombarded Stephanie's mouth.

She leaned over and looked down at her Bible still open on the table. The words blurred the harder she focused. She sat back with a frustrated sigh.

Perhaps God had already answered her prayers, and she'd missed it.

Or maybe it was time to expect the unexpected.

A miracle from God.

FIFTEEN

"Are you sure you guys can do this?" Stephanie swallowed back her nerves and stared across the top of the glass counter at the young woman who beamed at her. *Melissa* was engraved on the tag pinned to her apron. The sweet aroma of chocolate and confectioneries scented the quaint shop as Stephanie breathed in and out, breathless from the slippery walk over this morning from the B&B. But she'd been happy for the exercise in the warm winter sun. Thursday's weather was shaping up to be a great day.

"Aren't you overworked with the festival going on? Do you have enough people to handle an order this size?" Stephanie's questions tumbled together as quickly as the tempo of the Christmas tune playing through the shop speakers. "I mean 250 little boxes is a lot. There's what? Three truffles in each?"

Melissa nodded. "No worries, Ms. Clark. We're always prepared at festival time for unforeseen circumstances. We do everything in house so there shouldn't be a problem with getting you the chocolates this week." The confidence in her voice eased the strain in Stephanie's shoulders. "If you're okay with a variety of truffles and molds, we can get it to you that much faster." Inquisitive eyes stared back at Stephanie.

Stephanie blew a strand of hair from her face. "At this point I don't really care." Stephanie smiled weakly. "Whatever you have will be fine."

The bell above the entrance to the store chimed, and a rush of cold air pushed a customer inside.

"When do you want to pick them up?"

Stephanie glanced at her phone and scrolled through her schedule. She frowned. This would be so much easier if she knew what was going on with her car and when she was leaving town. *How* she was leaving. She could always call her father to rescue her, but she preferred her independence to the subjugation of her father's reprimands. Nope. She needed to bite the bullet and ask Jason to drive her over to the garage today. She vaguely recalled something about the garage and her car being towed. Enough of this procrastination. She loved Old Red, had the car since college, and if the mechanic told her Red was unsalvageable, it'd break her heart. She kind of expected it though, considering the sign had fallen through what had been left of her windshield. Stephanie smiled in spite of herself. Expect the unexpected... like having to order party favors for a Christmas party in D.C.

"How soon can you have them done? I just don't know my schedule yet."

Melissa pulled a clipboard from a hook behind her and flipped through pages. "How about Saturday?"

Two days from now. That quickly? Impressive.

"Saturday works. I'll stop by first thing in the morning to get them." Stephanie zipped up her coat and stuffed her phone in her purse.

A group of women bustled into the shop, their chatter competing with the Christmas music playing in the background. Melissa waved at them and turned back to Stephanie. "Are you that reporter that's been writing all those stories about the missing Christmas decorations? My aunt's been clipping your articles. She was one of the people you interviewed. Missing Christmas wreaths?"

Stephanie nodded, recollecting the telephone exchange. "Your aunt is a lovely woman, and I hope everything will be sorted out soon." If only the chief of police would give her an interview sooner than Christmas Eve. A customer with a store basket full of items sidled toward the counter. "Thank you *so* much. You have no idea how much I appreciate you guys doing this."

Stephanie gave a little wave to Melissa before turning to leave. She yanked open the door and side stepped an elderly couple entering the shop. The bell chimed goodbye as she stepped into the frigid, but bright morning. She shivered and pulled up the white scarf tucked in her jacket, covering her bare neck from the frosty air.

The street was already busy with tourists and shoppers milling the festival booths. Twinkle lights, mistletoe wreaths, and tastefully decorated evergreens covered every conceivable place around town. The air was just as saturated with the scents of Christmas spices from baked goods wafting from the bakery and outdoor kiosks.

She paused outside the chocolate shop and enjoyed the scene in front of her. There was something special about this town at Christmas. She'd miss it when she returned home.

She turned to the left and spotted Jason coming toward her on the sidewalk. His Santa hat slouched over one eye and a golden bell at the white tip jingled with every step. Ha! He'd finally caught Christmas fever.

Her smile widened, and her pulse pumped at an insane rate.

"Don't you have a story to write?" Jason righted his hat, a crooked grin on his face.

"Already done." Her hand flew to her fluttering stomach as big, gorgeous eyes beamed at her.

Unless her blood sugars were going haywire, she was definitely in trouble.

Jason Miller had managed to wiggle his way into her heart. Again.

He could woo a pig, that man.

Stephanie giggled at the memory of Mrs. Sweeney's description of her own newspaper man.

Jason paused in front of her, his expression full of questions.

"Can you woo a pig?" Stephanie's teeth pulled back her bottom lip.

Jason lifted his face skyward. A finger tapped against his adorable chin. "You'll have to ask Rosie." He lowered his chin, and his eyes twinkled.

"Who's Rosie?"

His face grew serious as he averted his eyes and seemed to focus somewhere behind her. A prickle of apprehension crept down her spine. In the slowest of motions, she pivoted and searched over her shoulder. The sandwich board for *Chocolate Chocolates* advertised their festival specials and next door, patrons passed under the decorated arbor over the library's entrance. Was one of those women with a book bag in her hand named Rosie? Stephanie turned back and looked up at Jason. He lowered his gaze to look at her.

"Butcher Brown's pet pig." His voice was solemn and so low she'd barely had time to register his words. Stephanie swatted at him and laughed.

He probably could woo a pig.

"So, if your story is already done, how come I haven't seen it yet?" Steam rose from his mouth into the morning light. He shoved his hands into his pockets. The warm look he gave wrapped its soft fingers all around her.

She shivered and stomped the cold from her toes. "Had to take care of party favors first." She cocked her head back toward the chocolate shop. "Daniel's P.A. called yesterday and delegated that task to me for his Christmas Eve party."

Jason seemed to study her for a moment. "Isn't that her job?"

Puffing out a flimsy sigh, she shrugged. "Yeah, sure." Her shoulders drooped as the familiar knot twisted in her gut. It was Becka's job, not Stephanie's. Yet she kept getting pulled into the campaign despite being on vacation. Would it always be this way with Daniel? All work, all the time. Would she ever have time to herself?

Stephanie swallowed the uneasy feeling. How was it that she could go from such an elated happiness to the depths of sticky mud in one minute?

Jason fixed his stare behind her and cleared his throat.

She hated the awkwardness that sprouted between them every time she mentioned anything to do with the campaign or Daniel. Her head said it was the sensible thing to do for her career, the fastest way to the top. The easy solution for gaining the clientele she wanted.

But her heart—and stomach—said something completely different.

If only she could get them all to agree.

Jason didn't have to say it, she could tell from his rigid shoulders that the topic made him just as uncomfortable. The sooner she could get her car fixed and running the better for both of them.

"I guess things are moving along then?"

Stephanie watched visitors emerging from Santa's Village, arms loaded with colorful parcels, and listened to the happy chatter drifting their way.

"You could say that." Her lungs filled with frustration before she blew a perfect steamy 'O' from her lips. "Seems like plans are in motion as if I've already taken the job." She squinted at the crowd. At least some people were happy this morning.

Gravel and sand crunched beneath Jason's boots as he stepped closer. Stephanie pressed her lips together and focused on a Christmas bow above the crowd, tails swaying with the light morning breeze.

No matter how hard Stephanie prayed, the answer wasn't clear. She'd promised Daniel a final decision on the job, yet the closer Christmas came, the more suffocating her promise was.

"But you're going to take it?" Jason's question sounded hopeful.

Her breath caught.

"Do I have a choice?" She nearly spat the words to the cracked sidewalk.

Great. Not only was Daniel pushing her to take the job, Jason expected her to take it.

That's it? After all the work she'd done, he was ready to write her off. Fine. Let him. She had a campaign to win and a dream to pursue.

A wave of heat surged through her body. Jerking her gloves off, she pulled at her zipper and loosened her scarf. Too many layers. Too many bossy people. She needed to shake the snow off her feet from the little town.

"So, now that that's done, I'll go back to the B&B and send over the story." Stephanie's chest stabbed with cold as she drew in a long breath. She aimed a thin smile at Jason, the best apology she could manage for now.

"Steph…" Jason touched her arm, and she stepped back. Anything he had to say wasn't worth listening to. The sooner she could lock herself away in the B&B, the better.

A dull ache started in her temple. She squeezed her eyes shut and rubbed the throbbing spot.

"Steph, look at me." His boot scuffed the ground, sending chunks of gravel skipping across the sidewalk where small patches of ice still clung to the cold pavement. She shook her head.

This was ridiculous. She didn't want him to tell her all the reasons why she should or shouldn't take the job with Daniel. Didn't anyone understand it was her decision and hers alone to make?

She wasn't going to listen to what he had to say.

And no, it didn't matter she was falling for him all over. She still couldn't trust him. No trust, no future. No point in listening.

"Your car is totaled."

Stephanie's eyes flew open. "What?" Old Red was totaled? As in unusable, finished, destined for the junkyard? Now how was she supposed to get to D.C.? The last thing she wanted to do was call Dad or Daniel to come get her like she was a helpless little girl.

"I thought I told you Roger stopped by a few days ago when he'd towed it. Didn't I? Anyway, he said he'd try to get to it later this week. He called earlier and confirmed what he'd already suspected. It's going to cost more to fix your car than to buy another decent used one." Jason shifted, moving to stand beneath the shadow of the overhang of the chocolate shop and out of the foot traffic.

She stared at him, mouth ajar. It was going to cost more to fix than buy another one? But she'd had Old Red since college, and it had never failed her before. Granted, her parents and Daniel had been urging her to trade it in, but she just couldn't give up on her car when it had been so reliable. She'd have better luck shopping in the D.C. area than here, but it would take time to find what she was looking for. Time. She should have already asked her dad to be on the lookout. "When did he stop by?"

"Mmm… Monday." He rocked on his heels, the bell on his hat jingling.

A boulder of dread plunged in her stomach. Right. The day the green monster decided to make an appearance. Her brain was trying to suppress that memory. And everything else that had happened since then. But still, that was three days ago. Surely he could have found time between then and now to tell her about her car.

"Today's Thursday and you're just telling me now?" She clenched her teeth. "I could have done something about it already!" Her hands fisted at her sides, and she stomped one foot.

"I'm sorry. It must have slipped my mind, but—" Jason grimaced.

"When did he call? And why did he call you and not me?" She inched closer. It seemed everyone was conspiring against her. The mechanic called Jason instead of *her*. It was her car, not Jason's. Which meant that Jason was keeping her trapped here on purpose. She could have been home already.

Jason frowned. "He called just now. I stopped by the B&B to pick you up, but Tilly said you'd come down here." His brow furrowed. Another excuse.

Her winter jacket *swished* as she crossed her arms, and she glared at him.

Typical.

215

He'd withheld information to keep her here in the hopes of printing her story. He'd make a name for himself if he printed the one she wanted to give him. With a police cover-up, his newspaper would rise from the slump, and Jason would become the town hero. Why not? Kill two birds with one stone. He could manipulate her and keep her trapped in this measly little mountain town far away from reliable cell service and the conveniences of the city. It was a perfect crime. He was probably even in cahoots with the chief.

Stephanie's chest heaved. Jason remained motionless next to her.

Apparently, Jason Miller hadn't changed one iota. He'd had no qualms using her in their college days to dig up some sort of story on her dad's political connections, and he still had no remorse for using her now for another story.

The man was insufferable.

This was the last time Jason Miller would ever use her for a story. She was done with him and done with this crummy place. She had a life in Washington and all she had to do was get there. Somehow.

"I'm sorry about your car, but I can…"

"Save it, Jason." Her tone trembled with fury, and she glared at him. "If you had really wanted to help me, you wouldn't have forgotten to tell me I was stuck here in Santa Land indefinitely." She shouldered her way past him and stomped away, her boots clopping across the sidewalk, kicking up sand behind her.

"Steph, don't—" His voice was lost behind her as she picked up the pace.

Her eyes burned with tears, and her vision blurred. She took longer strides, no speed was fast enough to escape.

Jason's voice called out behind her, propelling her down the street. "Steph!"

Stephanie heard his shout before she felt the ground slide beneath her.

And then her world went black.

SIXTEEN

She'd only blacked out for a few seconds after hitting her head on the light post, but it might as well have been a lifetime the way his heart still pounded. That, and carrying Stephanie the short distance back to the B&B. Seeing the woman he loved slip, knock her head, and then crumple to the ground was something he hoped to never witness again. Jason wrapped gauze around her swollen ankle and taped the end with medical tape.

"Really, I can do it myself." Stephanie whined for the umpteenth time.

Tilly handed him an icepack. He looked up at her from the ottoman where he sat and smiled. Jason lifted Stephanie's heel onto the couch and pressed the pack against her leg, ignoring her protests.

"How's your head?" He lowered his voice and pointed at Stephanie. She'd been complaining of a headache.

She pouted and touched the bump on her forehead. "Still there."

Jason chuckled.

"I'll go find something for that headache of yours." Tilly sauntered out of the room.

Stephanie wiggled her toes, and the icepack slid from her ankle to the floor. After reaching for a fluffy decorative pillow from the wingback chair, Jason slid it beneath her foot and repositioned the ice on her leg.

If only he had the right to cuddle in beside her on the couch, he'd wrap his arms around her, willing the aches away. Except he'd thrown away that chance years ago.

He dragged himself to his feet and found a place next to the roaring fire. He watched the logs glow orange, the flames dancing and embers floating into the flue, and wished the secret he carried would burn in the fireplace.

"Jason?"

His whispered name swept across the hollow places of his lonely heart. He angled his face, heat painting the right side of his jaw.

"Thank you."

He dared not look in her eyes but focused on the subtle pattern of the pillow beneath her head. He knew what he would see there, and nothing was left in him to resist loving her the way he wanted to.

God help him, he loved her.

The seed of friendship planted in college was firmly rooted, though life and circumstances had stunted its growth. He had been a foolish kid, ignorant of the treasure Stephanie was. They'd been rapidly crossing the line of solid friendship into a more intimate relationship until the day she'd collapsed and her family had forced him away. But now?

She deserved to be loved and valued for the amazing woman she was. She needed someone who would fight for her.

Not a backslidden Christian duty-bound and chained to a struggling family business in a small mountain town, who couldn't even fight for himself.

Jason turned his face back to the mantle and stared unseeingly at the greenery arranged on the surface.

The sins of her father beat against Jason's conscience. Stephanie's absence from his life had made it easy to bury the secret, to almost forget how he got here. Trapped in a promise to hide the truth from the woman he loved. How could he keep living this way when Stephanie stoked the charcoals of desire to be a better man? An honest and trustworthy man. A man who didn't keep secrets from her.

Tilly returned with pain medication and a glass of water before settling into a nearby chair to chat quietly with Stephanie. Jason stared at the hissing flames and leaned his arm on the mantle.

His throat constricted.

Was he a man or a coward?

The question had tormented him from the first moment he'd confronted the senator about everything. Discrepancies Jason had uncovered during the campaign would have cost the senator everything if Jason could have proven the allegations. Then Jason had found the evidence he needed to make his story credible.

Could he be a coward when everything he'd done since that moment had been to protect those he loved? The senator's actions spoke of impenetrable power, and so Jason had done the only thing he could do. He buried the story.

And with it, he'd lost his very best friend, and the only chance he'd ever wanted at a wife and family of his own.

Jason could never have a romantic relationship with Stephanie now as long as he kept lying to her. And even a friendship couldn't last for long with that type of foundation. If they have any chance at the kind of future they'd wanted back then, he needed to tell her the truth. All of it.

"Jason, about what I said earlier..."

The fire snapped, and Jason looked over his shoulder toward Stephanie. She was seated now, a pillow behind her back and her legs resting on the couch.

When had Tilly disappeared? She must have helped Stephanie sit up.

"It's just... I..." Her voice cracked.

Please don't cry. I don't know what to do when you cry.

He cringed at her muffled sobs. Tapping the mantle, he pushed from his spot and lowered himself to the floor next to Stephanie with his back to the couch. He stretched his legs across the gleaming hardwood and crossed his ankles beneath the coffee table.

He'd waited long enough to tell her the whole truth. Jason rubbed his neck. And as soon as she was done crying, he'd do the one thing he never wanted to do. He'd break the promise he'd made over a decade ago. And in the process, he would shatter her heart.

#

Stephanie could hardly believe she was about to say it, but it was time. She'd avoided the topic for days, but if she were about to leave town, she had to tell Jason how deeply he'd wounded her when he'd abandoned her. And she had to know the truth. Why did he leave her and cut off all communication? What really happened after the hike in the mountain the last time she was here, in Winterberry Falls? Had their relationship really been just a ploy to uncover a story?

She sniffed and pulled the tissue box over from the coffee table on to her lap. The fire cast an orange glow across the top of Jason's messy hair, flecks of golden strands dancing in the fire's light. He kept his back to her, a blessing. He was making it easier for her to speak.

"I need to tell you something because even after all this time it still hurts, Jason. You disappeared and it broke my heart. When I was sick, I looked for you every day." Her eyes watered again with the memories. She dabbed the tissue underneath her eyes, then wrapped it between her fingers. Stephanie drew in a long breath.

"I was so scared. I had no idea what was going on with my health, but I knew if you were next to me, no matter what the doctors could find wrong, it would be okay. *You* would make it okay." Stephanie's voice hitched as she watched his shoulders stiffen.

"Months went by and nothing. It didn't make sense. We were best friends. We talked about graduation and exploring the world together. I thought we meant something to each other. I needed to hear you tell me I still mattered. That you still cared." A sob caught in Stephanie's throat, and she lifted the crumpled tissue to dry her cheeks. "That despite what my mother said, I wasn't being used to get an inside story that would jump start your career."

The tension in the air grew thick. Jason's silence condemned him as far as she was concerned. The ugly fingers of hurt twisted into coils of anger.

But what of the story? She'd never actually read it and couldn't say for sure if that betrayal had actually benefited him long term. But then again, she had refused to read anything with photo credits or bylines by Jason Miller.

How many newspapers had her parents destroyed because of her insistence she see nothing of Jason's betrayal?

Stephanie closed her eyes, a waterfall of tears slid down her cheeks and dripped from her chin, soaking her sweater.

Please God… give me wisdom. Open my eyes to the truth.

Had their whole friendship been a lie from the beginning? The possibility he'd conned her hadn't lined up with his profession of faith in God, or the kind of man she believed him to be. Honest. Trustworthy. Loyal. Someone had to be lying. But who?

She gritted her teeth. *Please God. Make him tell me. I have to know… No matter what.*

"Where did you go? Why did you disappear?" Stephanie's nose stung, and she squeezed the soft cartilage between her fingers.

"Jason?" Keeping her voice level was impossible. Still, he kept silent.

Bracing herself for a painful answer, she forced enough coldness into her voice that could freeze fire. "Was getting your story worth it?"

She hated the question. Hated all of this.

The taste of tears on her lips mingled with the distress of her soul as her shoulders shook with her quiet sobs. Nothing was fair.

Stephanie hid her face in her hands. The couch shifted, as if Jason bumped it from his spot on the floor. She wept harder as strong arms wrapped around her, holding her and bringing comfort though everything within her wanted to fight against him. To pound her fists against his chest for leaving her crushed and confused. Her mind hurled violent accusations at him even as her heart yearned to stay in his embrace.

"Why, Jay?" Her voice shook with all the angst she'd kept locked inside these past twelve years. Her fingers grasped the taut muscles of his forearm, and her body trembled.

Could she bear the truth?

The heat of his breath swept across her neck as he buried his nose in her hair, and his forehead pressed against the top of her head. He swayed with her and pulled her close to his chest.

God, I love him.

How much she wanted to be with him, but it had to be in God's timing, in God's way.

And right now, the way she was hurting, a relationship with Jason was hopeless. He still hadn't answered her, and as much as she wanted to believe in his innocence, her gut told her he was holding something back.

Something that could tear them apart forever.

Her throat seared with misery as she controlled her sobs. This moment and his tender embrace would end too soon. Just when they'd found each other again.

God… Yes. She was selfish. She wanted him to be innocent of the accusations she'd been foolish to believe for so long. Was it too late to go back and search the newspaper archives herself to discover the truth of what he had written?

Stephanie sucked in a noisy breath and leaned into his embrace as the fight left her. A sense that this was all part of God's plan grounded itself in her mind. She had asked Him for direction, and He'd brought her here.

Back into Jason's arms.

Perhaps, if He was as gracious as she knew Him to be, He'd finally give her the answers she was searching for.

#

A log snapped in the fireplace behind him, stoking his resolve.

With one final brush of Stephanie's back, Jason pulled away and let his gaze wander the lines of her face. He'd pictured her a thousand times in his mind over the years, and, despite the red puffy eyes, she was beautiful. And would always be that way to him. It was a picture he wanted to savor one last time before he annihilated whatever this was between them.

Jason dropped his arms. The moment of truth was here, but where should he start? The beginning was always best.

"Do you remember our first day of Journalism 101?" He smiled as the scene replayed itself in his mind, love at first sight. "I didn't know who you were, but I was determined to get to know you." He moved to the wingback chair.

"I didn't know your father was running for Senate. I didn't find that out until…" Jason shifted his gaze and stared at the fireplace.

Perhaps a different approach would be better.

"I always wanted to be a photojournalist in my own right. I knew *The Independent* would be here, but I didn't want a free pass because of my heritage."

Somewhere down the hall, a muted telephone rang, and footsteps sounded across the floor. Jason rose from the chair and retreated to the mantle. He reached for the fire poker and shifted the logs. The flames billowed and settled back to a slow burn. He replaced the poker and faced her, his arm draped on the mantle.

"There was a political rally an hour from here in Burlington a couple of weeks before our graduation ceremony. I went to it and stumbled on some... interesting information. I heard about stuff that shouldn't be happening and if it was true, I was ready to blow the lid and get my byline. After all, the public deserved to know the truth about the people running for office." A spark flashed in her eye. There was no way she'd miss the connection he was making to the Christmas Caper culprit. He'd believed that sentiment then, and he still believed it now. Sadly, life had taught him truth wasn't always appreciated, nor was it always cut and dried. "I was trying to process what I'd uncovered and wanted to talk to you about it, but I didn't know how. That's why I called the same night, practically begging you to come here the next day and when you did, I didn't know what to say." Jason resumed his spot on the chair.

"After you fainted on the trail, I got you to the hospital here in town. But since I wasn't family, they wouldn't let me stay with you. I was told the medical staff would take care of you until your family was contacted." His heart thundered. She would hate him for this next part.

"The next morning, I confronted..." Jason leaned forward on his elbows and cleared his throat. "I confronted those involved. Of course a heated discussion followed and denials made, but I knew there was a cover up. It was huge, and I was going to blow the lid off their campaign." His adrenaline pumped the way it had when he'd uncovered the story.

"I was close, Steph. So close." He clasped his hands together and licked his lips. "I found documents and all kinds of details supporting my theory. No one would have questioned me if I'd printed the story." His knee bounced as the intensity of his discovery raced back up to the surface.

"After the interview, I went to the Winterberry Falls hospital where I'd taken you. I had to see you, to make sure you were okay and to tell you what I'd discovered. When I got there, they wouldn't disclose anything and only said you'd been transferred somewhere else. I couldn't even get them to tell me the name of the place you'd been taken to."

He huffed. "That last week of finals, I tried leaving you messages at the dorm and even asked the administration to contact you for me. I didn't know what was happening with you or where you were." He jumped to his feet and paced in front of the fireplace.

"So, I did the only thing I could do. I focused on the biggest story of my nonexistent career." He stopped pacing and fiddled with the evergreen garland draped along the top of the mantle and pushed a golden candlestick back and forth between his fingers. Jason's gaze flitted across the room to where Stephanie sat.

"That time is still fuzzy in my mind, but I remember it was May, and I didn't go to the graduation ceremony. I finished my courses at distance." She sucked in a loud breath. "It was the May rally. You said you had gone to it and had something to tell me, but it was too big to say over the phone. That's why I drove two hours to come here. You started to tell me on the trail, but I passed out before you could get anything out." Her voice was distant, and Jason hated the heavy shadow of hurt that darkened her features.

He squeezed his eyes shut. The truth would devastate her if he divulged the rest. And what he'd spent the last twelve years protecting, he'd destroy in two minutes.

God, I can't do this. I can't ruin her life.

He pressed his fingers against his temples. A futile effort to banish the rushing memories. Every nuance and insinuation of the men involved were carefully recorded in the recesses of his mind. Their vivid voices lived on and refused to be pushed from his head.

He'd been pushed into a corner. His family had been threatened. His blossoming relationship with Stephanie discovered.

"Jason." Stephanie's voice whispered through the tortured flashback.

He opened his eyes, and she gaped back at him. "I killed the story. I had to promise, Steph, and I wasn't given a choice. If I'd printed the truth, they would've

230

destroyed my father's business and made sure none of us would work in this state again. My brother and sister's futures were on the line." Jason swallowed hard and turned from her pleading look. He gripped the rounded edge of the mantle and leaned back on his heels as fire spit and sputtered an angry dance, matching his own fury.

His chest heaved, and his breaths grew shallow with the memories of every angry word tossed his way and every threat uttered.

"How do you know that?" Her question begged him to be wrong.

Jason clamped his teeth down hard and sucked in a nose full of sulfur. "Two days after the interview with the main party involved, my dad called me." He closed his eyes, the disbelief still pummeling his gut all these years later. "The IRS was searching through the files of *The Independent*. They'd received a tip from a reliable source the night before that things weren't all they appeared to be."

Stephanie gasped.

Jason's chest rose and fell, desperation, helplessness and all the emotions he'd held at arm's length came rolling over him. He opened his eyes and turned toward her again, pleading with her to figure it out on her own, without having to speak her father's name. "I wish to God I'd never gone to those rallies." His voice shook with a thousand regrets as he banged a fist on the wood, sending evergreen needles falling to the floor.

"Who was it, Jason? Who made you promise not to print?" Stephanie's unsteady tone was laced with fear.

Jason clenched his hands and shook his head.

"Who was it, Jason?" Her voice was stronger now.

He looked at her, fear and certainty blazing from her eyes.

She knew. She had to know, yet he still couldn't voice what she demanded.

God forgive me, I can't tell her.

#

He wasn't going to do it. He wasn't going to tell her.

Stephanie clenched her fists and resisted screaming her question again. She knew that look. Torn and tortured by their shared past. A secret he carried so heavy it was destroying them.

"It was my father, wasn't it?" She choked back a sob, heat throbbing through her veins. Her father had been campaigning all over Vermont in May that year. That's why he'd been so quick to get her transferred from the hospital in Winterberry Falls to Montpelier.

Jason's Adam's apple bobbed as he stood next to the fireplace, staring at her with eyes full of grief. He didn't flinch with her question but kept silent.

He was still the man of integrity she'd known him to be. He'd made a promise, and he wasn't going to break it.

"I didn't know who you were, Steph." His fractured whisper threaded with remorse pierced her heart.

He hadn't known because she'd never told him who her father was. The appetite for independence back then had been just as strong as it was now. She hadn't wanted to be known as the daughter of the state's biggest insurance provider, or part way through her schooling, the newly elected state senator's daughter. She wanted to be known for who she was.

Deep down inside, she believed Jason had always been loyal to a fault. That he'd never abandon her by choice.

If he kept his word not to print the story, it never saw the light of day.

Stephanie's back sagged against the arm of the couch, and her chest tightened. She focused on the throbbing of her ankle and the pounding in her head. She'd rather deal with the physical pain than the opened wounds of the past. She closed her eyes and wished this was just a horrible dream she could claw her way out of.

Why tell me all this now, God? Wasn't it better when I didn't know?

Moisture slid from the corners of her eyes, leaving a wet trail across her cheeks and dripping from her chin.

Every confusing emotion of the past week and a half had been upended by Jason's confession.

Jason refused to give her a name even after he had been blackmailed by a crooked politician. But he was still part of a massive cover-up even if it were for noble reasons. He didn't write what he knew and instead buried the truth. And quite possibly, her father had been lying to her all these years.

Was no man to be trusted?

Stephanie covered her face.

How much she hated herself for falling for Jason. This was huge. He had intentionally swept the story under the rug, like the chief of police he was so adamant in protecting. It all made sense now, why Jason fought her on that one. No. She couldn't love someone she didn't agree with or someone who lied by omission. Why hadn't she kept her distance?

"I have a few things to wrap up at the office." His tone was void of the angst from moments before.

Stephanie pitied him, but was angry at herself for her foolishness. While she'd been enjoying spending time with Jason again and writing something other than politics, he'd known the truth all along. No wonder he'd been keeping his distance. She got carried away with the charm of Winterberry Falls and the excitement of solving a mystery he wasn't interested in pursuing. With his tendency to cover up hot button issues, Jason would never run the last part of her story. As far as she was concerned, he could take the Christmas Caper article and throw it in the fireplace.

She was done with Winterberry Falls.

And she was done with Jason Miller.

"I'll take you to D.C. in the morning." His voice was hoarse and lacked enthusiasm for taking her home. It was just as well. They'd likely not speak the whole way back anyway.

Stephanie was anxious for him to leave and dreaded his return.

She slid her fingers through her hair when Jason's steps paused next to her. She refused to open her eyes and give him the opportunity to see her pain.

"Forgive me? I never meant to hurt you. Ever."

Stephanie listened to the sound of his retreating steps, then tugged at the hem of her shirt. When the front door opened and closed, she released the rest of her tears, emptying herself of everything she had ever stored in her heart for Jason.

SEVENTEEN

The flickering light from the fire threw a warm blanket across Stephanie's face, and she wished the hammering headache would subside. Judging by the growling of her stomach and the sun's rays brightening the grand room from the picturesque window, it should be close to midafternoon, snack time. She must have fallen asleep after Doctor Hudson's quick house call to make sure she was okay and eating the sandwich Tilly had provided for her lunch.

Stephanie pushed up on her elbows and winced at the pain shooting through her right shoulder. She must have injured it, too, along with her head and right ankle when she fell outside *Chocolate Chocolates* earlier that morning.

Jason.

He'd been there to rescue her. Again. She didn't like feeling helpless, yet she'd gotten more than she bargained for when her little car crashed into this small town. She sat up fully and wedged the pillow behind her back, resting her feet on the cushions of the couch. Stephanie surveyed the room. The place didn't hold the same charm it had earlier in the week. Too many painful moments would forever be engraved in the confines of this room. Her gaze settled on the coffee table. Tilly, bless her heart, had left a cookie and some tea for her. Stephanie picked up the tea cup. She savored the comforting warmth of the beverage as she sipped before replacing the cup next to the shortbread. How could she be so well cared for here and yet, be so desperate to run from the pain Winterberry Falls brought her?

"God, what are You doing?" Stephanie shivered.

That morning He'd given her the answer she'd been looking for—the truth of what happened in the past.

But Jason doesn't trust me enough to reveal his source, or the details of his conversation. How can I trust him to be completely honest with me always?

Even as she grappled with her weak argument, fingers of slimy guilt slithered across her skin. Of course he wouldn't reveal a source. If their roles were reversed, she likely wouldn't tell him either. How could she continue to point her finger when she was just as guilty? Keeping sources confidential was all part of the job.

A lump fused to her throat, making it cumbersome to breathe.

Hypocrite.

Liar.

Someone who was very close to her defined those very words. Her journalistic gut told her it wasn't Jason.

Stephanie laid back down and massaged her scalp. If she didn't know any better, she'd swear the pounding in her temples sounded like knuckles wrapping against the door.

She breathed in a long draw of air through her nose. A hint of cranberry—the candle on the mantle a likely source—blended with the comforting scent of the hearth.

With God's help she would be able to face one challenge at a time.

But where to begin?

She adjusted the pillow behind her head.

Forgiveness. She'd blamed others for so long she'd lost sight of the part she played in her past with Jason. She believed a lie even though doubt assailed the validity of the story she'd been told. Yet, it had been easy for her parents to fulfill her demand of keeping any printed story from her, because Jason had never printed it. There was no story to read. And she'd paved the foundation for the lie by insisting she be kept in the dark.

Oh, why didn't she search out the truth?

Shame washed over her.

She was just as much to blame as Jason. She'd never told him her father was a state senator or that he was running for the U.S. Senate. Her parents had tried hard to keep her out of the scrutiny of the press and out of the limelight while he served in office. Stephanie covered her face with her hands.

She'd let fear lead her instead of God. She trusted in everyone else, but God. No wonder she couldn't see the answers He'd plainly given her.

"Stephanie?"

The touch on her sleeve startled her. She dropped her hands and stared into a pair of dark eyes she hadn't seen for some time. His face was hazy, but she didn't need to rub the sleep away to know who belonged to the square jaw hidden by the neatly trimmed beard, or the slightly crooked nose.

Her stomach cramped.

Daniel Walker. A classy guy and one who turned the heads of every single female whenever he entered a room.

Except her.

"Hey there." A genuine smile lit up his face. His warm fingers stroked her brow, avoiding the goose egg on the right side and leaving a ripple of longing for someone else's touch to soothe her.

Stephanie reached for his hand, squeezed his fingers, and gave him a shaky smile. "What are you doing here?" Her voice cracked.

"Heard my star player was stranded in a pokey mountain town, so I came to bring you home." He winked.

Stephanie stiffened at his assumptions. Oh, there were just too many things wrong with that statement, but there wasn't any fight left in her to tackle the thorniest of issues. "Winterberry Falls isn't pokey."

Daniel glanced at his wrist and adjusted the diamond cuff link on his jacket sleeve. A pang of guilt struck and fled just as quickly. The bracelet Daniel had given her was tucked at the bottom of her duffel bag, something she'd done after this morning's shower. It was a gift and she could do what she wanted with it and shouldn't feel any obligation to wear it, though the giver wanted her to. That, and the knot in her stomach was relentless every time she looked at it.

"William was anxious to get some hours in so he offered to fly me here and bring you back since nothing seemed to be happening with your car." Pride for Daniel's younger brother's accomplishment shone in his eyes. William was quite the aerobatic pilot, and she'd been impressed with his ability on more than one occasion. Except today. The churning in her stomach was back with a vengeance, and the thought of flying all the way to D.C. with William's occasional tricks didn't alleviate the nausea.

"Can you believe it's going to happen, Stephanie?" A grin tugged the smooth edges of his beard up. His gaze swept over her and focused on her forehead. A stern frown erased his smile as he sunk into the wingback chair.

She touched the bump and flinched.

"What happened?" What? No sympathy? And he hadn't even noticed her foot with the melted ice pack yet. Then again, if she were to agree to his job proposal, perhaps it was better if they kept it professional.

Her stomach recoiled.

"I was taking care of the party favors for your Christmas party this morning. I stepped on some ice and fell." It wasn't necessary to tell him she'd practically been running from another man when it happened.

Daniel dragged the chair closer, knocking against the coffee table and sloshing her tea. He swept her hand into his. Stephanie resisted the urge to squirm and pull away, clutching a fist against her stomach instead.

"We'll have to be more careful in the future. Don't want to have bumps and bruises while the cameras are on you." His lips formed a thin smile.

His continued confidence in her commitment to his cause disturbed any peace of mind she had. Hours of rest on Tilly's couch wasted.

She dislodged her fingers from his grasp. "I haven't given my answer yet, Daniel."

A muffled beep sounded, and Daniel patted his suit jacket. Barbs of annoyance scratched her skin as he pulled his phone from his pocket. He slid his finger across the screen, his expression intensifying. He looked like he had stepped away from the office dressed the way he was.

Daniel sighed and replaced the phone in his pocket, fixing his softened gaze on her. "I know I said you didn't have to give me your answer until the twenty-fourth, but I just started thinking about all the possibilities if you came on board." He adjusted his yellow silk tie and leaned his elbows on his knees. "You've lived the political life, and you're a fantastic journalist. Who better to have working on my campaign than you?" The glow from the embers of the fire was no match for the light in his eye.

Stephanie's brow furrowed as a million reasons why, on both sides of the argument, fought to be heard.

She stared at her swollen ankle. Visions of Jason tenderly wrapping it flashed through her mind.

"Once I'm elected, we'll see where God will take us." His voice grew quiet, infused with all the certainty Stephanie felt the same way he did.

She swallowed back the frustration and counted silently to ten.

"Let's not get ahead of ourselves." Stephanie's attempt at humor fell flat. "Actually, Daniel, there's something—"

Daniel flicked his wrist and frowned. "Look at the time. I need to get back to D.C. pronto. I've got a conference call at seven, and I'd rather be in my office than in the air. I left William at the airstrip filing a return flight plan." Daniel looked around the room before he launched himself from the chair, pulling his phone from his pocket again.

Stephanie sighed. Perhaps there would be time on the plane to discuss her decision. And it would be nice to get back to D.C. without any inconvenience to herself and to put some fresh clothing on. There was a cashmere sweater in her apartment closet calling her name. "I'll grab my stuff." Stephanie wobbled to her feet and supported herself against the arm of the couch. She grimaced at the sharp pain in her foot.

Daniel made his way to her side. "Stephanie, you're hurt. Let Ms. Miller pack your things." Daniel's voice was low, commanding.

"I can pack my own things. Tilly's not a maid." She steadied her trembling limbs. If only Daniel would lend an arm for a minute or two, she should be strong enough to make it the rest of the way upstairs on her own.

He stared at her for a moment before he nodded. "Well, if you're sure. I need to return a couple of phone calls. I'll just wait in here until you're done packing." Daniel resumed his spot on the chair, his focus fixed on the device in his hand.

A wave of fatigue pummeled her as she hobbled to the door.

A long nap until Boxing Day sounded refreshing.

Stephanie rolled back her shoulders and lifted her chin.

She could do this. She could put the last ten days behind her and leave everything that happened as a slice of history where it belonged.

And she could definitely ignore the bulging knot in her stomach.

Maybe.

She would work hard to get Daniel into office, and she'd work even harder to launch her PR firm in D.C.

Stephanie ignored the churning of her gut.

A future in Daniel's office meant leaving Winterberry Falls and its fine citizens behind forever, including her blue-eyed best friend of yesteryear.

She supported her weight against the wall and shuffled down the hall to the grand staircase, sidestepping greenery and Christmas decor in her way.

After what happened with Jason, she was tired and just wanted to go home. Being back in D.C. would remind her of all the reasons she needed to say *yes* to Daniel and *no* to Jason. Wouldn't it?

Stephanie slowed her turtle pace. She definitely needed to check her sugars and then give herself some time to get better. Once back home in her little apartment all by herself, she would rest easier and be able to think without distraction. And sleep. She always slept well in her own bed.

The bottom step creaked under the weight of her weary body. She paused and focused on the landing above.

She barely had energy to make it to the top of the stairs.

If she didn't have the strength to walk a flight of stairs, she certainly didn't have the strength to face whatever was next.

God help her, because she couldn't escape the foreboding she wasn't done with heart-wrenching confessions.

At least not yet.

#

The smells of toast and coffee drifted from the breakfast room as Jason entered Champlain House B&B, the happy chatter of early rising guests a testament to his cousin's hospitality.

A crash and Tilly's shrill voice thrust Jason down the hall toward the kitchen. Half hidden by the center island, Tilly crouched over a metal bowl on the floor and scooped up white powder with her hands.

"Everything okay?" Jason tried not to startle her.

Tilly's head popped up above the counter, her hand clutched at the apron strings strung around her neck. "Yeesh, Jason. You could've given me a heart attack!" Her cheeks were red, and spots of white dusted her face and hair.

Jason grabbed the dustpan and broom from beside the pantry and began sweeping up the white flour. "Sorry. Didn't mean to scare you." He gave her an apologetic smile as the hard bristles swished against the stone tiles.

Tilly moved the mixing bowl to the end of the counter and brushed the fine powder from her hands. She pressed her foot on the pedal of the garbage beside the counter, sent the lid flying open, and dumped the contents into the trash. Jason emptied his dustpan at the same time and replaced the broom.

"Thank you for your help." She placed the bowl in the sink and grabbed a fresh one from the cupboard. "If you're looking for Stephanie, she's gone." Tilly carried the bowl to the island and opened the bag of flour still sitting on the counter, the measuring cup nearby, and started scooping.

"What do you mean gone?" His heart tripped. "Gone for a walk?" His midsection filled with unease as he braced himself against the island. It couldn't be more than just a short jaunt to town. He'd told Stephanie he was coming this morning to drive her home.

He had even stopped by the diner and got them food for the road.

How could she be gone? And with an injured ankle?

Tilly's lips pursed as she leveled off the flour and emptied it into the clean bowl. He watched the methodical way she scooped and dropped her ingredients, his impatience growing with every step of her process.

"Tilly." His voice was louder and more aggressive than he'd intended.

His cousin glared in return.

"Where did she go?" He toned it down. He would get more bees with honey if he tried hard enough, or so they said.

Tilly wiped her hands down her apron, smearing the cute Christmas reindeer design in a layer of white. "Coffee?"

Jason rubbed his face. Sometimes his cousin was downright infuriating. She was stalling, and he was tired. "Sure." Jason sunk onto a stool on the opposite side of the island where his cousin worked.

"Do you remember when we were in Mrs. Sweeney's class?" Tilly readied a cup for him as he recalled that school semester. It was the year after his aunt and uncle had moved to town and his younger cousin was placed in his grade two-three split class.

"A bit. Why?" Why did Mrs. Sweeney's name keep coming up? Stephanie had talked to the woman who was somehow mixed up in the Christmas caper story Steph was so adamant in pursuing. Jason scratched his arm. He could tell from the quirk of Tilly's brow he was in for a classic cousin rant.

Tilly slid a mug across the counter. "The Secret Santa project. It was my second Christmas in Winterberry Falls, and I was still having a hard time making friends. Mrs. Sweeney, bless her heart, saw how I was struggling and decided to help me out." A smile lit up Tilly's face as she retold the story.

Scenes from childhood stirred in Jason's mind as she reminisced. At first he wasn't sure he liked the idea of his younger cousin, a girl no less, hanging around. He could count the number of times his friends teased him about her. But after Mrs. Sweeney's project, Tilly's popularity had skyrocketed, and it made him proud to be connected to her.

Tilly grunted as she hefted a club-sized bottle of vegetable oil onto the counter. His cousin had grown out of the shy, pig-tailed seven-year-old girl.

"Because of Mrs. Sweeney's Secret Santa project, you and I became more than blood relation. We became friends." Tilly's round eyes filled with kindness as she glanced up from her bowl, and Jason nodded.

"I remember." His voice mellowed as Tilly's attention returned to her baking. She knew of his love of photography even back then and had planted the seeds for his professional pursuit. The project was to find something of value in another person and express it in a creative way. Tilly had created a photo frame from popsicle sticks, glitter glue, and ribbon. In her own seven-year-old script she'd scrawled *World's Best*

Photographer across the middle and had drawn a picture of him. She had always believed in him and had become a valued friend over the years.

"And because we are good friends and cousins to boot, I feel I have every right to tell you when you're being an idiot."

Jason gulped back the coffee and coughed. "Excuse me?"

"You're being an idiot." Tilly scraped the edge of the bowl as Jason gripped the granite countertop, his chest heaving from nearly choking. Of course he had been an idiot in the past, but that was in the past. He'd already established that, several times this past week already. Tilly didn't have to point that out to him this morning.

"Do you love her?" Tilly's voice challenged him as much as her knowing stare.

A nerve in his eye pulsed. "What?"

"Answer the question." She rested her hands against the counter and leaned forward. "Do you love her?"

Jason opened his mouth and abruptly closed it as he scrutinized his cousin. She stared at him, wide-eyed and waiting for his answer.

It didn't matter he loved Stephanie. She was determined to stay in D.C. She had plans that excluded him.

And then there was the senator's decade-old ultimatum to think about.

249

Jason weaved his fingers through the handle of the mug and stared into the creamy brown center.

Still, a life without Steph was no life at all. He couldn't return to being the man he was before God gave him a second chance to love her.

He needed Stephanie as much as the air he breathed.

"Yes." His voice cracked as he lifted his gaze.

Tilly smiled. "Then fight for her." She straightened. If he wasn't mistaken, that gleam in her eye told him she knew more than she was letting on.

"Why do I get the feeling you have more to say?" Because she always did.

Tilly shrugged and picked up the spatula. "I don't see how such a charming man in designer clothes and fancy shoes showing up here midafternoon yesterday after flying around in his own plane would appeal to Stephanie."

Jason tightened his grip around the Christmas mug.

Daniel. That's how she got to D.C. How in the world was Jason supposed to compete with that?

"Go after her, Jason." Tilly's words came fast and loud. "Whatever promise you made back then to Senator Clark was a promise he never should have forced on you. If you let her go, you'll never have another chance to get her back." Tilly stared at him.

He shook his head. "You don't know anything about it." His knuckles turned white. "Not really."

Tilly stirred the batter, her movements as clipped as her words. "I know who you were when you left for college, and I know that whatever happened in Senator Clark's office changed you. I know the IRS showed up on *The Independent*'s doorstep two days after you met with him. And I know how broken and miserable you were for years after. I know how much you cared about Stephanie back then, and I can see how much you care about her now." She slid a muffin tray next to her bowl and paused her mixing. Her face softened, and Jason shifted on the stool.

"You did what you thought best, but you didn't let God take care of things for you, Jason. You took care of things yourself and then blamed the rest on God. You walked away when you needed to go to Him." Tilly's hands rested in the dust of flour as she leaned forward. "God brought Stephanie here, I'm sure of it. She needs you as much as you need her. You'd be a fool to let her get away when it's evident it was God's hand that's been working all along."

Jason dropped his head and stared at his jean-covered knee. Yesterday's almost confession had ripped open a new wound that hurt just as much now as it did back when it all began.

He'd had no choice but to walk away from the story back then.

To walk away from Stephanie. But what about now?

Tilly pulled a tray of finished muffins from the oven and a rush of heat warmed the space. "I know there are things about your job you can't share with others." Tilly turned from the steaming tray and tucked her hands in the apron pockets. "But Stephanie's a reporter, too. She understands all that confidentiality stuff."

Jason lifted the mug and sipped. Tilly's point was valid, but it didn't ease the tangled mess of his stomach.

"You were a kid trying to protect his family. No one could ask anything less of you, but now you need to forgive yourself for things you had no control over." Tilly released a slow breath. "And forgive her dad for backing you into a corner in the first place."

Jason cleared his throat and busied his hands with the mug, avoiding his cousin's stare.

She moved to the tiny desk in the corner of the kitchen, and Jason looked out the window at the snow-capped mountains in the distance, his mind already heading beyond the southern tip to a world away from here.

"Stephanie asked me to send her order from *Chocolate Chocolates* to this address tomorrow via courier. However, since Melissa sent an email early this morning saying they were ready to be picked up any time, it might be a good idea to deliver the goods yourself." Tilly pulled the stool from under the wall desk and sat. "The shop opens up at eight. She's probably already there and will let you in if you're a bit early. I'll call and tell her you're on your way over." Tilly pulled her phone from the charger.

"Tilly, I—"

"Shh! It's ringing." Tilly turned her back to him and pressed the phone against her ear.

Tilly was right about everything, but he hated to admit it. She was right that he'd run away from God instead of to Him and in doing so, Jason had walked away from his faith and had been stumbling ever since. Tilly was right that he needed to chase after Stephanie and tell her he loved her. He'd fight the senator if he had to in order to be with the woman he loved. There wasn't anything holding him to Winterberry Falls today since he'd already made arrangements at the office to be away and had rushed to get tomorrow's edition ready for print, without Stephanie's article. He pursed his lips.

Jason knew Stephanie needed to be reassured of the truth, to know exactly why he'd disappeared from her life. He told her what he could yesterday without breaking any code of ethics and endangering his family again.

He knew it hadn't been good enough for her.

Steph still doubted him. And he didn't quite know how to fix that.

Tilly laughed at something on the other end of the line, and Jason glanced at his cousin. How blessed he was to have family that cared about him.

Stephanie's family cared, but somehow it came out twisted and cruel.

She was a senator's daughter, but being one didn't define her. Nor did it mean she was privy to the secrets of the politician's office. It was obvious her father had been trying to protect her at the time.

Given the same set of circumstances, Jason would do anything to protect the people he loved, too.

And when you love someone, you tell her the truth. Ugly stuff included.

Within minutes Tilly replaced the phone and turned, a satisfied look on her face. "Like I thought, Melissa said she'd let you in early." Tilly's smile couldn't be more triumphant if she tried.

Jason chuckled.

She crossed her arms and tapped her foot, a Miller habit. "You've got eight hours of road ahead of you, give or take. Just as soon as I get some snacks ready for your trip, you'd better get going, cuz." Tilly stretched across the counter and slid the box of resealable bags closer. She pulled two out and began filling them with muffins and treats from the various containers on the island.

God was at work. And if it was His will to give Stephanie and Jason a future together, nothing was impossible to overcome.

Jason had deceived himself into thinking he could control his circumstances all these years and lost sight of the One who controlled the universe. He hadn't believed God was bigger than his problems in a very long time. If God intended a future for Stephanie and Jason, then it was time he started trusting Him to make it happen. Jason was going to D.C. to fight for his future with the woman he'd always loved, and he'd give her a name if she demanded it this time. And he'd let God control the outcome.

Tilly sealed the bags closed and slid them across the counter. Jason downed the last of his coffee and reached for the treats.

Yes, he had a very long ride ahead of him and lots of time to spend with God. He had hours to forgive himself... and the senator, too. It was time to finally let go of the past, surrender his anger, and swallow his pride.

God was leading and wherever He went, Jason would follow.

Jason stood and rolled his shoulders back.

Yes. He would follow God. Even to the dark corners of Senator Clark's office.

EIGHTEEN

Stephanie curled deeper into the plush pillows and adjusted the Egyptian cotton sheets of the guest room in her parents' D.C. home. She scrolled through the endless list of missed texts and messages accumulated on her phone over the two weeks she'd been in Vermont. Apparently people in D.C. never took a vacation, or left anyone alone who was.

There was a soft knock at the door before it was opened. "Here you go, Ms. Clark, hot and black, just like you like it." The maid's voice interrupted Stephanie's lazy morning as she set a cup of coffee and a plated muffin next to the bed, then drew the drapes. Stephanie's stomach growled. The muffin would be enough to take the edge off her hunger. Light spilled into the room from the picturesque slider windows, and Stephanie squinted.

The maid was a fairly recent hire, and her mother already raved about her.

"Thank you. Am I expected downstairs for breakfast?" Stephanie's ankle still throbbed, the pain killers worn off through the night. Descending the two flights of stairs to join her mother for what would surely turn out to be a lecture with light fare and more coffee didn't exactly thrill her.

A soft laugh filled the room as the maid turned a kind smile to Stephanie. "Senator and Mrs. Clark ate several hours ago and have since left for various engagements this morning. We can prepare something more substantial when you are ready for breakfast. Mrs. Clark would like you to plan to eat on your own for lunch, but intends to be back in time for tea. The senior Walkers and their son will be joining you later for dinner." Her planned day of laying around the house in her pajamas wouldn't suffice. And the Walkers were coming here today?

Stephanie winced. Great. She could recreate her failed attempts at telling Daniel exactly what she thought of his job offer. He'd been more absorbed in his laptop and telephone than he'd been interested in chatting with her the entire way back to D.C. He barely waved goodbye when his car service dropped her off at her parents' house and zoomed away, leaving her standing alone on the front sidewalk with her luggage.

Stephanie placed her phone on the side table, threw back the covers, and massaged the bulging mass of her ankle. She frowned. It should be better by now. The maid moved closer to the bed, and Stephanie glanced up.

"Your parents didn't mention your ankle injury. Perhaps I might send someone up to help you downstairs when you're ready?" The maid wrung her hands as she dutifully waited for a response. If only Stephanie's parents had an elevator installed in their eight bedroom, three story home, last night's climb up to the corner bedroom wouldn't have been so excruciating.

Stephanie shook her head. "No, thank you. But you could bring me an aspirin or something for the pain. It seems I more than twisted my ankle yesterday though the doctor didn't think I did when she looked at it." Doctor Hudson had made a quick house call at noon, saying Jason had stopped by the medical clinic on the way back to the office and asked her to check on Stephanie. Even after everything that was said yesterday morning, he still thought about her well-being. Her eyes watered.

The maid furrowed her brow. "Is there anything else I can bring you with the pain medication, Ms. Clark?"

"I need to check my sugars. I left my glucometer in the bags downstairs. Maybe bring a glass of juice with the meds and the glucometer. And please, just call me Stephanie. There's no reason for you to be so formal with me. It makes me feel…" Stephanie grinned. "Old, like my mother."

The maid lifted a pale hand to her mouth, but not before Stephanie saw the curl of her lips and the twinkle in her eye. She smoothed the front of her apron, turned on her heel, and pulled Stephanie's door closed behind her.

The bed sagged as Stephanie leaned across the mattress and brought the still steaming cup of coffee to her chin. The nutty aroma filled her nose as her lips curled over the white porcelain cup. Her gaze drifted around the room, the smallest bedroom of her parents' home tucked into a corner of the uppermost floor. Her mother had turned the bedroom that would have been Stephanie's—had she chosen to live here after college—into a library. So, whenever holidays came around, Stephanie found herself relegated to this room. She relished the privacy the space afforded. The closet had been left open after she changed for bed last night, exposing the selection of clothes brought over from her apartment for her arrival. She scanned the tailored and colorful outfits. It would be nice to wear something different other than the jeans and sweaters she'd grown accustomed to while in Winterberry Falls. Stephanie sighed. Somehow the excitement of fashion had dulled and been replaced with a desire to dress in comfort instead. But with her ankle the way it was, she'd have to forego the stilettos and tights any way. Something her mother would disapprove of considering the engagements they'd been invited to over the next few days.

She'd discovered this room when her father first came into office and moved the family to D.C. Nothing could bring her out of the funk she lived in after months passed without a word from Jason. Her parents thought introducing her to an old family friend's son and the newly minted lawyer, Daniel Walker would help.

And it had. Daniel had helped her walk through the sketchy waters of her newfound faith, helped her find a church family, and encouraged her to grow as a Christian.

Daniel became a good friend, but not nearly the friend Jason had been. They attended events together that required dates and visited during the holidays when their parents would get together. He'd told her on a number of occasions he'd like to upgrade the status of their relationship, but she'd continually resisted his advances. A professional relationship was all she had to offer Daniel and even that thought had her stomach churning once again.

Stephanie's ankle ached, and her head throbbed a dull tempo, but it would be nothing if she went out on a limb and did her own thing, opposing God's will. She'd been missing God's peace with every thought of working for Daniel. With every glance of the bracelet she'd hidden and every text from Daniel's P.A., her stomach begged to be freed from the coils that twisted it.

She'd prayed for a sign and received one. Though it had destroyed Old Red for good, she'd missed the bigger meaning. She was meant for someplace else.

"What am I doing?" She shook her head and blew a frustrated sigh across the top of her cup.

This wasn't her. A grand home with servants waiting on her hand and foot wasn't her thing.

Did she really want a PR job immersed in the very same political arena she said she wanted to avoid?

"This is a mistake, isn't it, God?"

The room answered with a sullen silence as Stephanie traced imaginary circles on the side of the mug with her thumb. A heavy winter wind rattled the corner windows drawing Stephanie's attention outside. A light dusting of snow covered the barren branches of the trees lining the fenced yard. It was a sprinkling compared to the blast of snow she'd just come from. And she missed it. Or rather, one special person who lived there.

Jason was right. She could open a PR firm anywhere. She didn't have to cater to clients in the D.C. area or even need high-profile clients to survive. When her family lived in Montpelier, there were several high-profile events that benefited from skilled PR personnel. And politicians and entertainers had people working for their brand while working in the state capital, too. Not to mention a town like

261

Winterberry Falls with a festival as big and long as theirs could use help with their PR campaign.

What was holding her here anyway? Her parents had their social circle, one she'd rather not mix with. And if she worked for Daniel, she'd end up with stomach ulcers in no time. No. It was best to decline now before Daniel's plans passed the point of no return. It wasn't good for her health even if it might be good for her career. She rubbed her bare wrist with one hand as she clutched her mug on her lap. As pretty as the bracelet he'd given her was, she'd never put it on again. Perhaps she'd have a chance later to return his gift, along with her answer. Why wait until the 24th when she knew she couldn't follow through?

The tension in her stomach eased. Yes, it was the right thing to do even without knowing the full truth of what really happened during the May rallies of her final year of college.

If even an inkling of what Jason had hinted at was true, only one other person knew what had happened after Jason had left the hospital.

Her father, she was sure, was a huge chunk of the puzzle.

Stephanie placed her cooled coffee mug on the bedside table and burrowed into the pillows. She sucked in a deep draw of air, pungent with polished wood and fabric softener.

Two men she loved more than anything in this world had kept the truth from her for much too long. It was high time to set the record straight.

Stephanie's cheeks moistened as she stared at the ceiling and felt the pounding of her heart against her chest. She squeezed her eyes closed and wished life had turned out differently.

If only things weren't so complicated.

Her breath hitched as she let despair envelop what was left of her faith in men and in herself. She'd trusted Jason and trusted her father. She'd even trusted in her own abilities to get things done.

Somewhere along the road, she'd forgotten to trust God.

It's better to trust in God, than man.

As the verse looped through her brain, she prayed in the stillness of her attic room.

No matter what happened next, she would trust God and lean on Him.

Even if it meant she had to walk away from a dream job, the only man she ever loved, and from the only family she had.

#

Jason shifted his SUV into park and stepped out of the vehicle. He removed four large paper bags filled with chocolate boxes from the back seat, locked the doors, and turned to admire the opulent house.

The tiny evergreen bushes lining the pathway up to the address listed on Tilly's paper shimmered with light. Strands of little bulbs cast a white glow through the greenery while evenly spaced solars peeked above the freshly powdered snow. The sun was setting in the early evening sky, behind the slanted roof of the colonial-revival-style home. The mature trees and the varied character of houses in this wealthy suburb on the outskirts of D.C. provided a welcome diversion from hours of driving along the interstate.

Jason mounted the short three steps and shifted all four bags into one hand. Taking a deep breath, he pressed the ornate doorbell and stared at the fresh wreath hanging on the door.

Faint footsteps could be heard inside approaching the front door. A woman dressed in a pale gray uniform opened it.

"Hello. I have a delivery for Stephanie Clark." He smiled wide.

Her brown eyes studied him as the maid held the door slightly ajar. "Is Ms. Clark expecting you?"

He shook his head. "No, but she ordered some chocolates for Daniel's Christmas Eve party, and I've brought them from Vermont." He pulled one bag from his loaded hand and held it up for the maid's inspection, hoping she wouldn't notice the twitch in his fingers or the waver in his voice. She glanced at the bags in his other hand, no doubt noticing the emblazoned *Chocolate Chocolates, Winterberry Falls, VT* in black lettering.

"I will be sure to set them aside for him. Thank you kindly for taking the time to deliver them. I'm sure you will be compensated adequately." The maid held out a hand to retrieve the bags. Jason stepped back and lowered the chocolates to his side.

"Please. Is Stephanie here?" He softened his voice. "I've come all this way to see her." His heart pounded a deafening performance as the young woman eyed him suspiciously. "I promised to deliver the chocolates to no one but Stephanie. If I don't give them to her personally, then I'll have to take them back."

The woman didn't flinch, nor did she seem sympathetic to his cause.

Jason heaved a sigh, the puff of air misting in front of him.

Perhaps he needed to change tactics.

"At the beginning of last week, Stephanie crashed her car outside my office. It was the worst and best thing to happen to me." He put the bags on the ground and massaged the tender spot on his palm from the weight of the chocolates. "But Stephanie left before I could tell her—"

The maid pressed her finger to her lips, hiding her smile. "Ms. Clark is upstairs resting and is not to be disturbed." Her hushed tone was firm, but the door moved an inch at a time wider.

Jason's breath accelerated, time slowing to a stop, until the maid stepped aside and gestured for him to come in.

He grabbed the bags from the porch, crossed the threshold into a Christmas display that rivalled Tilly's, and placed the chocolates on top of the foyer table between silver candelabras and silver framed Christmas scenes. He quirked an eyebrow as the maid took a step back.

She glanced behind her, and Jason inspected the grand entrance. Draped evergreen boughs were strung through the painted banister, standing out against the muted yellow walls. Muffled laughter trailed from somewhere deep in the house and footfalls resounded away from them in the equally decorated hall before she directed her stare back at him.

"Ms. Clark is not to be disturbed unless it's of great importance." She pressed her lips together and clasped her hands in front of her as she tipped her chin up, her eyes narrowing as if she could assess his true reason for calling.

Jason released the breath he didn't realize he'd been holding and chuckled.

I trust You, God.

"I do have a matter of great importance to discuss with Steph." He shoved shaky fingers through his unkempt hair. He should have made the effort at one of the many rest stops to tame it.

A creak at the top of the carpeted stairwell sounded at the same time he heard a familiar gasp. He turned and took in the refreshing sight.

Stephanie stood with her hand grasping the railing, dressed in an outfit belonging to a woman of means, and one he'd never seen before. The burgundy of her shirt brought out the auburn flecks in the waves of brown hair draped across her shoulders. The mahogany depths of her incredulous stare were intense and full of questions he intended to answer this time.

"Jason?" Stephanie stepped forward and winced.

Jason took two stairs at a time as she grabbed for the railing and stopped herself from falling down the stairs. He reached out and supported her.

"Are you okay? You shouldn't be putting weight on your ankle." He looked down at her bulging foot, better than drowning in those gorgeous eyes and forgetting why he was here. The beige tensor band fabric peeped from beneath her white pant leg, a snug fit into her fuzzy slippers.

Her soft laugh was music to his ears as her breath tickled his cheek.

"I'm okay. I'm…" Her voice cracked, and he met her earnest gaze.

His blood pumped faster.

God, she's beautiful. And I never want to let her go.

"What are you doing here?" The question came breathless, sending his pulse racing faster than Santa's sleigh on Christmas Eve.

He swallowed hard, nerves buzzing while cotton stuck to the roof of his mouth.

Her brows knitted with worry.

"Chocolate." His voice dipped and he chuckled. So, Tilly had neglected to call her departing guest about a special delivery coming ahead of schedule. Good old Tilly. "Tilly asked me to bring your order for Daniel's party."

Her forehead relaxed as a sparkle of understanding, and perhaps something more, glinted in her eye. What he wouldn't do to spend the rest of his life making her look at him like that every day.

"You drove all the way from Vermont to bring me chocolate?" A teasing smile touched her lips.

"Not just chocolate." He gave her his killer coy smile. "Only the best chocolate you'll ever taste in your life."

Her smile widened, and a lovely shade of pink colored her cheeks. Soft hands captured his, her gentle touch sparking a fire within. She laced her fingers through his, and Jason lifted their entwined hands to his heart. A perfect match.

"I asked Melissa to pack a special sugar-free box for you." Jason glanced down the stairs to where he'd left the bags of chocolates. The foyer was empty, along with the bags he'd brought all the way from Vermont. Oh well. Melissa had placed a different-colored box with a red ribbon containing Stephanie's 90 percent cacao treat. It'd be easy for her to find later. He turned back to Stephanie.

"That's very kind of you." Her long lashes lowered, and Jason squeezed her fingers gently, her hand still pressed to his chest.

"I'd do anything for you."

Her expression clouded. "Are you sure about that?" The hint of uncertainty in her tone paralyzed him for a moment.

He'd done that. He was responsible for the hurt in her voice, and God was giving him yet another chance to fight for her this time. He lowered his eyes and stared at the perfect fit of their hands together. Jason breathed a prayer this wouldn't be the last time he wrapped her hand in his.

He wanted to be with her. His heart trilled with every dream of making Stephanie his, but as long as their past stood between them, it could never be.

"I have something important to tell you." He looked back up from their entwined fingers and offered a sincere smile, feeling oddly at peace with what he needed to say.

Her shoulders heaved with an audible breath. She squeezed his fingers back and nodded.

"Well, well, well." The booming statement from the bottom of the stairs sent the hairs on the back of Jason's neck standing.

His stomach jolted. He turned his attention to the impeccably dressed older gentleman standing erect at the foot of the stairwell.

Blazoned eyes fixed on Jason.

269

"Dad, you're home!" Stephanie's welcome sent a layer of ice through Jason's veins. He'd just stepped into the lion's den.

NINETEEN

"Jason miller. This is an unexpected surprise." The senator sounded anything but pleased, and his stare was void of any warmth from the sentiment. Jason held the man's cold gaze.

"Dad! When did you get home?" Stephanie's happy greeting sliced through the building tension.

"I've only just arrived. Your mother wanted to supervise the unloading of your Christmas presents before all our guests arrive, so she asked me to drive around back to make sure nothing gets broken. And so that you don't see what you're getting either." The older man's face visibly relaxed. "Your mother's maid said you wanted to talk to me."

The senator's gaze followed Stephanie as she tugged on Jason's arm, pulling him up to the step beside her. She leaned into him as they started her limping descent. Her steps were slow, and Jason was in no rush to go down the staircase, at any speed. No wonder her dad did well in politics. That frowning stance would intimidate even the naughtiest on the naughty list.

Her knuckles whitened with every stair they descended, and Jason sensed she was in more pain than she let on. He looked at the senator who observed his daughter's careful steps, his jaw set and his gaze sharp. Jason spread his fingers across her hand, hoping she'd rest easier with him next to her.

At the bottom of the stairs, Stephanie let go of Jason's arm and embraced her father.

"Daniel said you'd hurt yourself. How are you feeling?" The senator's voice filled with tenderness. It was a stark contrast to the man who threatened Jason at his last visit.

Stephanie dropped her hands to her sides. "I'll be fine in a day or two. Just a little twist of my ankle. Nothing to worry about."

Jason pressed his lips together as he watched them and hung back. Senator Clark's face held a fondness he'd never witnessed before, an obvious place in his heart for his only child. It wasn't a surprise he'd fought so hard to protect her.

The senator turned, an icy glare sharp enough to pierce Jason. "I didn't think I'd be seeing you again. Especially in my home." His gaze narrowed as he seemed to size Jason up.

"No, I don't suppose you did." Jason stepped forward, a thin smile on his face.

God had this. He was in control. Now all Jason had to do was remember that fact and trust God to do the rest.

"Actually, I'm glad you're here, Senator Clark. I wonder if I might have a few moments of your time." The muscles in his abdomen contracted. The older gentleman stared hard, but Jason refused to be intimidated this time and took courage in God's ability to do the impossible.

Stephanie placed a hand on her father's forearm. "Dad?"

His face softened at Stephanie's quiet prompting, and he nodded curtly at Jason. He heaved a long sigh and glanced between them. "I suppose we have some time to talk before our guests arrive for dinner." He motioned for Jason to follow them to a sitting room off the main foyer.

After Stephanie was seated, the senator pulled the French doors closed, the gentle click blocking out the chatter filtering down the hallway. His strides were clipped as he moved to a sideboard table, silver candlesticks and more evergreen filling the spaces between canisters.

"Can I offer you something to drink?" He picked up the carafe and glanced at both of them. "Our cook makes a mean cup of coffee and it's always hot."

ANN BRODEUR

At the rate he was drinking coffee today, the stuff would start running through his veins. Maybe he should quit. Better yet, make it his New Year's Resolution. Just not yet.

Anything to distract his fingers from holding Stephanie's hand again. "Coffee sounds great." Jason spotted a footstool and slid it over to Stephanie's chair.

"What do you take?" Her father's voice could command an army.

"Sugar, cream."

Satisfied that Stephanie sat with her ankle elevated, Jason offered up a silent prayer and surveyed the no-expense-spared room.

A fire glowed and pumped warmth into the large space. The fireplace mantle dripped with evergreen, twinkle lights and silver bows creating a celebratory touch to the old Colonial. A much too large spruce towered in front of the bay window, its branches weighed down with matching decor. Plenty of seating was provided for those who cared to enjoy the festive space.

If he'd felt worlds apart from Stephanie's luxurious lifestyle, this room only exacerbated the distance. He would never match the senator's salary, nor would he ever come close to giving Stephanie a taste of what was contained in this room. But he could give her his heart, and he could become the man of God she needed him to be.

He looked at Steph as her father set the mugs down on the antique coffee table. She seemed so at ease in this rich setting. Jason sagged into another one of the many chairs. What was he thinking by asking her to leave all this behind? He hadn't voiced the question yet, but would she even consider it?

The senator leaned back in his chair, crossed a leg over his knee, and folded his hands against his belly. The seasoned politician's stare narrowed. "Before you say anything Jason, I think I know why you're here."

The seriousness in his dark gaze did nothing to unnerve Jason, a tactic he remembered well from his college days. God was on Jason's side, he had nothing to fear. Not anymore.

"I believe we have a great many things to discuss, and the sooner we get things on the table, the better." His brown eyes looked at Stephanie, and he held her gaze for a long moment.

He turned back to Jason.

It was now or never.

#

Twenty minutes later, Stephanie didn't know whether to scream, laugh or vomit all over the Persian rug under her feet. Her father, in his designer shirt and tie, sat across from her in the wingback chair, his age-spotted hands clasped in his lap and his thinning head of hair bowed.

Stephanie watched the crackling fire, a snapshot of what had just gone down. Her life as she knew it was gone up in flames with the whole sorry confession from her father, complete with added bits of commentary by Jason.

She placed her long-emptied mug on the ornate coffee table and gripped the arms of her chair. Stephanie shivered despite the heat blasting at her from the fireplace. From the corner of her eye, she saw Jason slide from his chair and crouch down beside her. His hand covered hers, infusing warmth and reassurance.

"God's in control, Steph." He squeezed her hand with the whispered assurance.

She blinked moisture from her eyes and relaxed in the comfort of the man who had done everything humanly possible to protect her. Stephanie's head spun. Jason hadn't abandoned her at all. He was forced from her life.

Her dad cleared his throat. "If I had known then what I know now, I never would have hired my Campaign Manager. It's no excuse, but I had no idea what was going on behind the scenes until Jason confronted me." Defeat shadowed her dad's face, his body limp from confession.

A solitary tear slid from her eye.

"I did what I had to do until I could get to the bottom of it." Her dad's words faded.

Stephanie swallowed hard, her emotions threatening to suffocate her. "But you didn't fire Frank. You let him finish the election." Her voice trembled. "If you knew he was doing things behind your back, why didn't you let him go?"

His shoulders sagged with a huff of frustration. "I'd known Frank for years, and Jason was just a kid—no offense, Jason—still in university chasing a story he thought he'd found." The senator rubbed the back of his neck. "Who was I going to believe?"

Anger simmered beneath the surface and waited to explode as her thoughts and words scrambled together at an exhausting speed. "But, didn't you think maybe there was some truth to what Jason told you? Didn't you want to know why he thought your campaign was tainted? Didn't you—"

"Enough, Stephanie!"

Her eyes widened at his outburst. Her dad's face reddened, and his nostrils flared. He slipped a finger behind his silk tie and loosened the knot, his movements stilted. She'd never witnessed this side of her father before. It's no wonder then, that Jason had kept his end of the bargain and stayed away. The man in front of her coupled with the IRS showing up at *The Independent* would have been enough to send braver men running.

"I did what I thought best. Asking these questions now does nothing to change what happened. You can't blame me for a situation that was forced on me. I had to do damage control the best way I knew how." He swiped at a line of sweat beading across his hairline. "I was able to work quietly with the Feds and Frank…"

He fixed the determined look she knew so well, on her. "I had a wife and daughter to think about. A daughter who was very sick at the time."

Stephanie dropped her gaze and stared at her ankle. She didn't need to be reminded how sick she had been. It only served to rip the wound wider. She had wanted to see Jason, and he'd been prevented from contacting her because of a stupid campaign. Jason's thumb rubbed the back of her hand, encouragement from someone who had also suffered at the hands of a crooked politician.

"But the IRS showed up at the paper." Her throat hurt with the raspy statement.

"Frank did that to ensure the story was dead. I didn't find out until after he'd done it."

She closed her eyes.

You've got to help me on this one, Lord.

"I wasn't prepared to have my campaign hit the fan when I was so close to getting into office and sacrifice the future of my family for the sake of a story." A heavy sigh swept across the table.

She lifted her eyes and watched the hardness from his stare fade into love for her, radiating from the tough exterior of a skillful senator.

"Steph?" The consoling tone of Jason's voice waded through the sticky mess of her emotions. "If there's one thing you need to remember, it's this. We did what we thought was right at the time."

Stephanie's breathing shallowed.

"That's right, Stephanie Grace." Her dad straightened in his chair and tightened the knot in his tie. "Assess the risk, find a solution, and move on."

The practiced expression of empathy used in front of television cameras and public appearances crossed his face. Of course, her dad was ever the politician. And how easily he seemed to slip into that role.

Tears pricked her eyes. How could she stay angry at her dad when it was obvious he'd been sideswiped from the beginning? But he had lied to her and kept her from the man she loved.

"If I had to do it all over again, I would have told you before we even started that hike, when I had the chance." Jason's voice cut into her thoughts. "I would fight for you, Steph, and wouldn't stop. I wouldn't let twelve years, let alone one minute go by without you knowing the truth."

Stephanie was helpless against the tears in her eyes. Jason's words spoke healing to her heart.

He was fighting for her and fighting hard.

God, I don't deserve him.

"I'm sorry I didn't tell you everything back then, Steph. I'm sorry I didn't fight harder." Jason's eyes glistened as he dropped to his knees, his hand still clutching hers. Stephanie held back a sob.

"But most of all, I'm sorry I didn't tell you 'I love you' when I had the chance. I've always loved you, though I didn't show you back then."

Goose bumps cracked over her arms as her heart leapt.

Jason loved her!

"Stephanie." Her dad cleared his throat.

Tears rolling down her face, she angled toward her dad.

Humility brushed the hard lines of his face. "Everything I've ever done has been for you and your mother."

Stephanie nodded and wiped her cheeks dry with the cuff of her sleeve. Her eyes burned, but her spirit longed to be free. "I know."

She would never understand the sacrifice both men had made for her, but she knew it was for love.

Despite their letting her believe a lie for far too many years, there was no way she wanted anger or unforgiveness to take root in her heart.

Justified or not, God had also shown her grace and mercy when she didn't deserve it. God had paid the ultimate sacrifice in giving his Son to nail her sin to that lonely cross on Calvary. God loved her. God forgave her when she asked, and He knew she never deserved it.

She smiled through the subsiding tears.

Stephanie would forgive with all the love and grace of a woman forgiven by God.

The freedom of forgiveness had woven its way into Jason's life. She didn't need to ask to know that somewhere between yesterday's encounter at Tilly's and now Jason had run back to God.

With God's help, she could do the impossible.

Stephanie released Jason's hand, leaned over the table and grasped her father's fingers. "Dad, I've been stuck in a "what if things were different" cycle for years, but I can't base my life on that. All I can do is live in the moment and trust the rest to God." He dropped his chin to his chest, and Stephanie released a tired breath. "I love you, Dad, but you were wrong."

His shoulders straightened, and his eyes flashed defiance as he looked back at her.

"I know I can't change the past, but I can change my direction now." A soft smile pulled at her mouth. The welcome sense of certainty filled her heart, the one she'd been looking for on the road to Washington. "I thought I'd be happy staying in D.C. and taking the PR job with Daniel, but since I've been back here, I know this isn't the life I want." She shook her head. "Politics is your life, Dad, not mine."

Her dad nodded and released her hold.

She turned toward Jason. "A wise friend told me I didn't need to stay in D.C. to start my own PR firm, I could work from anywhere."

Jason's lips turned up in a half grin.

"But for now, I want to write about gingerbread house contests and missing Christmas decorations."

Jason laughed, and her heart skipped at the thought of exploring life with her best friend, far removed from the politics of D.C.

"Dad." Stephanie practically sighed his name. "I forgive you… for everything."

He rose from his seat and crossed the room to where she sat. She wrapped her arms around her dad.

"I love you, Stephanie Grace." His voice cracked, and Stephanie felt, rather than heard, the apology he gave.

"I love you, too, Dad." She closed her eyes and savored the warmth of her father's love. Too many years had passed without these kinds of moments, and she was determined not to let more go by without telling him how much she loved him.

As her dad kept his arms around her, Stephanie's heart soared. *Thank You, God for answering my prayers. And thank You, for showing me what I'm supposed to do next.*

"As much as I love you and Mom, there's somewhere else I need to be this Christmas. I don't belong here, and I think we've both known that for a while." She pulled back and smiled up at him.

His warm gaze rested on her face for a moment before he turned and nodded at Jason. "Then I guess you'd better go with him and make sure you tell him how you feel." A soft smile played on his wizened lips, and he chuckled. "Especially since he's already told you he loves you."

Another wave of heat rushed to her cheeks, sending tingles across her skin.

Her dad placed a gentle kiss in her hair and helped her stand. He draped an arm across her shoulders.

With his protective embrace still around her, he turned to Jason, who stood, and held out a hand. Jason winked at her and shook the senator's hand. Her heart bubbled with joy as she watched the men make amends. God was so good to her.

"You know, the first time I met Jason I could see how he felt about you, and maybe I wasn't quite ready to give you up back then." Admiration radiated from his dark eyes, releasing a flood of happiness in her soul. Her dad accepted Jason.

God was definitely at work doing the impossible.

"After all this time, Jason, you have proven yourself a man of your word." He cleared his throat. "I couldn't be pleased to see my daughter with any one more worthy."

Stephanie's hand flew to her chest, a flurry of emotions filling her heart.

"Love her with everything you've got, Jason."

Jason nodded. "I will."

Thank you, God. You're amazing! If her ankle didn't hurt so much, she'd dance.

With a firm handshake of Jason's hand and one last childhood kiss on her nose, her dad turned and left them alone. When the door finally shut behind his towering figure, Stephanie fell into Jason's open arms. Her ankle still throbbed, but it was nothing compared to the pounding of her chest and the joy of her soul. God was giving her the life she'd always longed for.

And this year, with her dad's blessing, she would spend Christmas with her best friend, the man who had captured her heart.

TWENTY

Jason glanced in his rearview mirror and blinked for the thousandth time in the seven hours since leaving the grand old house in the D.C. suburbs early that morning.

How incredibly blessed he was.

Stephanie sat sideways in the backseat with her injured ankle resting on the bench. A pillow was propped between her back and the car door, her arms crossed in front of her. She looked so peaceful sleeping there, like an angel, with her dark lashes pressed against pale cheeks.

His own Christmas Angel.

Ha! She wouldn't stand it if he dared call her that.

Jason smiled. Whether Steph liked it or not, she *was* his Christmas miracle, and he couldn't wait for the special holiday to arrive in four more days. And this year, he would share it with her and his family all together.

Winterberry Falls wasn't much farther, but the needle of the fuel gauge hovered close to empty. He could use the break to stretch his legs, too.

Jason rolled his shoulders and stopped next to a pump at the well-lit station. He reached for his wallet in the glove compartment, careful not to wake Stephanie, and withdrew his credit card.

Movement in the back seat caught his attention.

"Where are we?" A groggy Stephanie stretched her arms above her head and yawned.

"New York. Not much longer and we'll be home."

A soft smile painted her lips. "Home."

The whispered word wrapped ribbons of hope around Jason's heart. Anywhere Stephanie was would be home to him.

"Do you want anything?" She pushed down on her seat belt buckle.

Jason tossed his wallet back in the compartment and looked at her in the mirror. "I'd say coffee, but with the amount I've had in the past week, I won't sleep ever again."

Stephanie grinned and reached for her purse. "A surprise then. I don't want to hear any complaints when I get back."

The chill of the December air shocked his eyes wide as they exited the car. Jason watched Stephanie cross the parking lot with a slight limp and disappear inside the convenience store. He stomped his feet and shoved one hand into his pocket. The fuel apparently thought it was on holiday for the length of time it took to fill his tank.

He checked his watch. Another hour and bit before they arrived in Winterberry Falls.

He finished refueling the vehicle and then parked in a spot near the door so Stephanie wouldn't have far to walk. He'd get her set up at the B&B when they returned and head into the office to put the last touches on the New Year special edition and review the assignments for the concluding days of the festival. Jason sighed. The work never ended.

He really needed a news editor. Despite Kimberley's qualifications and eagerness to start in the coming week, she was a bit too flirty for his liking. She'd have the heads of all the single guys in the office spinning. All he needed was one good candidate, and while he'd love for Stephanie to take the job, she was focused on her PR firm, and he wanted her to achieve her dream. Jason adjusted the strap of his seat belt across his chest. God had given him one huge miracle already, there wasn't a reason why He wouldn't provide the perfect solution to *The Independent*'s staffing issue.

Stephanie emerged from the store and hobbled back to the SUV, hands and arms burdened with packages. Jason leaned over the console and opened the passenger door for her. His blood hummed as she smiled at him. What was it about this woman that captivated him?

He looked at the pile of snacks Stephanie piled on her lap after settling in next to him. "Hungry?"

She chuckled as she buckled up, and they made their way back to the highway. "Famished. I think I bought everything I could eat in there."

Jason slowed as he hugged the curve in the highway.

"You wouldn't happen to have—"

"Your favorite?"

Stephanie's hand shook a snack sized bag of sour cream and onion flavored chips, her wrist conspicuously bare of the bracelet she'd worn the entire time she'd been in Winterberry Falls.

Jason grinned. "You remembered."

She grimaced. "How could I forget the stench of those things? Honestly, I don't know why you love them so much."

He snatched the bag from her hand, keeping his eyes on the road. "You just don't appreciate the benefits of convenience foods."

She threw her head back, her laughter filling Jason's heart. "Well, if there's one thing I do appreciate, it's breath mints." She pulled a small tin of mints from her pocket and tossed them onto the dash. "Humor me when you're done."

Jason opened the bag with his teeth and crunched a chip. Stephanie snickered.

He marveled at how easily they slipped back into their friendship and how comfortable silence could be with her. He was incredibly blessed.

"So, what happened to your bracelet?" Jason dug into the chip bag on his lap and focused on the road ahead. "I haven't seen it for a while."

"I gave it back last night after the dinner party when I told Daniel I wasn't going to take the job. He'd given it to me, and I didn't think I should keep it, all things considered." Her quiet response assured him truly nothing held her to D.C. anymore. "I can't say he was pleased about it, but at least this time he actually listened to me." Her soft laugh brought a smile to his face.

So that's what happened after I left her parents' place for a hotel. Thank You, God.

They drove on and the crunching of snacks filled the comfortable silence, Stephanie with her cheese and crackers and Jason with his junk food.

"How'd you manage to get away from the paper for two days on such short notice, especially when you don't have a news editor yet?"

Jason drew in a breath and leaned back against the headrest. "I spread the work around a bit and some were more happy than others to take an extra load for a day or two. But, it's just not sustainable the way we've been going. I really need to get someone in place soon, so I spent part of the evening on Thursday reviewing the resumes that came in. I have three interviews lined up for Monday." Jason pulled another chip from the bag.

"Well, I hope for your sake you get someone pronto. I'm sure it will work out. God's got this, Jay." She bit into her cracker. After a minute, she took a sip from her water bottle and replaced it in the drink holder. "Um, so, what about Miss New York? She's certainly qualified and seemed... eager."

He grinned before crunching on the last chip and wiping his hand on a napkin Stephanie had brought with the snacks. So he'd been right when Kimberley had come to the office. Steph *was* jealous of the young reporter.

"She's willing and likely capable, but I don't get the feeling it would be a long-term thing for her. I'm keeping an open mind, though. I want to interview a few more before making my final call. It's a decision I'd rather not repeat any time soon." He glanced at her, and she smiled back at him. Her hand slid across the console and grasped his.

"Anyone else in mind for the job?"

He turned his head at her question and held her look for several seconds before concentrating on the road.

"Yeah, but she's got big dreams of her own. And I want her to have that chance to live it. She'll always have a place at *The Independent* though if she wants it. All she has to do is ask." Jason steered the vehicle around another short curve.

"You're incredible." Her voice caught as she squeezed his hand.

No. She had it wrong.

"I don't deserve you, Steph," he whispered and lifted her hand to his lips. Slowly, he planted a tender kiss on her knuckles. His anger and fear had cost him too much, and he was done with wasting time. He promised himself he would show her how much she meant to him every day.

Starting now.

He lowered their clasped hands and cleared his throat. "You know, you could make things easy on me and just take Emily's job until I find a more permanent solution and you get your PR firm off the ground." He lightened the tone and shot Stephanie the most convincing grin he could muster.

Stephanie's lips tugged into a smile, and she shook her head.

"I've got a ton of stuff to do. I need to find a car, sell my apartment in D.C., and move to this little out of the way place I recently rediscovered." Jason smiled at her trail of thought already leading her to a more permanent stay in Winterberry Falls. "Oh, and I still have one final article to write about missing Christmas decorations in this same small mountain town. Town's on edge because no one knows who's behind the thefts." She scrunched the snack bag in her free hand and lifted her chin. "I've got a source who says she knows what's going on. And that the police are in on it."

Jason released her hand to grip the wheel again. "Yeah, about that. You missed the deadline for this morning's edition, so I pulled your spot." She was not going to like that one.

"You pulled the spot?" The question was laced with an edge. "What about the rest of the story? Did you pull that spot for Tuesday's edition, too?"

"You gave me nothing before you took off to D.C., and I have a paper to run. I pulled your spot and promised readers a better story on Tuesday. So, you've got a lot of work to do before Christmas Eve. Which is in three days by the way in case you've forgotten." Jason reached for his take-out cup and took a drink. He stole a look at Stephanie as he replaced the cup.

"What is a better story than the one I'm working on?"

Jason forced his face into a stoic expression. "How Santa delivers all those presents in one night." He bit down on his inside cheek and waited.

Stephanie slapped his arm and groaned. "Right. I haven't lost yet. You'll see. *Where Did Baby Jesus Go?* is the biggest Christmas story *The Independent* has ever published."

Jason chuckled and pulled the sun visor down.

"I can't believe you still think there's no story there." He barely missed her mumbled response.

"All right, Ms. Smarty Pants Reporter. Finish your article and then start on mine. But in all seriousness, could you at least think about filling in temporarily?" Jason checked his mirrors and changed lanes.

Stephanie leaned forward and placed her garbage in a plastic bag on the floor. "Of course, Jason. I'm not crazy about a reporter's job long term, but you know I'll help where I can."

Jason nodded. "I know, but I don't want to take advantage of your willingness to help. And I know you have dreams of starting up your PR firm. I don't ever want to stand in the way of that." He stared into the distance.

"I have everything I've ever wanted right here." Her quiet words sucked the breath from him.

If he were anywhere else, he would have twirled her in the air and kissed her better than the actors did it in those romantic movies women loved. He'd have to settle for a smile and a brush of her cheek.

"Me, too, Steph." Her skin was soft and warm beneath his fingertips. "Me, too."

#

Jason hung up the phone and rubbed his face. He'd finished interviewing the three applicants that morning and started calling references after lunch. There was one potential candidate from this morning's pool, but he'd much rather be taking event photos or searching for a new vehicle for Stephanie than tackling interview protocol.

An irregular *rat-a-tat-tatting* interrupted Jason's Monday afternoon. He stood, crossed the room, and opened the door.

"Dad, what a nice surprise." Jason pulled the older man's hand in for a shake and a hug. His dad hadn't lost his hearty handshake nor his jovial laugh since his stroke.

Jason patted him on the back and offered him a drink.

"No, thanks. Your mother has me on a strict diet, and she has spies everywhere." He winked as he settled into a vacant chair.

Jason chuckled. "I'm sure she does." He nudged his office chair closer and sat.

"Anna tells me you've made some changes."

Jason lifted an eyebrow at his dad's remark and laughed. "Speaking of spies, right Dad?"

The older man chuckled.

"Anna's right." Jason rapped his knuckles against the arm of the chair. "With some changes to the way we do things around here, we should be able to stay in the black and maybe even increase the bottom line."

Dad stroked his chin as Jason shared details of the plans he'd made for the coming year, fresh energy pulsing in his veins the more he talked.

"Good, good." His dad stared at the floor.

"Dad?" Jason's heart skipped a beat at the confused look on his dad's face.

"I must have drifted off there, son."

Perhaps he wasn't as well as Jason initially thought. "Is everything okay? You seem out of sorts."

"Perfectly fine."

Jason frowned. Why was his dad really here? He'd barely visited since he got sick, and by all accounts from his mom, Dad was finally resting and enjoying time off after all these years.

"Have you found anyone to replace Emily yet?" His dad crossed his arms.

"I've interviewed four candidates, but the first one was a disaster." Jason's muscles tensed at the recollection of Kimberley's interview. Or rather, more accurately, Stephanie's show down. "One has potential, but I'm not convinced he's the best choice." His indecision likely had something to do with a brunette out on assignment who had his heart and brain all tied up in knots.

Jason pinched the bridge of his nose. "I still can't believe Emily left."

Dad chuckled "Love makes us do crazy things."

Jason grinned as the image of Stephanie filled his mind along with memories of a very long drive and a car full of chocolates. "Isn't that the truth."

His gaze drifted to the lower corner of the wall of photos. Peace settled over his heart. God was good, had always been good to him. Jason was just sorry it took him so long to recognize it.

"How is she?"

ANN BRODEUR

Jason flicked his gaze back to his father. Who? Oh, right. "I haven't talked to Emily since she left on the ninth. I suppose she and her new husband are off somewhere on their honeymoon by now."

His dad shook his head, a cheeky grin plastered on his face. "How's Stephanie?"

Jason's smile refused to be contained. "Happy to be back, I think."

The subtle laughter in his dad's eyes told Jason everything. He had never been good at keeping things from his dad. "So, she's staying?"

"It appears that way." Jason's thoughts scattered with the notion of sweeping Stephanie off her feet and making her happy for the rest of his life. All because God was granting his heart's desire.

Dad's face grew serious. "And Senator Clark is really okay with her being here?"

Jason's heart pounded. Despite giving his parents the short version of his trip to D.C. in the lobby yesterday after church services, his dad still wanted reassurance. After all, the last time he'd been with Stephanie, the senator's staff had all but destroyed the paper's reputation and left their family reeling with the aftermath of the surprise audit by the IRS. Fortunately, his father was a man of integrity who lived as honest as they come and nothing was found. Jason only hoped he could live up to his example.

"He is." The corner of his mouth crept up. "God is good, Dad. There's nothing to worry about anymore."

296

His slapped his knee and straightened. "Good. Then you'll be happy to hear I'm planning on coming back in the New Year."

Jason's eyes widened in surprise. "Really? Doc Hudson thinks you're ready to jump back in?" With both Jason and Stephanie starting all over from scratch, how would he have the means to support her? Granted, he hadn't been taking a salary, but with streamlining staff responsibilities and implementing cost saving plans, he would be in a position to start receiving pay again.

His dad's signature chuckle rumbled through the office. "She didn't approve full-time work. Thinks this job is too hard on my heart. But, she did approve part-time hours as your news editor, assuming you think I'm qualified to do a job I did when your grandfather ran this paper." His eyes twinkled.

Jason tilted his head. He'd been hoping his dad would be well enough to resume his most-recent position at the paper for a while, but..."What are you saying?"

His dad's eyes filled with pride. "You're the boss, Son. You can make whatever changes you want. I'll be here to help if you need it. With the way the staff loves you and all your ideas, you'll be in charge until Megan graduates and afterward until you decide differently. The projected numbers will enable you to start taking a full-time salary again. I know you left a job you absolutely loved to come home and keep your grandfather's legacy going. And I can't tell you how proud you've made me because of that."

Jason's breath caught as the room seemed to freeze in front of him.

"You've proven you can run this ship without any guidance or interference from me, and you've got plans to move this business forward." He rubbed the scruff on his chin. "Megan still has schooling to finish, and even when she graduates, she won't be ready to take over. And she's perfectly happy to work under you until you are both ready for changing hands." He pressed his lips together. "*If* you want to change hands should you feel God is calling you elsewhere."

It had been his grandfather's wish that the generations following would keep the paper running. But even more than that, he'd wished for his children and grandchildren to follow the Lord's leading. Had God led Jason back to the paper so he'd be here when Stephanie crashed into his life again?

Jason's vision blurred. His dad was giving him the management of the paper, carte blanche to do what was necessary to survive, giving him a future, and a way to provide for Stephanie and any little ones they might have.

He was giving him a choice to stay or leave.

No strings attached.

It was more than he'd hoped for. God was answering even his unspoken prayers.

He puffed his cheeks out before letting go of his breath.

"I don't know what to say." Jason's voice cracked.

"Say you'll take it, if that's what you want." His dad's voice lowered. "I know you had other dreams and the paper wasn't really a part of those plans, but I'd be honored if you agreed to lead *The Independent* into the future."

Jason's eyes stung

What would Steph think? Would she be happy staying here with him in Winterberry Falls?

Jason covered his mouth and listened to the faint chatter of the newsroom. He cared about these people, had grown up with many of them. They were like family, and he'd missed the hometown feel when traveling the world with his camera chasing a youthful dream. Did he really want to go back to the life he had? His dad was giving him an opportunity for stability, a way to provide for a family and a chance to settle down, with the flexibility of moving on in the future. With his renewed relationship with Stephanie, he had no desire to go anywhere any time soon.

Somehow, he was sure Steph would feel the same way, too.

He smiled and swiped the back of his hand across his eyes. "I'll make you proud, Dad."

His dad's eyes glistened as he pushed to his feet and pulled Jason in for an embrace. "You already have, Son. You already have."

TWENTY-ONE

The sun shone gloriously Christmas Eve morning behind the Fallsview Retirement Center as Stephanie's cross-country skis sliced through the cut trail pushing her into the open meadow of Mrs. Sweeney's home. Roger had recovered her skis for her when he examined her car and had them delivered to *The Independent*. It was like an early Christmas present seeing them sitting in Jason's office yesterday. She paused at the edge of the forest to scan the flattened peak of Bread Loaf Mountain, her heavy breaths curling into wisps above her head. She reached for her goggles and slid them up.

This view was worth taking the trail from town. She'd have to remember to thank Tilly for telling her about it.

"Thank you, God." She panted the prayer and smiled. Her ankle was feeling better, thanks to the weekend of rest. And with the weight of her D.C. decision behind her, Stephanie hadn't felt this healthy or strong in a long time.

If only she could share this moment with Jason. Except, he'd been so busy playing catch up, she hadn't spoken to him since yesterday morning. He was hoping to get through the essentials today so that he had a clear slate to take two days off for Christmas celebrations.

Besides, he'd given her time to finish her article yesterday and to search for a more permanent living arrangement. She had one more interview to conduct for Saturday's final installment before she could declare her running story the best series of Christmas articles *The Independent* had ever printed. But until then, she had other plans for her day.

Stephanie pushed off on her skis, the *swish, swish* of the blades gliding through the snow blended with her scrambling thoughts. After turning down Daniel and returning the bracelet to him at her parents' dinner party on Saturday evening, she had finalized and sent her resignation letter to the magazine. It was reluctantly received, but her boss was happy for her new endeavor. He'd wished her well. Cutting all ties that linked her professionally to D.C. was liberating. She couldn't wait for January 2nd when she'd move into the little bachelor apartment she'd found right above the chocolate shop. For now, she'd booked a room at Tilly's for the rest of the holidays.

She ground to a stop in the middle of the field, spraying snow in an artistic display. She lifted her face toward the warmth of the sun and reveled in the peace of following God's will.

"You are so good, God!" Stephanie lifted her arms high.

She adjusted the straps of her backpack and slid through the blanketed field toward the main building. Christmas Eve had arrived, and Stephanie was exactly where she wanted to be. Mrs. Sweeney was expecting her for lunch and had asked for help in preparing the Christmas surprise. She was eager to help Mrs. Sweeney execute her plan, gleaning a firsthand account for her last article. Jason had promised to stop by later to take photos, despite his contrary opinion about the truth of the missing decorations.

She snapped off her skis and leaned them against the wall of the wraparound porch, leaving the poles next to them. She stomped the snow from her boots and opened the door to the retirement center.

"Good morning, Stephanie. What brings you here on Christmas Eve?" The receptionist looked up from her desk. Stephanie smiled at the woman she'd met the first time she'd come to visit Mrs. Sweeney last week.

"Merry Christmas, Judy." She pulled her woolen hat from her head. "Mrs. Sweeney asked me to spend the rest of the day with her, so I'll be hanging around here this afternoon if you don't mind." Stephanie grabbed at her flyaway hairs.

Judy smiled. Leaning on her forearms, she glanced up at Stephanie. "What a lovely way to spend your afternoon. I'm sure she'll have stories to tell you. By the way, I've been enjoying the series of articles in our little paper. Have you solved the mystery yet? Do you know where the decorations have gone? I'm dying to know."

Stephanie chuckled. "Mum's the word and I have a feeling it'll be more than just listening to Mrs. Sweeney today. I came prepared to work."

Judy tilted her head, and Stephanie drew a finger across her own lips, throwing away the imaginary key. "Sworn to secrecy. But I have it on good authority, you will be in the know by the time Santa is loading his sleigh this afternoon."

Stephanie was sure the petite woman's laugh was the stuff of fairy dust and sugar plums. "Well then, I shall leave you to it. Lunch is served in five minutes, so I'll let them know upstairs that you'll be joining her."

Stephanie thanked Judy and made her way through the stark hallway to the elevators.

After spending time in downtown Winterberry Falls, the lack of decorations stood out like a reindeer's red nose. It was disheartening to see, but Stephanie knew Mrs. Sweeney would do her best to bring some cheer to this blank space. And she was more than willing to help her get it done. If anything the chief had said about his mother was true, she was sure to find a way to bring Christmas to her neighbors.

The elevator announced Stephanie's arrival, and she paused as the doors parted. On the other side stood a smiling Mrs. Sweeney, erect and dressed as festive as one could get. Her Christmas sweater was outdone by her Christmas patterned skirt and her reindeer antler barrettes topped off the ensemble.

Stephanie stifled a laugh as she stepped into the dining room.

"Stephanie, right on time. Good girl. Let's sit. We have much to discuss." Mrs. Sweeney tapped her cane, the silver garland wrapped around the shaft shimmering in the sunlight.

"We have plenty to do today to be ready to unveil our surprise." Mrs. Sweeney's eyes shone brighter than the star at the top of Stephanie's family Christmas tree, sparking an excitement that only Christmas could bring. They ordered a simple lunch and ate, Stephanie losing herself in the old schoolteacher's hushed plans.

Stephanie's phone buzzed from her backpack on the floor.

"Go on, dear. But don't be upset if another brie goes missing while you're checking your messages." The older woman shoved her glasses back up the bridge of her nose.

Stephanie pulled her phone from the backpack.

Jason: WHERE ARE YOU?

Stephanie grinned at the text from Jason, her heart wildly skipping. What was she, in eighth grade again?

The retired teacher put down her fork, the brie missing from her plate. "You should have come for breakfast, dear. Crepes, sausage, and eggs. It doesn't get better than that."

Stephanie: HAVING LUNCH WITH MRS. SWEENEY.

Stephanie sent the text, placed the phone on the table, and attacked her bowl of soup before the older woman finished her own.

Jason: BE THERE SOON.

"You better eat up, Ms. Clark, before your mouth falls off from smiling. It would be a shame to let good food go to waste." Mrs. Sweeney's eyes scanned the plate in front of her.

Stephanie laughed and replaced her napkin on her lap. "Yes, ma'am."

Mrs. Sweeney guffawed before slicing through the last tomato on her plate. "It will do just fine that Mr. Miller is coming. We can use an extra set of hands, especially strong ones like his." She shoved a forkful of food into her mouth. "Looks like the Good Lord answered our prayers and gave us a marvelous day in order to give these folks a Christmas they won't soon forget." She turned happy blue eyes toward Stephanie and winked. "And just think, I have you to help me with it."

Stephanie lifted her glass to her lips and downed the last of the water. "And I am more than happy to be Santa's little helper."

A few minutes later, Mrs. Sweeney covered her lips with a wrinkled hand and giggled, her eyes locked on something beyond Stephanie.

"Did I miss anything?" The heat of Jason's minty breath swept her neck as he spoke in her ear. His strong hands slowly brushed the sides of her arms and sent a cascade of delightful shivers shooting through Stephanie's spine.

Mrs. Sweeney's brows arched in amusement as she rose to her feet. "Now that you're here, Mr. Miller, our work can begin."

Jason scooted to his former grade schoolteacher's side and handed her the cane. With her pulse still speeding at an incredible rate, Stephanie gathered her things and bit the inside of her cheek.

Would it always be like this with the love of her life?

Would Jason still send shivers down her spine with just one glance when they were Mrs. Sweeney's age?

Stephanie hoisted her backpack around her shoulders and stole a glance at Jason as he helped steady the sweet old lady. Her heart melted with a picture of their future together. Stephanie would not take him, or his love, for granted.

Thank You, God for Your blessings.

Jason stopped beside her with a wink and tugged her hand free from the backpack strap. She smiled up at him, and his gaze warmed. He entwined his fingers with hers, stealing her breath and weakening her knees.

"Quit mooning over Ms. Clark, Mr. Miller. We've got work to do." Mrs. Sweeney's matronly voice riddled the air. She stood at the elevator doors, cane tapping the floor.

Jason laughed. "Yes, ma'am." He leaned over and pressed a quick kiss to Stephanie's forehead before pulling her along to follow Mrs. Sweeney.

As they slipped into the elevator after the retired schoolteacher, they found a place behind her. The doors closed, and Stephanie breathed a happy sigh.

God had answered her prayer the minute she'd crashed into the town's sign.

If only she had been paying attention.

Jason squeezed her hand before mouthing, "I love you."

Her heart nearly burst with love.

Yes, God was good, and His mercies were new every morning.

As she inclined her face heavenward, she closed her eyes, wrapped in the love of her heavenly Father. God saw her, even in this cube of an elevator, just like He'd always seen her.

The bell chimed, the doors swept open, and Mrs. Sweeney shuffled forward. Stephanie let Jason guide her out of the elevator.

She couldn't have asked for a better gift this year than the one God had given her and Jason.

A second chance at forever.

TWENTY-TWO

Later that afternoon, Stephanie had never seen so many smiling faces, nor had Christmas been so tightly wrapped around her heart.

Mrs. Sweeney floated through the games and recreation room hugging neighbors from town and from the residence, laughing while Christmas music drifted through the speakers of Fallsview Retirement Center. How she had managed to convince the management of this one little concession was beyond Stephanie, but she imagined the retired schoolteacher had worked her illustrious charms.

"Well, Ms. Clark, care to interview me now?"

Stephanie turned at the sound of Chief Sweeney's voice. "I believe instead of interviewing you, I owe you an apology."

His eyes danced as she held out her hand. He covered her hand with his large one and pumped, lips parting in a jovial smile. "No need. You were just doing your job."

Stephanie shrugged. "As were you."

He winked. "One can't exactly say *no* to my mother. She rallied the aid of the center's youth volunteers and their friends. They willingly lent her pieces, mind you without the consent of their parents. When she explained what she was doing, I thought I'd better help her. There was no real harm done and after this party, all property will be returned to their rightful owners before the live nativity is finished tonight in town."

"I can't say I approve of your aiding, but I can't say I approved either of management's decision to ban Christmas. I mean, look around you. The place was bare this morning and now it's like we're in the North Pole." Stephanie surveyed the crowd. Residents and their guests held plates of Tilly's Christmas baking and sipped on eggnog provided by Blitzen's Diner. And one glance around at the wooden reindeer, bows, and even the baby Jesus solved the mystery of the missing decorations.

The chief nodded his agreement and headed to his mother's side. She watched him help her to the makeshift stage where a microphone and speakers had been set up.

Mrs. Sweeney's master plan played out before her very own eyes, and Stephanie held the exclusive rights to the story that would be printed in *The*

Independent's special Christmas online edition and again in Saturday's print paper.

A camera snapped and Stephanie spun on her heel.

"Now there's a picture worth a thousand words." Jason grinned behind the lens.

"Not like the photo in your dad's office." Stephanie's memory of the first time she'd visited Winterberry Falls was rooted firmly in their history. She no longer would look back on that time with heartache, but would choose to remember it as a necessary chapter of their happily ever after.

He held out a hand, beckoning her to draw closer, then brushed his knuckle across her cheek, his eyes shining with love. Her heart twirled with the music.

She could get used to him looking at her like that. Stephanie shivered. He had such a soothing touch it made her feel cherished.

"That was the day I truly fell in love with you."

Heat throbbed in her cheeks, and her lips twisted into a grin. She was loved by a wonderful man who found his way back to God.

A flash of mischief sparked in his eye.

Stephanie's gaze narrowed, and she nearly shrieked when he dragged her to the treat table. Thank goodness Mrs. Sweeney's amplified voice covered her little outburst.

"I made sure there would be something you could have at the party tonight." He moved to the end of the table and lifted the lid from a box conspicuously set apart from the rest of the Christmas cakes, cookies, candies and squares.

What did she do to deserve someone who cared about her, right down to the details of what she could eat?

"For you." Jason dramatically bowed, arm circling through the air in front of him. He held the lid behind his back. "I ordered it specially from Tilly's kitchen."

Stephanie's hand flew to her heart as she eyed the silver platter. Stalks of broccoli rose up from cauliflower snowbanks, gathered around a veggie dip pond, creating a beautiful winter wonderland.

"This is…" Stephanie laughed. "Pretty amazing. Thank you, Jason for thinking of me."

He straightened after placing the lid beneath the table. "I'll never stop thinking of ways to make you smile."

Stephanie swatted his arm. "I never knew you were so cheesy."

Jason chuckled. "Well, I can't help that part, but I guess I have to keep my star reporter happy and healthy. And part of Christmas party fun is food. Although, most of the food on this table would have us repeating some history I'd rather not."

Stephanie raised an eyebrow as laughter erupted behind them.

"You concede the victory then? I was right and you were wrong about the Christmas caper."

Jason shrugged. "I wasn't entirely wrong. It was still high school kids, but I'm wise enough to recognize your talent to find a good story. I have to be able to give my staff room to follow their hunches, since I'm taking over the paper permanently."

Her eyes widened. "That's amazing!" She vaulted into his arms, loving the feel of him against her. A girl could get mighty used to that. "Are you happy about this? I mean, what about photography and your dream of traveling the world?" She pulled away, keeping her fingers locked behind his neck.

Jason's hands slid to her waist, leaving a delicious trail of tingles along her torso. "I am. I'm exactly where I'm supposed to be."

Stephanie examined his face. Yes, he really seemed happy with taking over the paper. Her heart did an excited flutter, and she drew her fingers through his dark hair, the applause behind them barely registering.

"Besides, I can take photos in Winterberry Falls and travel for fun instead of work. Maybe I'll even find my Pulitzer here." He smiled and nuzzled his nose against hers, pushing her core temperature higher. Her heart thundered like the hooves of reindeer landing on a shingled roof.

"I've a new dream now." He rasped, desire welling in his eyes.

Stephanie's eyes fluttered closed, and her teeth gripped her bottom lip. This was it. The moment she'd longed for since Jason declared he loved her in D.C. One tilt of her chin. One purse of her lips. One—

"And without further ado, I'd like you all to meet the reporter behind the fun series of articles about my little escapades and your participation in this Christmas surprise."

Stephanie's eyes flew open as her body grew rigid. Horrified, she pinched her lips into a smile and turned slowly to face the room. Stephanie offered a slight wave to the hundred pair of eyes directed at her. She swore the color of her cheeks must match the red of her dress she'd brought in her backpack for the afternoon's event.

Jason released her waist and clutched her fingers. He chuckled as he led her to the front of the room where Mrs. Sweeney stood beaming, the microphone quivering in her hand. A wrinkled arm slid behind Stephanie's back as she stopped next to the podium.

"Ms. Stephanie Clark came crashing into our town." Mrs. Sweeney was rewarded with a few chuckles, and Stephanie tamped her lips tighter, heat once again creeping up her neck. "And we're so very thankful she did. But with her arrival, our beloved town sign suffered irreparable damage. I am pleased to tell you, the Clark family has donated a magnificent new sign with big, bold lettering and everything."

Thunderous applause broke out, and Stephanie nodded at the crowd. She'd been able to pull a few strings to have a temporary sign installed today.

When warmer weather arrived, a more permanent structure would be put in place.

Mrs. Sweeney's eyes glistened as she looked at Stephanie. "But what I really want you all to know about this remarkable young woman is that without her help, tonight would not have been possible. Thank you for bringing Christmas back to Fallsview Center, Ms. Clark." Jason remained next to them and wore a striking smile, his eyes bright with pride.

Something stirred deep within Stephanie's heart, and she squeezed the frail woman's waist.

"We hope you'll find it within your heart to call Winterberry Falls home." Mrs. Sweeney's words were drowned in the answering applause, but still floated to Stephanie's heart. Never in her wildest dreams had she thought this place would be—would feel like—home.

Mrs. Sweeney released Stephanie and clapped with her fellow residents before raising her arms and quieting the audience. "Just one more thing before we all go back to celebrating the birth of the King."

As Mrs. Sweeney jumped topics, Stephanie felt a nudge on her elbow.

Jason stepped over to the Christmas tree they'd pulled from its hiding place in the janitor's closet earlier in the afternoon. Multicolored lights twinkled, sending spurts of color against Jason's cheeks. He gripped her fingers and stepped back, putting a modest amount of space between them.

"We've been so busy getting this room ready for Mrs. Sweeney today, we haven't had a private moment for me to do this next part. As my first act of publisher in chief, I want to offer you a part-time permanent position of news editor. My dad wants to come back part-time, but I need a full-time editor. If you take a part-time position, you'll still have time to get your PR company up and running. You could still live your dream."

Stephanie took a long draw of air, her muscles relaxing. Hints of gingerbread and chocolate flavored the air.

God indeed had a purpose in bringing her back to Winterberry Falls.

Had it only been two weeks?

"There's no one I'd rather have next to me than you." His voice dropped a notch. He lifted her fingers and brushed his lips across them. "At work. At home. Every moment in between." With each declaration his kisses lingered longer.

"You're truly impossible." She nearly gasped as his lips pressed against one knuckle at a time. He looked through heavy lashes, the heat from his breath sweeping across her fingers like a fresh dusting of snow.

How could she resist this man?

"Is that a yes?" His eyebrow cocked, and Stephanie's feet slid closer.

"Yes."

The corner of his lip lifted, and with agonizing slowness, he placed her hands around his neck, his body moving in time to the relaxing music piped through the speakers. He touched his forehead to hers, lips so close she could smell the hint of Tilly's baking he'd eaten earlier. Her body listed against his as her hips swayed, and her feet followed Jason's lead. Stephanie's breath caught as she breathed in everything Jason. Everything Christmas.

Everything home.

"Well done, Mr. Miller." Mrs. Sweeney's voice croaked, distracting her from Jason's warm embrace. Again.

"However, it seems, young man, you've forgotten one thing."

Jason stopped moving and turned his head toward Mrs. Sweeney, his arms still wrapped around Stephanie.

"And what's that, ma'am?"

The stern look she gave couldn't hide the twinkle in her eyes. She lifted her cane upward and cleared her throat. Stephanie followed the line of her cane to a dangling bough of mistletoe. She laughed and glanced back at a blushing Jason.

"Go on then. What are you waiting for?" Mrs. Sweeney leaned forward and winked. "Christmas?"

Jason laughed and turned the bluest of eyes to Stephanie. With the touch of his finger, he tipped her chin up. "Merry Christmas, Steph."

Blood hurdled through her veins, nearly stopping her beating heart. The hard contour of his nose grazed hers, anticipation threading through her. The heat from his lips radiated across her parted mouth, hovering and teasing her until she was cookie dough in his embrace.

Stephanie closed her eyes, blocking out the gathering crowd, and relaxed in Jason's arms.

Jason loved her and wanted forever with her.

To everything there is a purpose. The dizzying thought God had given them this moment sent heart songs of praise upward.

For one last agonizing second, Jason's lips lingered above hers before his mouth claimed her like a thirsty man in a desert, leaving her breathless and wanting to kiss him forever.

Her eyes fluttered open at the cheers and applause.

"And that's how it's done, gentlemen." Mrs. Sweeney's voice cut through the good-natured teasing.

Stephanie grinned up at Jason. He looped a stray hair behind her ear, his tender touch turning her insides to melted marshmallows.

Yes, God definitely gave her a sign that stormy day two weeks ago, but He'd given her so much more.

He restored her faith and gave her back something she'd lost on the way home.

Hope.

With one final glance at the mistletoe above their heads, Stephanie gazed deep into Jason's eyes.

"Merry Christmas, Jason."

ABOUT THE AUTHOR

ANN BRODEUR is an avid reader and inspirational romance novelist. She's happily married to her own French Canadian Hero and is the proud Maman of four. After years of writing nonfiction for a variety of nonprofits, and placing in a handful of writing contests, Ann is pursuing her dream of publishing stories that encourage and inspire hope. When she's not reading, writing or chasing after her kids, Ann can be found drinking coffee, that's been reheated several times throughout the day. She aspires to drink a hot beverage in one sitting.

Blog and exclusive reader news:
http://brodeurwrites.com
For more reader fun:
https://www.facebook.com/annbrodeurauthor
Find me on Pinterest:
https://www.pinterest.ca/brodeurwrites/

www.anaiahpress.com

Printed in the USA
CPSIA information can be obtained
at www.ICGtesting.com
LVHW090214031023
759980LV00017B/49